HIDDEN AGENDAS

BY

KAREEM TORAIN

Published by:
LOCK THE GLOBE PUBLISHING
P.O. Box 23639
Philadelphia, PA 1914-3

ISBN: 978-0-615-70368-8
Copyright: June 29, 2010
Library of Congress Catalog Card No.

HIDDEN AGENDAS CREDITS
Story by Kareem "K-Gotti" Torain
Written by Kareem "K-Gotti" Torain
Edited by Ja'Ron, Ro'gier Roger, and Mikell Davis
Graphic Design by Clash Graphic Flyers, Eli Schein, Owner

Printed in the USA

DEDICATION

CONTENTS

CONTENTS

ACKNOWLEDGMENTS

Al-hamdulillah—All praises be due to Allah for allowing me to have the mind frame and energy to write this classic novel.

To my mother, Carolyn, who I love with all my heart; my two sisters, Marg and Meeka, who always had my back, love yaw. Mimi, Khadijah, Deon, to my Pop Talib Alim, Uncle Shakur, Larry, Aunt Sharon, Aunt Evelyn, Aunt Milly, Ms. Amina Shirl, Nina Ross, Dee Dee.

My cousins: Debbie, Pratt, Ronda, Big Hawky, Robert Speed, Nana, Big Kiya, Lil Kiya, Mil Mil, Sha, Taheerah, Ronny, Stacy, Sonya, Shirley, Amy, Regina, Roro, Larry, Joe the Boss, Mookie, Stafakhan, Beez, Migel, Dew, Lexus, Mercedes, Lil Derrick, Boo Boo, Waleisha, Damon, Bert. My nieces Steph, Bree, Delly, Tyree, Tyhir, Tammy, Cece, Reema; my nephew, Lil Lib, my heart.

And to my daughters, Sobby and Ranisha and my beautiful grandchild, Autumn.

To Halimah and her girlfriends Big Lex, Taheerah, Feesah, Crystal, Judie. To my 56th and Master family Khari. Glad we buried the nonsense that broke us up. Azim, Lester, Nafis, Unc Blue, Dennis, hold ya head homey, Insha-Allah you'll be home soon. Lil Tone, my Youngin and Rappy who road the wave. Fatta Banks, my brother from another mother, Toddy, J-Rock come back man. You went too far Insha-Allah. Hilly, Pooper, Turtle, Baby James, Chicken Wing, L-Gravy, Fat Mike, Dinky, Diddy, Lil Vinny Bronco, Shawn Brise, Kidney Keith, Kasheem, Ronny James, Vern

AKA Vedo, my Rappy Hassan in the Feds, Nelly, Black Magic, Saboo, Yaya, can't forget the Bottom. Lou, Cutty Raw, Fat Ed, Yotti, Chante, Wicked Wanda, ladisha AKA Key Key, Malarie, Lazette, Nafeesa, Lil Kiya, Kita, Reese, Shanice, Aishah, Carla, Shante, Rowe, Hassan, Tank, Monk, Jerry, Earn, Twon, and my no good baby mom, Sabriya, Lucy, Khalil, Sadiq, Finks, sorry about your loss homey, Leroy, Spuddy, Locke, Mumu, 59th and Master, O-Dog and Black Delancy street, Bumpy Face Darnell, Laronda, Kisha, Bubbles, Antilive, Taheerah, Sheshe, Shelly, Lisa, Linda, Monica, Joyce, Amira, Janice AKA KuKu, Rafic Slim hold ya head homey. I ain't forget, Gene Bird Major love homey and I'm here for ya, Shake 62nd and Felton I owe you champ. You showed me crew love from the jail.

Feedy, Reefy, Lea Small, Saeed, Massi, Malik, Sunny, Rose, Kim, Ms. Terry Blanding, Khabir AKA J, La Sheeka, AB, Ike South Philly, Nah South Philly, Lou from the bottom's wife, Carmela, Tariq, Lil Wayne, RatRat, Michelle Parker, Lil Dennis, Sabrina, Teffa, Tanisha, Short Dog, Tiffany Harris, MVIC southwest, Rev Todd, Abdul Razzaaq, Sutton Chains, Abdussabr, Hamza, Newark, New Jersey, Sadeeq, Shirley Phelps, Joseline, Sunny, Saudi Carolina, VA, Ms. Shirley Amiaa, Bernard, Quessa.

Kiya get your life together. You know who you are, Big Merrel, "Titty" you showed me major love cuz, Lil Roc, Old head Haneef up the grove, Danielle, Yolanda, Mahasin.

To my man Tez Look out for Caught In the Life coming soon, and to my Stepping Stone Publishing Family and Brother Gabriel who brung you Black Mafia, Holding Court, Etc. Over 12 years strong. Shot out to all my brothers over New York. Big Girly, Lisa Sanchez, Nasheed up Fayette, Abdul Lateef, Abdurrahman, Mujahid, Akbar, Teeb, Abdul Salaam, Jaleel AKA Greenie, Big G, Khabir, Jihad, Tommy AKA the Wesel, Boony, Kiya, Yana, Big Maze, Old head Hop up Dallas, Old head Naim I ain't forget ya. Black Tiffany from Chester, Fitz.

To my man RO "ClosedMouth" is coming soon, Nasir my brother stay up on that Haqq. Sheed, Damarcus, Keith Lils, Jeff, Poo AKA Laown, Thatcher AKA Will, Free, Ste-Al, Poo Insha-Allah you give that L-Bow Back, Sadat, Kenny Bilal, Fees from 49th Street, 23rd and Diamond Ty my brother from another mother love ya homey. Cliff Vine Street, Mustafa Callow Hill, Trini, Jay Mississippi.

And to Yahya who took time out to type my book for free. If I forgot anybody, forgive me. Special shot out to Pretty Red.

CHAPTER 1

A GOOD CHICK IS HARD TO FIND

It was a cold winter night in Philadelphia and the streets were filled with fienes chasing their next fix. A hustler's best chance was to be indoors, but if you were about a dollar, you were out in the rain, sleet or snow. Saleem was definitely about a dollar. On this particular night, he had other plans, coming from T.G.I. Fridays' restaurant on City Line Avenue with Shay, a girl he started to catch feelings for.

"Are you staying at my house, or do you want me to drop you off?" asked Saleem, turning the volume down on the radio.

"Check you out, you don't waste no time always shooting from the hip," Shay responded smiling. She stayed over his house on several occasions, but nothing never happened, beside from them kissing. Tonight Saleem's hormones were kicking in. It never took him this long to get inside a girl's pants sexually.

"So did you like the food or what?" Saleem inquired.

"Yeah, it was good, especially the wings with the spicy sauce," Shay said, licking her lips as though it was still some there.

"I guess the answer is yes, because I'm not doing no more driving tonight," Saleem said, turning down Hunter Street, seconds from reaching his house on Conestoga Street, across from Bakers playground. Besides from the smokers

1

running up and down the streets, the stray cats and dogs were out digging through the block's cans.

"Boy, you know I'm staying over, that's why I didn't respond to your question," Shay said, looking over at Saleem, admiring how handsome he was. She knew what type of guy he was, and she was excited to be his significant other. They got out of the car, Saleem went around on Shay's side and grabbed the bag of clothes that were there since leaving the mall earlier.

"Shhh!" Saleem said, nudging Shay to silence as he closed the front door behind them.

"Saleem is that you?" a loud voice yelled from the top of the stairs. His plans of not waking his mother had failed. She had a habit of inquiring about his wellbeing, knowing the lifestyle he lived and how the streets had his best interest.

"Yeah mom, it's me," Saleem said, easing her worries. He then walked to the bottom of the stairs, making his presence known. He wanted her to know he was still alive in living color, not mentioning he had female company. He didn't feel it was necessary, being that this wasn't her first time staying over. The couch is where Saleem slept. He only had to go upstairs to use the bathroom, shower, and get dressed. *I hope tonight's my night*, he thought, flopping back on the couch.

Shay was Saleem's on and off girlfriend. And even though she stayed over on many occasions, he never had sex with her but he knew she wasn't a virgin. He met her a few months back at the Capri Bar on 57th and Master Street. When Saleem saw her, he was on her like flies on shit, even though he was high. He knew she was a looker when he ran across a chick that caught his attention.

The syrup and pills had him popping his wit like Goldy from 'The Mack,' and there were a lot of females coming through on the regular. But on this night all eyes were on Shay, and Saleem wasn't about to let this quarter piece slip through his hands. It didn't take long for him to grab hold of her attention with his talk being blunt and straight to the point. Shay was glued to everything Saleem was saying, even though it was hard to hear over the loud music coming out of the jukebox.

"Why didn't you tell her I was here with you?" Shay said, unbuttoning her coat.

"Some things are best kept secret," responded Saleem smiling, pulling on Shay's hair.

"Oh I'ma secret huh?" asked Shay grabbing hold of her purse, walking towards the door.

"Stop playing shorty. You know I'm joking. Look, I'm grown. I don't need permission to bring company over, plus she knows you already," explained Saleem. Shay would've liked to have been the center of his attention at all times. Saleem was the type of dude who had a variety of women at his disposal. Most were hood rats, with a couple of crumb snatchers, that normally neglected their children for the social life. Instead of standing on their own two feet, they depended on the few bucks Saleem provided them with.

It was qualities in Shay, that other chicks didn't have. She was a part-time employee at a local hair salon, dubbed as the shampoo girl. She also did hair on the side for extra cash, with hopes of graduating at the end of the year. To say the least, she had her stuff together. In addition to her work ethics, she had a helluva personality. She was soft spoken, thoughtful and kind hearted. Shay seemed to have a genuine liking for Saleem that the other girls didn't possess.

To compliment her above characteristics, she was a bonafide eye catcher. Standing at 5'10 and 165 pounds, Shay could've been a representative for plus size models. Her honey brown complexion blended perfectly with matching almond-shaped eyes. Her jet black hair was soft and silky, stopping at the length of her shoulders. The texture of it made her look Native American. The light peach fuzz that extended her sideburns and rested above her full lips accentuated her exoticness. As Saleem and Shay sat on the couch to watch TV, Saleem flicked through channels cutting his eyes at Shay.

Damn I wanna dick this girl's brains out, Saleem thought, not knowing how she would respond to his sexual advances. His eyes were fixed on her juicy lips. So he decided to lean in for a kiss. She showed no resistance, as to say what took you so long. While in the midst of a passionate kiss, he massaged her breast. *Damn her titties are soft as shit*, he thought. Within seconds his swipe stood erect like the Statue of Liberty.

Saleem then positioned himself on top of her. He slowly began unbuttoning her shirt, breaking the momentum of their kiss. Saleem took a minute to observe her firm double-D breast, bulging from her Victoria Secret bra. Next, Saleem gently lifted the bra, exposing the two succulent melons. Saleem drooled, craving the sight of his mouth watering appetizer. Licking his lips, Saleem palmed both of Shay's breasts, and began tenderly teasing her nipple with his tongue. Now in the swing of things, Saleem sucked on one breast and then the other.

"OOOHH Saleem," Shay moaned, grabbing the back of Saleem's head and burying it in her chest. Things really started to heat up and you could feel the tension in the air. Saleem removed Shay's shoes, before he started easing off her pants, with Shay assisting him by lifting up. *Shit, she must work out*, he thought, admiring the total package. Saleem was ready to knock the socks off Shay. He made his way down her whole body with his tongue doing all the work, stopping a little above the jackpot.

Saleem twirled his tongue in between her bellybutton and he could feel her body starting to tighten up. She laid back enjoying every bit of it. Saleem wasn't into deep sea diving, but he was willing to sacrifice for Shay, to fulfill her every desire. He wanted her to remember this night forever. It was only 11:30 P.M. and Saleem knew his family was upstairs dead to the world.

I'm going for the title, Saleem thought. He felt like his performance had to be top of the line, because a girl of Shay's caliber would put you on ice like a pair of skates. Saleem eased off Shay's panties. The sweet aroma of her coochie stirred up the lust in his loins. After licking her bellybutton, he traveled south, planting soft kisses around her half-trimmed vagina. Saleem's inexperience showed through. He thought, *I don't know what the hell I'm doing.* His tongue was all over the place. Unwilling to let a good tongue go to waste Shay decided to coach him along.

"Lick up here Saleem," she whispered directing him toward her clitoris, hitting the spot. Shay laid back enjoying the pleasure of Saleem performing oral sex on her. *Not bad for a rookie*, she thought. Saleem proved to be a quick learner, ultimately bringing Shay to a climax. *Now it's my turn*, Saleem thought, as he slid his pants and boxers halfway down. While mounting Shay in the missionary position, Saleem's manhood began slowly penetrating the entrance of Shay's vagina. He continued to push his pipe up in her, causing her body to squirm.

"OOH Saleem, it feels so good," she said cheering him on to continue to pound smoke out of her. Saleem was sweating like he just ran 8 miles. *Shit, the heat must be on a hundred*, he thought, taking his right hand and wiping the sweat off his face. *This pussy is good*, he thought trying to beat the one minute mark. Saleem got up off Shay, grabbing her hand directing her to turn around so he could hammer her doggy style.

"So you like doggy style position?" Shay asked, turning her head back to see Saleem's facial expression with her ass poked up in the air.

"What cat doesn't?" he asked, not really trying to hear what she was talking about. *My dick is harder than algebra, and she is asking me a stupid ass question*, he thought. Saleem grabbed Shay's waist, pulling her into his manhood as with each stroke they moaned in unison. A faint feeling came over him. "Ul . . . Ul. . . ohh shit," Saleem said, buckling over Shay's backside releasing body fluids into her vagina.

"Saleem I know you didn't just cum?" inquired Shay, looking back at Saleem expressing disappointment.

"What?" he responded wearing a sly grin like a cat who swallowed the canary.

"Ain't no what, you heard what I said," complained Shay.

"Girl I caught a Charlie horse," said Saleem.

"Boy get off of me," she said, pushing Saleem away from her in disgust. All Saleem could do was laugh, as he tripped over the pants that were left around his ankles.

"Don't touch me no more tonight," Shay said, as she began getting herself together. After wiping her private area with tissues and getting dressed, she tried getting comfortable on the couch.

"You tripping about a pipe leak, what can I say. I was in a heated situation," explained Saleem, trying to wrap his arm around her.

"This is my spot, move over there somewhere," she concluded, pushing him off with her feet.

The next morning Saleem woke up only to find Shay stretched out on the couch with her mouth wide open. *I should stick my dick in her mouth, the way she treated me last night*, Saleem thought, wiping the cold out of his eyes.

Saleem nixed his thoughts walking past her, heading up to the bathroom. You could hear a pin drop. Everybody in the house was asleep, except for Saleem. He took a shower and got dressed, putting on his black Guess jeans and his multicolor polo button up shirt, with his black Chukka Timberland boots.

He added a little fragrance to seal the deal. Saleem already thought he was every girls dream. And when he looked in the mirror his appearance affirmed his ego. Now Saleem was ready to drop Shay off, so he could go out and get his grind on. Saleem walked over to Shay and leaned over and began to gently shake her.

"Shay, Shay, wake up!" he said in a low voice. Shay turned over, yawning and stretched as Saleem's face now came into view.

"Ummh what time is it?" asked Shay in a raspy morning voice.

"Damn girl," Saleem said blocking his nose with his hand. Shay's breath smelled like she ate a bowl of poop loops.

"Yeah, whatever," Shay responded turning back over, pulling the covers over her head, not paying Saleem any mind.

"Sike naw come on Shay, I got business to handle," he said, trying to convince Shay to get up. She got up and went straight to the bathroom. Saleem's eyes were on her every step of the way, watching that apple bottom of hers. *I'ma make her my main chick*, he thought, falling into a daze. Shay was back down in a matter of minutes.

"Before you drop me off, take me to get something to eat," Shay said, grabbing her jacket and putting her shoes on at the same time.

"It's some cereal in the kitchen," responded Saleem, with a smirk on his face. Shay walked toward the door, rolling her eyes at him. He followed suit, locking the door behind him. Saleem jumped into his Olds black Delta 88 and they headed to the breakfast spot.

Chapter 2

Partners In Crime

Meanwhile, Wakil was at one of West Philly's known breakfast spots, Ace Diner, located on 56th and Lancaster Avenue. Ace's was known for their homemade bread and iced tea. This place stayed crowded and this day was no exception. Sitting in a booth by the bathroom, Wakil had his plate full with turkey bacon, eggs, and grits as well as a large orange juice to wash it down. He spotted Saleem and Shay standing by the entrance. He yelled for Saleem. "Saleem!" Once he grabbed Saleem's attention, he eased his way through the crowd with Shay glued to his back. Wakil was licking his fingers and wiping it off on his dickey shirt. He greeted Saleem with a handshake and a half shoulder hug.

"What's the deal player? I meant to get at you last night, but I was tied up," Saleem stated, looking over at Shay.

"Ain't Shit Fam, I see you was occupied," responded Wakil, cutting his eyes over at Shay, sucking his teeth as though a piece of bacon was stuck in between them. He ignored her presence.

"Fuck you Wakil! Saleem, I'm going up front to order," Shay blurted out. It's been an ongoing feud between them two, since they first met. With Wakil being one of his best friends and partner in crime, and Shay slowly becoming his significant other, they often fought for his time.

"Yo chill man, don't pay her no mind. She's mad right now 'cause I busted off and rushed off," said Saleem, sarcastically.

"Oh yeah, you finally hit the skins? I picked that bread up from Ms. Mary's crib last night," responded Wakil.

"What she give you?" asked Saleem.

"Two stacks. We should be ready to make a move in a minute," Wakil spoke.

"No doubt we gotta turn shit up an extra notch. Niggaz going to hate more than ever," said Saleem, grabbing a piece of Wakil's toast off his plate.

"Fuck 'em. It's whatever homey! I ain't got no problem with making a nigga famous," Wakil spoke cocky.

"You ain't never lied cuz." Saleem shook his head in agreement. Saleem was around to witness Wakil's work on many occasions. He never hesitated on busting his gun.

"I'm about to split," Wakil blurted out.

"Look, I'ma take Shay home and I'ma get at you later," spoke Saleem.

"No doubt, be easy fam," was Wakil's response as he got up to shake Saleem's hand. Saleem walked back up front behind Shay, smacking her on her buttocks. She turned around faster than a speeding bullet, with looks to kill. Seeing Saleem's face put her at ease.

"Boy you was about to catch a beat down," she said, slapping him on his arm in a playful manner. After waiting fifteen minutes or so, Shay's order was finally done.

"Come on you ready?" asked Saleem putting his arm around her.

"Yeah, let's go," said Shay.

They both walked towards the exit and the owner called Saleem's name as he was approaching the cash register.

"Saleem, hi you doing my friend," John spoke, pronouncing his name wrong. Saleem spent a lot of money there so when he reached in his pocket to pay, the owner informed him his money was no good and that his order was on the house.

"Good looking John," responded Saleem, leaving the restaurant. Shay was astonished by the Chinese guy catering to her man.

When they got inside the car Saleem blasted the heat and put AZ's 'Do or Die' in the tape deck. "Sugar Hill Baby," came through the six by nine door speakers, loud enough to throw a small house party. Shay lived in Wynnfield, which people considered the suburb's of West Philly, compared to the other parts of the city. Coming down Diamond Street hill, Saleem pulled right in front of her house. She lived across from Brynmar Tower Apartments. Saleem turned down the music.

"So what's your plans for today?" asked Saleem, turning around to face her.

"I gotta go to work at 12:00, but I get off at four," Shay stated, unlocking her door.

"I'ma make a few runs. As soon as I'm done we can get together. So hit my pager if you can't catch my cell," responded Saleem.

"Alright, be careful," she said, closing the door behind her. He waited for her to get inside the house before he pulled off, taking the opposite route from which he came. Saleem took a shortcut through Parkside Avenue. He came out on 52nd Street by the Sunoco gas station.

He drove straight to the block he hustled on—56th and Jefferson Street, right around the corner from Ace Diner. When he turned the corner, the fiends were lined up like a church giving out free cheese.

"Yo cuz, you stay sharp enough to cut something," said Bert, one of Saleem's cousins. They were related on his mother's side of the family.

"I try to champ, even if it's basic shit," blurted Saleem, feeling himself. He had a baby face, light complexion, smooth skin with hazel eyes, standing at 6 foot, 200 pounds, and medium build. He was a big young bull, and the females adored him.

"Where you coming from?" asked Bert, as he got up to serve a customer that was walking down the street.

"Dropping Shay off at her crib," responded Saleem, sitting on the steps next to the house where they sometimes used for a stash spot and to hustle out of.

"Oh yeah, that's the broad who's spending all your bread," Bert said.

"Not at all, but I keep her laced in the latest hot shit," responded Saleem.

"You ain't hustling today?" asked Bert, still serving the fiends. Jefferson Street was still running in a few thousand a day. But it wasn't doing no where near the numbers it use to do in the late eighties and nineties, when the block was known to do thirty grand a day. So do to the decrease in customers, catz started to migrate in other areas and put it down.

"I'm waiting to re-up, so I'ma holler at my man later as soon as I hit Wakil on his cell," Saleem said.

"I thought you retired from the game," spoke Bert, trying to be funny. He looked like a broke version of Martin Lawrence.

"All I know is the game! I'm far from up! Until I touch a million, consider me married to the game. Then, I can shine on the lames," said Saleem. Bert bust out laughing at what Saleem had said. He was known to have a slick tongue.

"Well, I'll be damn. You got deep on that one. I'ma be out here until the block burn down, and I don't see that happening any time soon cuz," responded Bert. Him and Saleem shook hands and departed. Bert went inside his grandmom's house who resided on the block.

＊ ＊ ＊ ＊ ＊

Shay was taking a shower preparing herself for work. As she stood naked, letting the soap suds drip from her beautiful body. She couldn't help but think about Saleem and what he was doing in the back of her mind. She knew she had a winner, but at what cost would Shay have to pay to be with him.

He would be the first guy she ever got involved with who was knee deep in the streets. And she knew how dudes of his status were more dedicated to the street life then their significant other. Shay's chain of thought was suddenly broken at the sound of her mother yelling from the bottom of the steps.

Shay stepped out of the shower and wrapped the towel around her body. She exited the bathroom reaching the top of the stairwell. She screamed back down the steps telling her mom she could hear and she didn't have to yell. She wanted to know what time she came in last night. Shay went to go get dressed, and afterwards decided to go confront her mother.

"I told you I could hear you!" Shay said.

"Girl, how you hear me with the shower running?" asked Ms. Lacey, sitting on the couch, blowing smoke from the cigarette.

"I stayed out last night. I came in this morning," Shay said, skipping past the last question her mom asked.

"Oh, you did huh? Where at?" Ms. Lacey asked, being nosy and sounding as though she was concerned.

"With a friend," responded Shay. *What the fuck is you my babysitter? I'm eighteen*, she mumbled under her breath.

"Don't get smart bitch," Ms. Lacey said, as though she was reading her lips. Shay just sucked her teeth and walked away. She knew her mom was probably coked up because she never really questioned her comings and goings.

"Ms. Lacey was a mother of four, but you couldn't tell. Age didn't creep up on her. She could've given Vanessa Williams a run for her money, on top of all the variety of different drugs she indulged in. She stood 5'8", 145 pounds, light skin with long straight jet black hair. So there was no doubt about where Shay inherited her looks from.

"Mom, I don't have time to be arguing with you. I'm already late for work," Shay said, with attitude heading towards her room slamming the door behind her. Ms. Lacey was grooving off of a few pills she had just taken, so she ignored the last words Shay had spoken.

Shay sprayed on some Victoria Secret perfume and looked in the mirror, making sure her attire was at its best from the matching bra and panties, to her outer appearance. She wasn't the type to get caught slipping, if she ever had to divest herself.

* * * * *

"Yeah bitch, suck daddy off, you like this big hammer don't ya?" Wakil said, pushing the girl's head further down on his manhood. She couldn't respond if she tried, since Wakil had her mouth hostage. She didn't mind the verbal abuse, especially coming from Wakil. She was in love with him.

Her name was Tiffany, but most knew her as Tiff. She was known to give the best blow job in the hood. Her body was well proportioned but wasn't attractive looking at all, due to the lazy eye and the scar on the right side of her face. But her sexual performance made up for the looks. Interrupted by the sound of Wakil's cell phone ringing— *Damn, who the hell could this be cutting into my session?* he asked himself, as he continued enjoying the pleasure he was receiving from Tiffany's mouth. The phone kept ringing. He pushed her head back to reach for his phone. She remained on her knees like a trained dog waiting for the next order to be given. Quickly recognizing the voice, it was Saleem.

"Yo Leem, what's the deal cuz? You still wit Shay?" asked Wakil.

"Naw, I'm at the crib. We gotta go handle business. I just left J-Street. Bert out there killing them," responded Saleem.

"My fault man, I'm sitting here fulfilling my sexual desires with deep throat," Wakil spoke. Tiff looked at him with death in her eyes. Even though she was labeled as the neighborhood slut, she expected Wakil to treat her better than all the others, especially being as though he was at her house.

"Who Tiff?" asked Saleem, knowing off the top who Wakil was referring to.

"You better know it," responded Wakil. Tiff still hadn't moved from the previous position she was in before Wakil's phone rang.

"Look, give that trash the boot. We got bread to get," said Saleem, feeling a little disappointed about Wakil, always lacking when it came down to handling business.

"Let me wash my swipe. I'll be there in twenty minutes," spoke Wakil. Tiff knew by the conversation that her performance was no longer needed. So she went to get Wakil a clean washrag with soap on it. He did a quick wipe and passed the rag back to her. He went in his pocket and pulled a fifty dollar bill off the wad of money he was carrying and threw it on the bed.

She didn't hesitate to snatch the money up. Wakil jumped in his Caprice station wagon and was pushing the pedal to the floor. He took 59th and Arch Street straight until he reached 55th Street and made a sharp left. Within a matter of minutes he was pulling up outside Saleem's house. Hearing a car pull up outside had Saleem peeping through the blinds. As soon as Wakil was about to knock on the door, Saleem opened it up.

"What you take, slow express? I damn near dosed off," said Saleem.

"Shit, I ran lights and stop signs," responded Wakil.

"Come on we taking my car. I hollered at Charlie already. He told me to hit 'em on his phone when we got closer," Saleem said.

"Where we meeting dude at?" inquired Wakil.

"On 62nd and Woodland Avenue. He said there's a McDonalds near there in the lot," explained Saleem, driving down 60th Street. He drove that route all the way to

Woodland Avenue. As they pulled inside the parking lot Wakil was looking around making sure there weren't any surprises. He just had a funny feeling about the boy Charlie, who Saleem looked up to and respected. Twenty minutes had passed. Saleem still didn't see no sign of Charlie, even though it was hard to see through the misty windows.

"This should be him right here," Saleem spoke. Charlie usually sent somebody else to meet anybody who was purchasing weight from him. But Saleem was an exception to the rule. Being as though they were doing business for over a year, their relationship was tight.

"I hope so, shiesty ass niggaz," blurted out Wakil. He just ain't trust the guy, but Saleem was his partner in crime and whatever move he made, Wakil was riding with it.

"Chill cuz," said Saleem, exiting the driver's side of the vehicle. Wakil reached inside the pocket of his Woolridge, pulling out his black six shot 357 revolver, placing it on his lap. *I'll be damn if I'ma let a nigga get stripes off me*, he thought, keeping his eyes focused on the green Taurus as Saleem entered the car.

"What's the deal youngin," Charlie said, extending his hand towards Saleem.

"Ain't shit old head. Trying to get this paper," responded Saleem passing him a brown paper bag that he pulled out from his coat pocket. It was twelve grand in stacks of thousands. Saleem stepped it up since him and Wakil cut into the other blocks to move their product.

Charlie put the bag between his legs without counting the money. He reached in the back seat, exposing a black duffle bag. When he opened it, the aroma of coffee grinds hit him in his nose like smoke from a barbecue grill. Coffee grinds were used to keep the K-9 dogs from sniffing out the drugs. Charlie knew that by being a season vet in the game, pulling out a Ziploc bag filled with white chunks of powder cocaine.

"It's a brick. Can you handle it?" asked Charlie, placing it in Saleem's lap.

"I only paid you for eighteen ounces," Saleem said, stuffing the bag inside his Polo down coat.

"Don't sweat it. Just give me fourteen grand back," Charlie spoke. Saleem just shook his head in agreement to what Charlie just said. Charlie could easily intimidate the average Joe, even the so-called killers. He was a darker version of Suge Knight. Saleem hopped back in his car, removed the drugs from his coat and passed it to Wakil. Neither one carried a license, so if the police was planning on pulling them over, they were gonna be in heavy pursuit.

"We gonna take that to your spot until we fry it up," said Saleem, backing up out of the parking lot.

"That's cool. Mimi won't be back for a couple more days, 'cause she be tripping all up in my shit," explained Wakil. Saleem followed the eleven trolley all the way to 56 and Woodland making a sharp left. It took them no more than thirty minutes to reach 61st Nassu Road. They parked in front of the building. When they exited, both looked around to make sure nobody followed them. Once inside the apartment, Wakil placed the drugs on the table.

"So what your old head pass off this time around?" asked Wakil, breaking the silence between them since leaving the parking lot.

"He gave up a brick and wants fourteen stacks back," spoke Saleem looking around inspecting the plush apartment that had changed a lot since the last time Saleem saw it.

"Well, that's cool. We'll be buying a couple of those in no time. Just gotta grind harder," Wakil said, taking the bag of drugs to the closet to hide it.

"I see you baller, you did the damn thing to this spot," said Saleem, flopping back on the black recliner.

"Man you know Mimi thinks she's a interior decorator. I ain't with that shit," responded Wakil.

"I gotta move out of my miz spot. You moved up like George and Weasey. You came a long way from being locked out of your miz spot and laying on my couch," Saleem said.

"Damn that was crazy right," Wakil said, laughing as they reminisced about old times.

Everything from the bathroom to the curtains was top shelf, and it was only a two bedroom apartment.

"We come a long way though cuz, and it can only get better. As long as we remain loyal to each other," Saleem responded, flicking the channels on the fifty-two inch floor model TV.

"Yeah, it's Death Before Dishonor," Wakil said.

"No doubt, I'ma get me a drink tonight. I don't feel right without my meds in me," Saleem shot back.

"I'm with ya. That juice is the best high ever made for catz like us," Wakil spoke. Juice was a nickname for syrup mixed with codeine and the majority of the hoods used it.

"Is Appletree Street secure? As far as work?" asked Saleem.

"We don't have nothing bagged up for down there," Wakil responded, stretching out on the sofa.

"It's like three grand worth of Nick's bagged up at my crib," said Saleem, cutting the TV off being as though it wasn't nothing to watch.

"Let's ride, drop me off at my car and I'll take the package down to Appletree so they'll have something pumping," stated Wakil, flicking the light switch off on his way out the door with Saleem right behind him.

"Yeah, I'ma go grab Shay. I know she on tilt. It's 5:30 already and I had my phone off," Saleem said, smiling with the thought of Shay in his mind.

"Man, fuck that bitch. She got you pussy whipped. Now you going to marry that chick," Wakil blurted out laughing while he was shuffling through cassette tapes inside the glove department.

"Watch your mouth nigga, That's my bitch. If a cat said something about Mimi you would faint," Saleem said. He was defending the woman he was falling in love with. He knew Wakil had a habit of coming out his mouth sideways. On the other hand, he took Shay personal. And he wouldn't have cared if it was any other girls besides Shay. Tension was in the air, it could be felt throughout the whole ride. Pulling up in front of Saleem's crib Wakil broke the ice before they got out of the car.

"Look, you my man dawg, my bad for ranking your broad, even though I can't stand her. Just don't let her break out bond," stated Wakil, with a serious look of sorrow on his face.

"Ain't nothing going to break our bond but death. I got love for shorty, no doubt. But bro's come before these hoes. So don't think I would cross you for her," said Saleem, stepping out of the car. He went inside the house while Wakil walked across the street to his mom's house which was directly across from each other. Minutes later both emerged from their residence.

"Here cuz," Saleem said, passing Wakil a small brown bag.

"Yeah, let me go handle this A.S.A.P.," Wakil said.

"Who you going put in there?" asked Saleem.

"Smoke, you know Ms. Cook want hers up front," Wakil said, stuffing the bag under his seat, letting it hang out a little bit for easy access just in case he had to throw it out.

"So give her a bean worth. Let her smoke until her heart bust," Saleem said, laughing with tears in his eyes.

'That's some cold shit. You shot out," Wakil said.

"All she wants is to chase her lungs," responded Saleem. Wakil had to pick Smoke up on his way. Even though Smoke got high, he always brung the money back straight. And people called him Smoke only because of his skin complexion, which was dark as tar. Saleem got back inside the car and pulled off, heading up to Shay's house. He grabbed a tape from the pile that was inside the glove department, placed it inside the cassette player. All you heard was Tupac's voice blast through the speakers. The song was "If I Die Tonight." Saleem went in the zone, as he cruised to his destination.

∗ ∗ ∗ ∗ ∗

Shay was in her room trying on several pairs of the jeans she had stacked in the closet. Some were so tight she could've caught a yeast infection. But that didn't keep her from admiring her physique in the mirror. Suddenly her phone rang. *Who could this be?* she thought, picking the phone up. "Hello?" she said.

"Hey babygirl. I'm outside your house," Saleem said, getting out of his car.

"I'll be right down," responded Shay, knowing exactly who it was. She had mixed emotions. On one hand she was happy that he was here, and mad at the same time 'cause she hadn't heard from him since he dropped her off. When she opened the door Saleem had a cool-aid smile on his face.

"What the hell you smiling about?" asked Shay, giving him the crooked eye.

"Don't act like that. I've been taking care of business all day, trying to get this bread for our future," Saleem responded, following Shay up the steps with his eyes glued on her butt.

"So now your business is more important than me? Are you out there with those sluts," she stated, with attitude.

"Stop tripping. You know the lifestyle I live and that's how I keep you laced," he responded.

"Don't throw that shit in my face. I work too," she said, folding her arms, leaning back against the bedroom door.

"Yeah, but come on, that part-time hair shit ain't getting it done. Plus, you should be trying to graduate," Saleem said.

"Whatever! I'm not worrying about school. I got that and I work full time now so kiss my ass." She was heated. You could've cooked a grilled cheese sandwich on her face, how red it turned.

"I came to see you 'cause I missed you, not to argue over nothing," responded Saleem, flopping back on her bed.

"I missed you too. My mom be stressing me the hell out. I gotta move out this crib." Shay's temper tantrum quickly faded and she settled down on her bed next to Saleem.

"Where is your mom at anyway? That's my buddy," he said, with a grin.

"Oh yeah, she only like you 'cause you bring her those damn pills, and I don't know where she's at," Shay said, slowly removing her pants that she previously had tried on. His eyes narrowed in and he became semi-hard. Shay knew exactly what she was doing. She had a body that no man could resist. Throwing the pants on a chair, she got up, locked the door and then turned around facing Saleem.

"Baby, I've got a surprise for you that you'll never forget," she said, speaking with confidence. Saleem didn't know what she had up her sleeve. He was shocked by the sudden change in her sexual episodes. If she had an alter ego he was all for it.

"I don't like surprises," he said.

"So, what do you think it is Mr. know it all?" she asked, pulling off his boots, then she slowly started to ease off his pants. She smiled at his manhood poked out of his boxers. She continued with her aggressiveness until she had him totally naked. She leaned over and kissed him seductively, causing his head to fall back on the pillow. Shay wasted no time going for the gusto, taking all of him in her mouth. She treated his penis like a prize possession as she began to massage it with her mouth. The feeling Saleem was getting from her pleasure was sensational. He tried hard to hold back from exploding. That didn't last too long. He released uncontrollably in her mouth like a water faucet.

He thought she would kill him after that last time they shared a sexual encounter and she almost had a nervous breakdown from him busting off inside her vagina. But she didn't pull back, instead she swallowed every drop like a vacuum cleaner. She had tired him out. He rolled over like a man trying to rest after a hard day's work.

"Oh no you don't. I'm not finished with you yet," Shay said.

"Dag what now babygirl? That was the bomb and the best blow job I ever had real rap," Saleem said, lifting his naked body up to lean his back against the wall.

"Now I want you to do something for me," stated Shay, as she started to massage his penis trying to bring life back into it.

"What babygirl? 'Cause I'm beat," asked Saleem. He knew she wasn't talking about performing oral sex on her being as though he covered that area.

"Fuck me in my ass," Shay blurted out causing Saleem to have an instant hard on. He was tongue tied. He thought he was dreaming. He didn't know where the animal was coming from inside her.

"Huh?" he said acting as though he didn't hear her the first time.

"You heard me. It's my first time and I want you to be the one I experience it with," Shay said.

"Shit, it's my first time too. I was taught if you fuck a woman in the ass you'll fuck a man in the ass," Saleem responded, confused and applaud at the same time to be the first to fulfill her sexual fantasy.

"That's not true. Don't listen to those jail stories, plus I know you're all man, and it'll be our little secret." Shay was trying her best to convince him to answer her request. It didn't take him long to give in. He asked for some petroleum jelly to moisten his manhood. She used her mouth instead. He bent her over backwards with her butt sticking up, giving him easy access to enter. As soon as he stuck the head of his penis in, it caused Shay to jerk forward.

"Oh shit," she screamed out in pain.

"I'm not even in yet," he said.

"Boy your dick is big. Even the tip, so be gentle," she said, burying her face in the pillow. He went deeper until he was halfway in, and started stroking. He felt her butt muscle tighten up on him. Her butt was on fire. He decided to push all of him in her.

But after a few more strokes she pulled away and turned to face him and took hold of his hammer and started sucking and licking all over it. She flipped back into the doggy-style position, reaching her hand back, grabbing his penis and directing it back into her butt hole. Saleem was in another world. *Damn she's an animal*, he thought, as he started cumming inside her ass.

Chapter 3

Party Time

Meanwhile, Wakil was back at his apartment getting dressed with the intentions of going out to party on a Saturday night, when he was interrupted by the phone ringing.

"Yo who this?" asked Wakil.

"It's your wife boy," Mimi said, calling from her native country of Ethiopia.

"Damn my fault Mimi. I thought you was going to call Sunday?"

"I didn't know I needed a special time to see my man?" she stated.

"Naw, it ain't like that. I'm glad you called. I miss you like crazy," responded Wakil. When it came to Mimi he was humbled towards her. She was different from all the other girls he mingled with. He seen her as the babymom type. And the others as just fulfilling his sexual desires.

"I miss you too. There's not a day that goes by that I don't think about you," she spoke, blowing kisses through the phone.

"When you coming home? I'ma catch blue balls," Wakil said.

"I need dick too Boo, my granny is real sick, and I just wanted to make sure she's well before I leave," answered Mimi.

"Well, I'ma be waiting for you sexy," responded Wakil making her blush.

"I hope so, and stay out of trouble, as well as away from those stink bitches," Mimi said, coughing like her grandmom wasn't the only one sick.

"I'm chilling, and ain't no broad like the one I got," Wakil said.

"Let me go Boo, love you and can't wait to see you," Mimi spoke.

"Love ya too," Wakil said, ending the conversation. As soon as he was about to place the phone on the dresser it rang again. *"Damn, who is this?"* he mumbled, frustrated due to the excessive phone calls that were stopping him from getting dressed.

"Hello," spoke Wakil.

"Yo Wah, what's the deal cuz," responded Boog overjoyed to hear from a person he considered a loyal friend. Even though they met through Saleem. Boog and Saleem were like brothers from different mothers.

"Ain't shit homey, I'ma take a trip down north and grab me a sucker shot of yellow and a few blue's," Wakil said, still sliding his socks on while holding the phone with his shoulder.

"Shoot past my crib, and scoop me when you're done. I'ma ride with ya," Boog said.

"No doubt cuz, give me less than a half," Wakil said.

Alright, yo I called Leems horn and paged him. He ain't answer neither one," said Boog.

"Man that nigga probably tied under Shay's ass," said Wakil laughing.

"You crazy Wah, I'll call him later. I'm laying on you," responded Boog. They said their peace and the line went dead. Even after Wakil hung up the phone with Boog, he still had Mimi on his mind. Although he loved her, his penis had a mind of its own. *"I'ma peel me a chick tonight,"* he thought. As he put dabs of Muslim oil on his body. Sealing the deal he put on his fresh six inch tan double sole's Timberland's with the collar.

He wore a black Fila velour sweat suit and the weather was just right for his waist length mink. He looked in the mirror, *I'm official,* he thought to himself, admiring the way he looked. Wakil was 6 foot 2, 210 pounds, medium build, and brown eyes that matched his skin complexion. And he mostly sported a dark fade. But on this particular night he let his curly hair stand out, even though he knew he desperately needed a hair cut. Taking a second look in the mirror, he grabbed his jacket and rolled out. It wouldn't take him long to get to Boog's house. He only lived five blocks away. As he pulled in front of Boog's house and beeped the horn, Boog came out and hopped in the car.

"Okay player, you got the mink on," Boog said.

"This is small shit to a giant," Wakil responded, stretching his hand out to shake Boog's.

"When you going to step your game up on the wheel side, this old ass car," Boog spoke searching for a tape. He found "Ready to Die" by Biggy Smalls, pushed it in the tape player and turned the volume up.

"Nigga those trees look like track sneakers, the way you walk around in them," Wakil shot back with a low blow. Boog couldn't do nothing but laugh. He knew Wakil was right. He didn't have no means of transportation. Saleem used to let him drive his car most of the time. Boog was a dark skinned chubby young boy with thin sideburns. He weighed 260 pounds. He was only 5 foot 11. Anyone who knew him, loved him.

"I'ma cop me a squadder soon, you know Leem going to look out for me," Boog said. He was right. Being as though he didn't hustle like that because his cousins, who were knee deep in the streets, didn't want that life for him. So he would sneak around to keep a few dollars in his pocket, on top of what Saleem and Wakil would pass off to him for helping them bag the product up.

"Give me a minute to win it, and a second to claim it. Best believe I'm be at the lot by next summer," Wakil said, driving down Lancaster Avenue, making a right on 47th and Girard heading down North Philly.

"I would've been up a little wit y'all by now, if my hating ass cousins weren't drawing on me all the time," Boog said, reclining his seat as he bopped his head to "One More Chance," by Big.

"Fuck them niggaz Boog. We got ya, all you gotta do is chill. Plus Leem's man Charlie just passed off a whole bird," Wakil said. Reaching inside his mink pocket he pulled out a Philly blunt, already rolled with weed.

"That's what I'm talking about cuz," Boog said, intercepting the blunt.

"This shit will blow your mind," Wakil said.

"Damn what you got in here?" Boog asked, choking.

"Only the best, that chocolate!" Wakil said, taking a few drags of the blunt. He turned down 17th and Jefferson Street which was known for selling syrup and pills. People called it pancakes and syrup. But this wasn't no flapjacks and Aunt Jamama syrup. It was cough syrup and pills mixed with Codeine that made the drugs more powerful. Wakil parked on the right hand side of the street where the pharmacy was located. He left the car running with Boog inside and walked up the street where he spotted Ant Live, who was Saleem's man.

"Yo Ant, what's the deal cuz?" spoke Wakil, shaking his hand.

"Chilling player, what can I do for you?" asked Ant.

"Let me get two ounces of yellow and fifteen blues," Wakil said.

"No doubt, here I got the blues now," Ant said, unscrewing a pill bottle passing him a handful of pills. He sent a younger guy in the alleyway to retrieve the bottles of syrup. The pills were three Xanax for five dollars. And the yellow ounce bottle was thirty dollars a piece. But Ant and his partner who wasn't around at the time, always gave them discounts. So Wakil gave him seventy dollars.

"Good looking champ," Wakil said, as he received the yellow ounce bottles.

"Anytime player, tell Leem I said what's up," Ant said.

"For sure." Wakil shook his hand and ran back to the car. Ant was a little short dude who always dressed like he was going to a party. To sum it up, he had swagger to his style and he always showed love to real dudes. When Wakil reached the car he gave Boog an ounce and seven pills and took what was left.

"I needed this shot," Boog said, wasting no time dissolving the controlled substance. Wakil turned the heat up in the car and pulled around the corner to the variety store on 18th and Master. He jumped out and ran in the store to buy two Philly cigars and a Pepsi soda.

"Here you dump these out now, so when we get to the gas station we can just drop the weed in there," spoke Wakil, giving Boog the cigars.

"I feel ya," Boog said. They turned up the radio and cruised back to West Philly crossing the zoo bridge. Wakil cut through Fairmount Park, taking a short cut to reach Parkside. When he pulled up to the gas station and garage that only sold a small amount of food and appliances that was used for a front to sell weed, the gas pumps didn't work. They occasionally used the garage for tune-ups and to change breaks.

"Grab four nicks," spoke Wakil, giving Boog a twenty dollar bill.

"Man, we need more than that," suggested Boog.

"Well, fatz come out your pocket. Nigga I bought the first bag and the juice and pills," Wakil said.

"You a cold nigga," Boog said, opening the door.

"I know, so close that door. My heat is getting out," Wakil said. Boog was back in a flash. They drove further down the block stopping at Sunoco gas station.

"Man, I'ma grab me two dogs. I'm starving like Marvin," said Boog.

"Nigga you always hungry," spoke Wakil walking to the last aisle where all the hot beverages were.

"A Wah, you sure you cool on these dizogs, these mother fuckers are banging," said Boog, stuffing half of the hot dog in his mouth before paying for them.

"Nah I'm good. This hot tea going put me on the planet like Janet," Wakil said, sipping his tea. You could tell the syrup and pills was starting to kick in how Boog's and Wakil's speech became sluggish. They paid for their items and left.

"Spark that blizz up," Wakil said, turning the heat down.

"Did you flip and call Leem again?" asked Boog burning the tip of the blunt.

"I'm telling you cuz he wit shorty. She got a spell on his ass," Wakil said, driving slowly down Landsdown Avenue and suddenly hearing a phone ring.

"Yo, that's your phone ringing," said Boog.

"Wah money at your service," answered Wakil.

"Yo, where you at?" asked Saleem, sounding serious.

"Goddamn player you came up for air," stated Wakil, feeling a little tipsy.

"Bert got knocked by task force," said Saleem.

"Oh yeah," said Wakil, as though he didn't really care. Him and Bert wasn't the best of friends.

"Mom P said they raided the block and her house earlier today," explained Saleem.

"Me and Boog are riding low coming down the avenue," Wakil said.

"Come through Mom P's crib. I'll be on the porch," said Saleem.

"I'm on my way." Wakil hung up and proceeded to drive turning down the block, parking on the opposite side of Mom P's house. Saleem came off the porch and climbed in the back seat.

"You niggaz twisted, yaw went down J- Street with out me huh?" Saleem asked, leaning between Boog and Wakil. They were mumbling with their eyes closed.

"Leem what's up bro?" asked Boog.

"Same shit fam on the grind to get this cheddar."

"You hustling now?" inquired Boog, with his voice sounding hoarse.

"Niz, I was shooting through the blizock. And Mom P called me. I was on my way to the spot," Saleem said.

"What time is it?" asked Boog.

"Anywhere near one or a little after," answered Saleem.

"Is there any dick suckers in there?" Boog asked, eager to get his rocks off.

"It's some smoker broad in there with a fat ass, I never seen before," explained Saleem.

"Let's go," Boog said, hopping out of the car.

"Hold up! You're high, plus the jakes are in there," Saleem said, stopping Boog dead in his tracks. Wakil was slumped over nodded. So Saleem rolled the windows down a few inches so he would be able to breathe and kept the car running with heat on low so he wouldn't freeze as well. Saleem took the keys out, being as though the car could run without them, and he locked all the doors. Him and Boog went inside the house. Once inside, you smelled the smoke burning from the crack pipes. The fumes were in the air. This smell stuck to your clothes. The house was in a desperate need of a makeover. Every piece of furniture looked antique.

There was a kerosene heater in the middle of the floor to heat the whole downstairs with a pot of boiling water on top of it. About a few years back this house was in good condition. And Mom P's house was known for giving out free lunches in the mid-80's to all the children in the neighborhood. But all that came to a screeching halt. Once the crack epidemic hit the streets, people lost their morals, honor and everything they worked hard for due to a drug that came with no remorse for human life. On Mom P's mantel piece set family photos of most of her children who were all grown now.

"Hey Starr, whup in Star," the voice yelled, a Jamaican accent coming from the corner of the house.

"Ain't shit B," Saleem said.

B was a Jamaican who hustled for another Jamaican named Slaughter. The only thing that saved them from getting murdered for trying to set up shop was keeping the block from being hot with police. Plus Mom P was in debt with them for messing up a package of theirs. So she let them set up shop from eight at night to seven in the morning.

"Where that smoker chick at, with the fat ass?" asked Saleem.

"Whata gwon, you wan mash it tup," B said, knowing exactly who Saleem was referring to.

"Boog tryna get his man ate up," Saleem said, as he moved towards the kitchen. There were a few people at the table burning lighters up to their glass pipes, but the woman he was looking for wasn't one of them. *Damn she must be upstairs,* he thought.

"Ear me Star, she upon the steps," B said, pointing towards the steps. The only thing that gave B away was his accent. He didn't have dreadlocks like most Jamaicans. And he looked as though he was born in the United States.

"Fuck that Bitch Leem," Boog spoke, leaning on the wall with his eyes shut.

"You won't say that shit when you see her," said Saleem, helping Boog up the steps. Every step they took you heard screeching noise like they were about to fall to the basement. They walked to the front room where Mom P resided and decided not to look in the other two rooms. Just when they were about to knock on the door it swung open with two women face-to-face ready to cut each others throat. Mom P cut in between them, bringing the altercation to a halt. Out the corner of her eye she noticed Saleem and Boog standing there.

"Mom P what's up?" asked Saleem, laughing at how she had her hat tilted to the side.

"Who let yaw asses in here?" Mom P asked, with raindrops of spit coming out her mouth, with every word she spoke. Mom P had to be in her late sixties. Old age was coming apparent and all the drugs and liquor she abused daily only added to it. She had black hair mostly covered in gray. A missing front tooth and she was light skinned with a naturally thin frame, minus the weight loss due to her addictions.

"We need to speak to her right there," Saleem said, pointing to the woman sitting on Mom P's bed, wearing a colorful sweater.

"Oh yeah, fast asses trying trick and get your little wee wees sucked."

"Nah Mom P, she has something for me. I was going to get it before I left," said Saleem.

To his surprise she bit the bait and they had convinced Mom P to let them speak to the lady. They all went inside the middle room where there was a bed, a wooden chair, a dresser and a pile of dirty clothes in the corner of the room. Boog set on the chair he was up now. The woman's body had his undivided attention. Saleem started to negotiate. She wasn't your average fiend. She still possessed some good qualities, which could be seen through her outer appearance. Her teeth was cocaine white and her skin complexion was caramel brown. The hips and butt complimented each other. Nice lips as well and long black hair.

"Do you smoke crack?" asked Saleem, finding it hard to believe she was a drug user.

"First, my name is Sue, and to answer your question I smoke laced turbs," Sue said. Laced turbs was weed and cigarettes mixed with crack.

"I know it was something that was making you stand out from the others," spoke Saleem.

"So what do you want from me?" Sue asked.

"How would you like to earn an extra few bucks?" Saleem asked.

"That depends on what you're asking of me," Sue said.

"My man is trying to get a blow job," Saleem spoke, turning to face Boog who was listening to their whole conversation, allowing Saleem to work his magic.

"Who gave the idea that I did those things?" asked Sue.

"Look, it's either you do or you don't. This ain't a debate!" said Saleem, getting frustrated.

"Give me twenty dollars and I'll suck the skin off his dick," Sue said, jumping at the opportunity to make a few dollars. Saleem gave her the money and took everything that was in Boogs pocket. So she wouldn't try to rob him blind, Saleem rolled out. Boog didn't waste no time dropping his pants to his knees. Sue got on both knees and went to work like a certified mouth surgeon. Boog got amped up and started pushing her head further down on his manhood. He knew it would take hours to cum due to the amount of drugs he had in his system. So after receiving a few more head strokes, he thought about having sex with her.

"Hold up, this ain't working. Take those pants off," Boog demanded with a hand signal.

"But you didn't pay me for that," Sue said, pleading her case.

"Bitch, give me my Dub Back," Boog said, trying to get the twenty dollars back Saleem gave her, if she wasn't trying to meet his demands.

"Okay, I'll do it," Sue said bowing out gracefully. Giving the money back wasn't in her plans. She dropped her pants down to her ankles. Her butt was firm and perfect with no stretch marks. Boog stood there with his penis still hard as a brick.

"Yeah Bitch you're gonna get Daddy now," Boog said, verbally abusing her every chance he got.

"Do you have a condom?" asked Sue.

"Nope, I'ma Raw Dawg Boy," Boog said, nixing the thought of mentioning protection.

"Just don't cum in me please," Sue said, bending over touching her ankles. She couldn't have been no more than in her late twenties, early thirties, how flexible her body was. Boog positioned himself to enter her. For some reason she was loose and wet.

"Who's ass is this?" asked Boog, holding her by the waist, slamming all of his penis into her. She was pushing back on his penis trying to do all she could to get it over with. Minutes later Boog reached a climax letting all his frustration out inside her. And he stayed inside her until he felt he was done.

"Why did you cum in me?" Sue asked, sounding like she was about to cry.

"Shut up Bitch. I'll cum in your mouth next time," Boog blurted out trying to pull up his pants. He had no plans of using any rags or towels to wipe himself off. Sue didn't respond to the verbal abuse. She only mumbled words that Boog couldn't hear. While she was using a sheet off the bed to clean herself out, Boog slid through the door. Saleem was downstairs with the Jamaican bul B.

"Bumba clot man, rude boy make luv to she," B said, speaking to Boog coming down the steps.

"Goddamn lover boy, I thought you was up there making passionate love to a crack head," Saleem said.

"That trick got some good twat," said Boog.

"You went raw dawg too, didn't ya?" asked Saleem, knowing for a fact Boog didn't strap up on the girl Sue.

"Dirty Dick Boog, you know my name. If it ain't raw, it ain't me," Boog said, with a sly grin on his face. When they left Mom P's house, Wakil was still unconscious inside his car. He managed to switch positions and let the seat stretch back so he was comfortable. Even though Boog was still a little twisted, him and Saleem had to move Wakil to the back seat. Being as though Saleem was the only one sober, he had to make sure his partners-in-crime made it home safe. He left his car parked on Allison Street. Boog only lived around the corner so he was the first to be dropped off.

"Okay player you cool. Go wash up dirty dick," Saleem said.

"Alright Leem. I'll holler later," responded Boog.

Saleem waited for him to make it inside before pulling off. It was a few hours short from sunrise. *"I'm tired as shit,"* Saleem thought to himself yawning. He drove past Overbrook and seen a police car parked on the corner, but he didn't pay no attention to it. He was hoping he didn't get pulled over. As he pulled in front of Wakils' apartment, he thought about the three flights of stairs he had to climb up. It took him ten minutes helping Wakil up the steps.

"Man you heavy as shit. Get your ass up these steps," said Saleem using all his manpower to push Wakil's body weight. Saleem opened the door to Wakil's apartment and helped him to the couch. He left the house keys on the table and locked the door and made his exit. He didn't bother going back to his car, parking Wakil's car on the pavement across from his house. Saleem went straight to the couch only removing his boots. Within minutes he dozed off. The rest of his family was upstairs sound asleep. It was so quiet you could hear a pin drop.

Chapter 4

Still Grinding

A few days had passed and business was good for Saleem and Wakil. Even with the competition they were moving a kilo a week. So Saleem met with Charlie on the regular basis to re-up. And their relationship grew tighter since they met a year or so ago at a crap game on 56th and Master Street, on the side of the Jamaican store. Saleem had won all the money that day including Charlie's five thousand dollars. Saleem tried to give half of it back but Charlie declined to take it. He let him know that it was something small to him. He passed Saleem his cell number and told him don't let it go to waste. Charlie took a liken to him. They had been dealing with each other ever since.

Saleem was waiting on Shay at her house to drive her to work when his phone went off.

"Hello, who this?" asked Saleem, not recognizing the voice.

"It's Spud, your old head," the voice answered.

"Damn Spud, you sound different," said Saleem.

"I got a cold, but look the 3-2 line is around the corner, and Titty is getting all the money up here."

"Yeah, I'm on my way as soon as I drop Shay off," responded Saleem.

"Where her mom at?" asked Spud, inquiring about Ms. Lacy's whereabouts. They had something going on that had

Spud chasing her down from time to time. Who could blame him. Minus the drug's she was a dime for a old head.

"I think she's upstairs asleep," said Saleem.

"Alright, look hurry up. I'ma be here," Spud said.

"I'll be there, trust me," Saleem said, clicking him off. It was the first of the month, so checks were being cut and the 3-2 center, welfare spot was a goldmine from the first to the fifteenth of the month. Seconds later, Shay emerged down the stairs.

"You ready Boo?" she said smiling.

"Yeah, like an hour ago," responded Saleem.

"It's not easy looking this good Boo. You got a bad bitch," she said, sounding conceited.

"Yeah whatever," he said, trying to get to that money he was missing, waiting on her to get dressed like she was going to a fashion show.

"What the fuck you mean whatever? Now, I'm not the wifey you claimed I was?" she snapped, losing her composure.

"I didn't say that, so stop putting words in my mouth. You are my wife," Saleem said, not trying to add fuel to the fire.

"Who was that on your phone that has you up my ass, rushing me? Tell that slut Kita to suck somebody else's dick," she said, walking out the door letting the screen slam in Saleem's face. *This bitch is tripping*, he thought, following behind her.

"Why do you keep bringing up other chicks every time we argue about some bullshit?" asked Saleem. Shay failed to respond and just got in the car. As she just stared out of the car window, Saleem threw in a tape and drove off. All you heard was "Shame on A Nigga who tried to run game on a nigga," from Wutang Clan. Within a few blocks from Headquarters Hair Salon, neither one spoke a word to each other. Saleem turned the radio down as he pulled in front of the shop.

"What you mad now?" asked Saleem, breaking the silence.

"No, I'm not. I'm just tired of a lot that's going on in my life," Shay responded, still looking out the window.

"Like what?" asked Saleem, grabbing her by the face so she could look at him.

"Getting out of my mom's house for starters. My sister had moved out a year ago, and I'm still there," she said. You could see the sincerity in her eyes.

"Look, give me some more time and I promise we will find us a place to live," he said, bringing a half smile to her face. She knew Saleem had more than enough to move. So she didn't know the reason for the prolonging. But just knowing he was considering it was good enough for her. She kissed him sexually on the lips and exited the vehicle. All the girls from the salon were in the window glued to the action as though Saleem and Shay were part of a soap opera. He drove off after seeing the shop door buzz open.

✳ ✳ ✳ ✳ ✳

Since Mimis' return from Ethiopia, her and Wakil have been overwhelmed by all the make up sex they were having. It was hard for Wakil to resist her beauty. She was on the level of a quarter piece, weighing in at 140 pounds, 5'10", dark caramel complexion and light brown eyes. Her hair came below her neck. She was every man's dream girl. Mimi was the housewife and the freak all in one package. Even though she never caught him red handed cheating on her, she knew he wasn't faithful. Something's were better left unsaid.

"Wakil, get up. You've been asleep for hours," she said, kissing all over his face.

"What time is it babe?" he asked, trying to wipe the cold out the corner of his eyes.

"It's after 12:00," she said, rubbing his hard on.

"You trying to get something started, and it's still early. I'm my own boss so I can afford to get my sleep on," he said, covering his face with the pillow. Mimi was still massaging the shaft of his penis. Wakil couldn't help but feel intrigued by Mimi's seduction.

By the time Wakil removed the pillow from his face, Mimi was booty ball naked. She climbed in between his legs and headed straight for his manhood, taking him in her mouth. She went down and up with caution, locking on like a pair of vice grips. Wakil was loving it, watching her head movement. *Shit, that's why I love her*, he thought.

Laying stiff as a board with his hand on the side, Wakil had a lot of women in his life that would provide oral sex. But he considered Mimi the best. She twirled her tongue around his pee hole, then she lifted her body up and slid her vagina down his manhood. Wakil instantly felt her muscles tighten up on his manhood. She rode him like the Kentucky Derby, with them both reaching a climax. Mimi fell face down on his chest. They remained inside one another. You could hear heavy panting. Wakil kissed her on the forehead and rolled from underneath her.

"Let me go hop in the shower," he said, smacking her on the behind.

"When you going to buy me a car? I'm tired of driving your big station wagon," she said, still laying in the bed with the sheet half covering her nakedness.

"Not the way you just drove that wagon," he yelled, from the bathroom. Mimi smiled. She knew he was being fresh. She loved his sense of humor.

"Stop playing Wakil, I'm serious. All my girlfriends have cars," she said.

"And all them suck dick for a living. That's their occupation," he said, entering the room with nothing on, dripping wet. Mimi stared at her man's physique as she passed him a towel to dry off. She had plans of having babies by him. She knew every man had a weakness, and women was his.

"Why do you have to take it there about my friends, with the dogs you hang around?" she said.

"I hang around players," he responded, while lotioning his body.

"That's why you can't keep your dick in your pants player," she spoke humming the pillow at him.

"I'll buy you a squatter this week for now, and when my cheese gets where I want it to be, you'll be able to pick anything off the lot," he said.

"That's all I'm asking for. I know you hate driving me to the malls to shop," she said. Mimi knew being Wakil's girl she had access to a lot of stuff other girls weren't getting. They might've had what was in his pants, but she had that, plus more. He made her feel secure, being as though he was her bread and butter.

They met at a skating party up Elmwood Skating Rink almost a year ago. After they went out a few times they decided to move in together because the living arrangements at her aunt's wasn't working out. She had to share a room with her little cousin and she had no choice since the majority of her family lived in Ethiopia. Besides from the few arguments they had once in a while, they really loved each other, and she considered him a lifesaver.

* * * * *

"You see the line is still long. Titty has been killing them all morning," Raheem said, pointing at the people standing in front of 3-2 center.

"It's nothing. I had a few runs to make first," Saleem said, shaking his hand.

"Where you parked at?" asked Raheem.

"On Edgewood Street, next to the tree behind your car," responded Saleem, sitting on the chair in front of the 99¢ Store. Saleem and Raheem rented the building to open up the store. But Raheem and his wife Donna usually run the business the majority of the time. Saleem would only work there if they both had to go out somewhere. Saleem and Raheem met a year ago when Raheem and his family moved two houses away from the block Saleem hustled on, and 56th and Jefferson.

Being new to the neighborhood, he tried to stop the younger guys from selling drugs on the corner. But temptation got the best of him. So he started selling off his porch, only serving certain customers he met through family members who were already involved with the use of drugs. That didn't work. He only ended up with the same money he started off with.

"I'm gonna catch what's left of the dough," said Saleem, walking across the street to the bank. It was so many hustles out there besides the drugs. You had the food stamp game that was pulling in almost a quarter million or more from the first t-o the fifteenth of the month. You even had the Muslim brother selling oil and incenses on his stand. On top of the several stores that were located in the area, they had a police officer who would occasionally walk the beat, due to all the recent complaints about the pocketbook snatching. The grind continued no matter what.

"Yo Titty, what's up playboy?" said Saleem, walking up on him while he was serving a fiend.

"Ain't shit Leem, out here getting this bread," Titty responded, placing the small plastic bag full of nick rocks between his butt cheeks. He was every bit of three hundred plus pounds. Him and Biggie Smalls could've been brothers. Saleem and Titty wasn't always good friends. He didn't like it when Saleem came up there and started hustling, being as though he wasn't from up there.

"I figured you should be done by now," responded Saleem.

"Just about," Titty said, counting his money.

"Yeah, I'm trying to get rid of this stack pack and I'm gone," said Saleem. He knew that would be easy being as though he had nick bags the size of a nickel, compared to the pebbles Titty had, and he was only copping four and a half ounces. The 3-2 center was his only means of accumulated funds. They started serving the fiends left and right. Some people even placed their orders while in line waiting to pick up their check.

"What you doing tonight?" asked Titty.

"Don't know. I might shoot down north and get me a little taste," responded Saleem, putting his package of nick rocks back under his testicles.

"Nigga I'm surprised you're not twisted now. When I saw you I thought you was on a sober vacation," Titty said, laughing. At times he could be hilarious.

"Naw cuz, I ain't drink in like two days. But I'ma get me a shot tonight," said Saleem.

"Oh yeah? Well, do you cuz, I'm about to break out. I'll catch you in traffic," Titty said, shaking his hand. He jumped inside his two-door brown Cavalier. Nobody knew how he squeezed into that little car, but he did.

Saleem was almost done the thousand dollar pack he had first started out with. So he decided to slide back over to the store and kick it with Raheem. Saleem was in a position where he didn't have to hustle hand-to-hand on street corners no more. He did so by choice.

"Hey Leem, Salaamu-Alaikum," said Donna giving him the Islamic greetings that meant 'May peace be upon you.'

"Walakium Salaam," Saleem said, returning the greeting. He was Muslim but he didn't practice his religion like he was suppose to. As for Donna she wore the Khimar, the Islamic scarf for women, the majority of the time. Raheem and her would offer the Prayers, as well their three children, but failed to complete the five Prayers a day, that were mandatory upon every Muslim. They had one foot in the life of the streets and the other foot in the religion.

"So what you been up to? I thought you would beat us here this morning," said Donna, knowing most of the time Saleem would be outside the bank at seven o'clock, even though the bank didn't open until eight o'clock.

"You know chilling the usual," Saleem said, looking out the store window watching Raheem talk to a fiend about changing the brakes on his car.

"Well, business was good today. We sold a lot of items, but it usually is good around this time of the month," Donna said, while she was attending to a customer.

"Don't I know it," Saleem said. Time was flying by. The bank was minutes away from closing.

"Raheem gave the fiend two nick rocks to change his brakes on his two-door Escort that Saleem provided him with. They shut the store down. Saleem and Raheem promised to meet up later. So after he drove off, Raheem did so seconds later with his wife following behind him in her black, eighty nine Jaguar, which fit her full figured body. Raheem was a little on the heavy side too. So the Escort was a tight squeeze for him, which he purchased after his black Cadillac caught fire inside a mechanic's garage.

Saleem really looked out for Raheem and even though they were ten years apart in age, he had a lot of respect for the way he carried himself. Raheem didn't have a steady job. He was out on workman's compensation after having an accident at the construction site. So his income was light. Saleem was always a phone call away if he needed anything. That was the type of relationship they established once they met.

CHAPTER 5

AT THE SHOP

"Turn it up that's the jam," one of the employees yelled out at the shop. Power 99 FM was playing all slow jams, and 'Stroke You Up' by Changing Face's was on. The song had everybody in the uproar, snapping their fingers and bopping their heads to the rhyme.

"So Shay what's going on with you and Saleem? Are you taking him serious?" asked Jane. She was Shay's friend. They met around the same time when both of them started working at the shop. People called her the gossip queen, but men and women were infatuated by her unique beauty. She was half black and half Chinese, five foot five, 135 pounds with an apple bottom shape, small chinky eyes and I can't forget she was pigeon-toed.

"Yeah, it's serious. He gives me anything I want and we just spoke about me getting my own place," Shay said, still shampooing her customer's hair.

"That's right girl, don't be a fool. Get yours now because a lot of them will hit and run," Jane responded, while giving herself a pedicure.

"He ain't going nowhere. I got his ass turned out on this snapper," Shay spoke.

"Because this pussy ain't free, and a dick suck is extra," Jane said, laughing at her own blunt remark. She was high maintenance so getting inside her pants came with a price, no matter what.

"You crazy as hell girl, but you don't bite your tongue, and I like that in you," said Shay.

"And where's that Wakil been with his fine ass? Shit, I'll fuck 'em for free," Jane said, smiling at the thought of having him her way. People at the shop looked at her like she was a lost child in desperate need of some help.

"Oh no you didn't just ask me about that asshole, knowing damn well I can't stand his ass," Shay said.

"Why you hate Wakil so much? What did he do to you?" asked Jane, not really understanding her hate for the guy.

"You don't know the half of it. He thinks I'm stealing Saleem from him, because we be together more than them, so he tries to say smart shit to me whenever I'm around," she said.

"I want to give him a shot of this good pussy, turn his ass out. Do he still live with that girl on 61st and Nassu Road?" Jane asked, handing over the customer's change. She was the desk clerk at the shop, but she could do hair if need be.

"Yeah, I think they do. I hear she's loyal to him," Shay responded.

"I bet you he ain't loyal to her ass, that's for sure. Plus, once he taste this, she won't stand a chance," said Jane, with determination. She had no problem with playing dirty to get what she wanted.

"No one knows what their man is doing when they're out on the prowl. Most think with the little brain, not the big one," proclaimed Shay, putting the finishing touches on her client.

"I need both of my man's brains to be big," said Jane. Even the clients in the shop had to agree to that one. They all smiled and shook their heads. Jane had a habit of speaking without thinking. She always came right out with it.

"You a freak," Shay said, taking a seat in the chair where her client just departed from.

"Come on Shay, keep it real. You know if they ain't packing in that department it's out the door they go," said Jane, being as though she didn't have a steady relationship, she was free to test the water with anyone she chose. And guys were lined up to get in her pants.

"I'm glad I don't have to worry about that. My man is good in that area," Shay responded, as her thoughts flashed back to the episodes she and Saleem had in her bedroom.

"Do you think Wakil's dick is big?" asked Jane, as though she was psychic.

"Stop asking me about him. You're going to have to find out yourself," Shay said.

"I plan to do just that as soon as I see his ass. He won't be able to resist me. No man can," Jane said sounding conceited.

"He'll be around, trust me. Wakil and Saleem are tied at the waist." Shay was right, they were inseparable.

"Let Saleem know I'm trying to holler at his man asap," Jane said.

"I'll do that, so don't have a heart attack. He ain't all that," responded Shay.

"Trust me, I'll fill you in on every detail," Jane spoke, feeling horny at the thought of sleeping with Wakil.

"Save me the drama of your little sexcapade," Shay said. But in reality her panties was getting wet and she couldn't understand why. She didn't like Wakil, but that had nothing to do with him being attractive.

"Whatever Shay," Jane said, rolling her eyes. They continued to talk most of the day. Being as though the owner wasn't around to stop them, they could get away with gossiping during work hours. Because Kim, the owner was a no nonsense kind of person, her mojo was business before pleasure. Majority of the time Shay and Jane paid her little attention. They did them by any means.

＊ ＊ ＊ ＊ ＊

On the other side of the city Saleem and KB his youngbul were at Bob Turner's barber shop on 55th and Landsdown, across from the Dominican store getting fresh cuts. Even though they had no plans of going anywhere, keepin' up their appearance was mandatory. Some people made appointments with their regular barber, but walk-ins were frequent.

"A old head, where Wah at?" asked KB. He was only sixteen, 5'4", dark skin and weighed 110 pounds soaking wet. The young and older girls were attracted to his baby face.

"I don't know youngin'. I seen him earlier," responded Saleem, sitting in the chair right across from KB. The barber shop wasn't that crowded, even though all eight chairs were being occupied.

"He came through earlier and dropped something off on Nell. I haven't seen him since," KB said, getting out of the barber's chair to check his cut out in the mirror.

"Oh yeah, because I know Nell said he only had something small," responded Saleem. As soon as Vaughn, the barber was about to remove the drape from Saleem's neck, somebody came from behind him and placed a gun to his back. Vaughn froze. He was petrified. Saleem seen through the mirror that a tall female with dark shades, long hair in a scarf wrapped around her neck was glued to Vaughn's back. Saleem didn't think nothing of it.

"Vaughn what's up with your chick. I see you like them tall," said KB, walking over towards Saleem until a short guy jumped up from one of the other chairs and pointed a gun to his head. KB figured it was a robbery so he stopped instantly and raised his hands in the air. Saleem hopped up to react reaching for his gun, coming up empty handed, after realizing that he left it in his coat pocket. The lady who had Vaughn at a standstill, pushed him to the floor and pointed the pistol at Saleem's head.

"Look baby girl be easy with that thing. I got a lot of money in my right pocket. Just let me and my youngbul go," said Saleem, trying to negotiate with the armed bandits. It was three of them no one would've expected the guy who was sitting by the entrance of the barber shop was a stick up man. He closed all the blinds in the windows and pulled a Tech 22 automatic out from his black leather trench coat.

"Shut up. You don't dictate nothing here. I'm holding the gun," the female bandit said. Snapping her fingers she ordered the guy who was holding KB at bay to search everybody in the shop. They made all the barbers and the customers lay on the floor, lined up in a row.

"Look sweetheart this ain't worth it. Take the money and roll. You can make a clean break," suggested Saleem, still trying to bargain himself out of an unfortunate situation.

"Didn't I tell you to shut the fuck up," the female bandit spoke. She snapped her fingers again, ordering one of the other guys to make Saleem stop talking. He took his gun and smacked Saleem across his head with blunt force, causing a small gash on the back of his head that immediately started to leak blood. KB was thinking about reaching for his gun that was underneath him in the waist of his pants. He was waiting for a window of opportunity to make his move.

After the guy hit Saleem, he continued searching pockets. When he got to the elderly lady who was trying to shield her son from the events that were taking place, she put up a little resistance until the gunman started getting aggressive by bending her arm behind her back.

When he got to KB he pulled a few hundred dollars out of his pants pocket. Then he tried to flip him over on his back. KB shot twice, hitting the gunman in his chest, then turned his gun on the lady who looked to be running the whole operation. He squeezed until the eight shot 380 caliber was empty. The lady bandit let off a few shots as she ran out of the barber shop with one of her assailants. The other one laid there barely breathing.

"Old head come on we gotta go before the police come," KB said, helping Saleem stand up.

"I'm right behind you. Vaughn keep our names out of it. I don't care what you guys say or do," said Saleem, throwing a hundred dollar bill on the chair before grabbing his coat and running out the door. Even though it was dark outside, it was only a little after seven o'clock, when Saleem and KB pulled off in his car.

"I might've killed that cat, old head," KB spoke, with his heart beating fast. He didn't know what to expect out of that ordeal.

"So what. You did good. That took heart and balls. That gun hurt. I think I'ma need some stiches in my head," Saleem said, touching his wound to see if it was still bleeding. It wasn't as bad as he thought it was, but he knew that it would require some stitches. Saleem took his gun and hid it in a vacant lot near his house, and took KB's gun off of him after wiping the fingerprints off it. He tossed it on top of an abandoned building three blocks down from his house, and headed to Presbyterian Medical Center on 38th and Powelton Avenue right behind Scooter's bar.

CHAPTER 6

THE DAY AFTER

The police were out looking for the barber shop bandits and someone to pin it on. Unfortunately, the third suspect didn't make it. Besides from Saleem getting hit in the head, everyone else was unharmed. Vaughn, the barber, as well as everybody else who were present during the robbery never mentioned Saleem and KB being there. Instead they were looked at as heroes in the victims eyes, on top of being one themselves. So KB was back on the block hustling and the hood was praising him for the work he had put in. Saleem was laying back in the house being cared for by Shay due to the migraine headaches he was experiencing off and on.

"Saleem," Ms. Cee yelled from her bedroom.

"Yeah mom," Saleem answered, walking to the bottom of the steps to see the reason for her calling for him.

"Give me a couple dollars so I can go to bingo?" Ms. Cee asked.

"Alright mom, I got you," Saleem responded. She could get anything she wanted from Saleem if he had it. Ms. Cee took care of him all his life including his three siblings. She knew he was hustling. With no father figure around, it wasn't much she could tell him to convince him that the lifestyle he was trying to live was the wrong road to take. Even though she tried on several occasions. Who could blame him, tired of seeing his mom struggle to provide for four kids. She moved from a town called Levittown, PA inside of Bucks County, where Saleem lived with his grandmom and grandpop along with his mom, two sisters and little brother. Living in a neighborhood predominately white, they all attended East Spencer Miller Elementary School.

Although racism existed, it wasn't popular around there. All their friends were Caucasians. As time went on Ms. Cee felt it was time for her to move on. She took her children and moved in a shelter for a couple of months. She put her pride to the side, determined to keep all four of her children together. That didn't last long after being packed in one room with three beds. So Ms. Cee moved back to Philadelphia where most of her family resided, after scoring a job at Woodschool the same place her mother worked, but different buildings.

This job consists of caring for disabled children. Securing income allowed her to move into her own house that was made available due to Saleem and his sister Hazel's grandmother on their father's side of the family. All four of her children attended Heston Elementary School, followed by Shoemaker Middle School and Overbrook High School with only her oldest child graduating. Being as though Baker's playground was directly across from where they lived, they didn't have to go far to play. But at times that wasn't good due to the amount of drugs that was being sold there throughout the mid-eighties.

By 1990 Saleem was introduced to the drug game. Majority of those involved was his family, so it was easy for him to get access to a package. Not wanting his mom to find out he was hustling, he lied and said he won the money gambling. He hustled on 56th and Jefferson, three blocks away from where he lived. So Ms. Cee never actually saw him selling drugs until he got arrested and she had to pick him up at 8th and Race, the Round House.

"Leem what's up?" asked Malik, Saleem's little brother. He was only two years younger than him but almost the same height, 170 pounds and brown eyes. They looked nothing alike. Malik favored his mother more.

"Ain't nothing youngin'," responded Saleem.

"Did you find out who these dudes were who robbed the barber shop?" asked Malik, sitting down across from Saleem and Shay.

"Naw, but now that I look back, the chick was tall as shit and cocky, like she had balls too," spoke Saleem.

"Yaw got robbed by a girl?" Malik said, shocked by hearing that one of the bandits was a female.

"Yeah nigga, a bitch with a gun! Ya know the first one who makes the draw, makes the law," Saleem responded.

"Nigga I just asked! Fuck you getting loud with?" Malik said, with aggression in his tone. They stayed arguing with each other. Punches were barely thrown.

"Curve your tongue young boy, before I have to spank ya," Saleem said, showing a sly grin.

"Yeah whatever sucker," Malik responded.

"Malik chill out, yaw fight too much," said Shay, intervening in the argument.

"Here you go, mind your business," Malik said, flagging his hand at her. She just rolled her eyes and leaned back on Saleem. Ms. Cee was coming down the steps on her way to bingo. The dispute between Malik and Saleem had calmed down due to Ms. Cee's presence, even though she witness them argue on a regular basis.

"Saleem I'm leaving. Debb just pulled up out front," Ms. Cee spoke, sticking her hand out in front of him.

"Hi Ms. Cee," Shay spoke.

"Hey Shay," Ms. Cee responded. She was one of the nicest ladies you would ever meet and would do anything to help you if she could. Ms. Cee was only in her early forties but didn't look it. She was brown skinned, 5'9", 190 pounds with chubby cheeks, and short dark hair.

"Here mom. You keep gambling, losing all your money," Saleem said, passing her a hundred and fifty dollars.

"Look at the kettle calling the pot black," Ms. Cee said on her way out the door. Shay and Malik started laughing. They knew Ms. Cee was right. Saleem was in no position to be pointing the finger, all the dirt he did on a daily basis. Seconds later Saleem's cell phone went off.

"Hello," spoke Saleem.

"Old head we out and the block is jumping," KB said, calling from a phone booth on Master Street.

"We'll come on through. Where's Nell at?" asked Saleem.

"He out here across the street," said KB.

"Alright, I'll be waiting on you," Saleem assured him, hanging up the phone. He got up from the couch and ran up the steps and went straight to his mom's room where his safe was. He opened it, grabbing a brown bag full of money and the zip lock bag that was next to it filled with small bags of crack. He dumped all the money on the bed, then reached back in the safe, bringing out more that was already counted in stacks of thousands. By the time he finished, and added all the money up, he had sixty seven thousand dollars. *I ain't know it was that much*, he thought. He put seventeen grand back inside the safe and left the rest out. It was time to call his connect. He dialed Charlie.

✳ ✳ ✳ ✳ ✳

Wakil and Mimi had been arguing for the last half hour, only because someone told Mimi they had seen a woman driving Wakil's car last night.

"Shit, I'm not trying to argue with you," Wakil said, walking towards the door.

"Every time I confront you about one of those sluts you run out on me," she responded.

"You keep listening to those dippy broads. They want your position, that's all," he said, flopping down on the couch. Even though he loved her, at times she could be a nuisance. He was good at turning the tables to make her out to be the guilty one. She never really inquired about his cheating. Her news came from her girlfriends.

"Boo, I don't want to keep going back and forth. Who cares what my girlfriends think or say," she responded, sitting beside him.

"Well, act like it," he responded, with aggressiveness in his voice. Even though it was a front, he couldn't let her know it.

"Dag Boo, you ain't gotta say it like that. No need to get mad," she said, reaching in to kiss him seductively, causing him to reach an instant hard on. The sound of the phone ringing broke the momentum.

"Yeah, who this?" asked Wakil.

"Yo player, where you at?" inquired Saleem.

"I'm at my spot chilling. I got the money from Mary and Kita was looking for you," Wakil said.

"Oh yeah, I know what she want. I ain't give her none in a while with Shay occupying all my time. I can't get to her," Saleem said.

"So how your head feel?" asked Wakil questioning his wellbeing.

"I'm cool. Look it's time to move on something else. I hollered at Charlie and he heard about the barber shop twist, so I told him you would be coming," Saleem said.

"Cuz you know me and dude don't twist at all," Wakil said, not trying to deal with someone he didn't trust.

"It took a lot of convincing him. he wasn't trying to meet no one but me," Saleem said.

"Where do I have to meet him at? I think dude is shady," Wakil said.

"He'll meet you on 60th and Arch Street at eight o'clock sharp. Look for a black Taurus wagon. Take Boog with you to watch your back, Charlie said. He'll be parked by the real estate building on the corner," Saleem said, giving him detail by detail.

"I'm take my 357 Magnum with me to watch my back." Wakil wasn't taking no chances of getting caught slipping.

"Cool, just be safe. Cop and roll out. You can't be bullshitting with two birds," Saleem said.

"Two, oh you stepped the order up." Wakil responded, surprised by the sudden boost in product.

"Nigga, it's now or never. We moving at a fast pace. Why not step it up," Saleem said.

"I ain't mad at ya. Let's do the damn thing," Wakil said, with other plans in mind.

"Well, come grab this fifty thousand," Saleem spoke, not mentioning the other he still had tucked. It really didn't matter Wakil had his own stash.

"I'm on my way as soon as I finish here with Mimi. She's tripping," Wakil said.

"Yeah, you know Jane is trying to get at ya," Saleem spoke, feeling elated about giving him the news. Believe it or not he fantasized about Jane many times, but never thought about crossing that line.

"From the hair salon, chinky eyes with the crazy walk and fat ass?" asked Wakil, looking in the direction of the bedroom to see if Mimi was coming back. He was astonished by the fact she was asking about him, knowing how he dogged women.

"That be her," Saleem affirmed.

"She must want some dick. I might gotta put that juice in my system just to secure my performance," Wakil said.

"Look, hurry up," Saleem said.

"My foot is out the door." Wakil hung up the phone. *This is the break I've been looking for*, he thought to himself. Massaging his chin, trying to plan his next move, evil thoughts were lurking in his mind. That wasn't good. Charlie was in for a surprise of his life and whatever was about to take place had to be done professionally, never tracing back to him. Saleem would never expect Wakil to cross him. He trusted him too much. With plenty of time left to organize a solid ambush on Charlie, Wakil went to inform Mimi he was leaving.

"Hey Mimi, come here for a second," called Wakil.

"What is it?" Mimi yelled back at him like she was asleep.

"I'm going to meet Leem. I'll be back shortly," Wakil responded.

"No, what time are you coming back?" Mimi asked, not wanting him to leave.

"Cool out. I'll be back in a flash," Wakil said, kissing her on the lips as she tried to grab hold of his manhood. He managed to slip away from her seduction, after convincing her he would be back and they would finish what she was trying to start.

"Okay, just hurry up," Mimi said, kissing him back.

Wakil was out. With no time to waste he shot straight to Saleem's house, with nothing on his mind but the come up. Still not sure of how he was going to lay the blueprint, there was no room for mistakes. He parked in front of his mom's house on Hunter Street. He quickly exited and ran on Saleem's porch. Before he had a chance to knock on the door, Saleem had opened it like he knew he was there.

"Let's move player," Saleem said, walking back to the dining room table where the money was piled up.

"You're home alone I see," Wakil spoke, looking around the house like it was his first time there.

"Yeah, my mom went to bingo and I don't know where Malik is at. Shay just left. She knew you was coming so she got ghost," Saleem said, sitting down and placing the money inside a carry-on bag. After he finished, he pushed it towards Wakil.

"Fifty grand huh? You made sure the count was right?" Wakil said, taking a look inside the bag.

"No doubt, I double checked. Plus it's put in stacks of thousands," Saleem responded assuring him the fifty thousand was all there.

"Where's Jane number at? 'Cause as soon as I handle this business, I'm at shorty," Wakil spoke, still not able to exit her from his memory bank. Saleem gave him the number. He concealed it in his back pocket with intentions of using it.

"She look good to Wah. If her and Shay weren't that close, I would try my luck," Saleem said.

"Man you might can still smash. These bitches is whores out here," Wakil said.

"That's too close to home. Can't shit where you lay at cuz, real rap," Saleem responded, not biting the bait Wakil was throwing at him.

"Leem you fooling man. That's the game stick and move, if you get caught deny that shit," Wakil said.

"Shay be trying to do everything to me that's freaky to turn a nigga out, so I won't cheat," Saleem responded.

"It's working too. I seen Kita earlier and she was looking like a million bucks and the jeans she had on were glued to that fat ass of hers," Wakil said, breaking out in a loud laughter.

"Nigga, you told me already, you stalking my broad," Saleem said.

"Cuz you know I got hoes by the dozen and I'm adding Jane to my list tonight." Wakil was speaking with confidence and he hadn't even spoke to her yet.

"Secure that Charlie business first, champ," Saleem spoke, putting his man back on point to what was more important.

"Yeah, it's done. Let me split now. Early bird always gets the worm," Wakil responded. They both embraced each other as always. With a half hour still remaining before he made the pick up, Wakil had to think fast. Boog was coming in as Wakil walked out. They both greeted each other and kept it moving.

"Where's speed racer going?" asked Boog.

"He's going handle some business. I'm going to go pay my water bill," Saleem said, with his mind set on going down North Philly to get a drink of syrup and pills.

"Man you think that's a good idea with that head wound?" Boog asked, thinking about his friend's wellbeing instead of using drugs.

"Boog, I'm straight homey. Besides, from the headaches, a drink will cure it, believe that," Saleem responded.

"Well Let's ride playboy," spoke Boog. He didn't need that much syrup and pills to comatose him.

"If you're drinking, I got you, so tuck your funds. We family and if I'm up, you're up. If you want the delt, you got it," Saleem said, shutting the TV off and heading out the door.

"Don't matter. I'll chill until you get that apartment, then we can shoot to the auction and buy a squadder," said Boog.

"Man when Wah makes the move he went to make, we'll be straight. Shit, I can get you a wheel now, but I'm waiting to see how this package turns out," Saleem responded, driving down Lansdown Avenue, with the Charlie and Wakil meeting still lingering in the back of his mind. He knew sometimes Wakil could screw things up, but this wasn't the time for mistakes and failure didn't exist.

"A little sucker shot, a ounce of yellow and about eight blues (Xanex), that'll smooth me over," Boog said, adjusting his seat, getting comfortable for the short ride.

"Damn you trying feel it for real. I ain't doing no babysitting tonight. A cop car is right behind me, so don't get up, just chill," Saleem said, a little paranoid because he was carrying a firearm with no driver's license. But the cop turned off, paying him no attention.

"You cool, or is he still behind you?" asked Boog, still laying down in the seat.

"He turned off," Saleem said continuing to drive to his destination.

CHAPTER 7

THE SCORE

Wakil had drove down 52nd and Girard Avenue, out West Philly, to pick up two of his young comrades who were known for putting in work. Wakil had the plan set up. Once the cocaine was secured and he walked back to his vehicle, Lil' Dizzy and Webb were to murder Charlie and take the black bag with the money in it. Parked on the corner of Dewy Street between Market and Arch Street, he ran the plot down several times to Lil' Dizzy and Webb as though he was trying to get them to perfect their craft.

"Listen Webb you come from the driver's side, Lil' Dizzy you got the passenger side. As soon as you see me exit the car that's your cue to move," Wakil said, making sure his plan was executed properly.

"We got you old head. This will be homeboy's last breath he'll ever take," Lil' Dizzy responded, pulling the chamber back on his chrome forty-five automatic pistol. Lil' Dizzy was only 5'9", brown skin, 160 pounds, with a bad scar under his left eye which he endured due to his stepfather abusing him when he was younger.

"No time to get stage fright now. It's all or nothing," Wakil said, trying to install confidence into them.

"Wah we got you! Don't keep acting like we don't ride. We ain't rookies," Webb said, sliding on his black leather gloves like he was preparing for warfare. He was 5'11", 165 pounds, dark skin and sported a 1960's afro. It was eight o'clock on the nose. So Webb and Lil' Dizzy got back inside their blue Celebrity station wagon. They watched Wakil drive up to 60th and Arch Street, keeping their distance, but still keeping him in eyesight. He parked on the opposite side of the street from where the Taurus was stationed at.

People were walking up and down the block on both sides of the street, women and children. *I hope these Niggaz don't do nothing stupid*, Wakil thought to himself, while placing his gun on the right side of his coat pocket for easy access. As he got out of the car, he looked all around him to make sure the police wasn't on him. You could smell the aroma of southern cooking in the air. He could see that the wagon, Webb and Lil' Dizzy was in clear view. Not trying to look suspicious, he quickly focused back on the Taurus. Tapping on the window, the door opened and Wakil got in, coming face to face with a man he despised for the second time and possibly his last.

"Come on youngin'. You got the money? This shit ain't legal!" Charlie said, in a demanding voice. Usually he would intimidate people with his size, but Wakil wasn't fazed at all.

"Here you go." Wakil passed him the money. Charlie placed it on the back seat and returned with a city blue clothing bag and gave it to Wakil.

"So do I have to count it or not?" asked Charlie, looking over at Wakil.

"Naw it's all there. Saleem made sure of that, alright Charlie," Wakil said, clutching the bag with his left hand and the door handle with the other, rushing out, not trying to get caught by police with a gun and coke.

"Hold up youngin'. Tell Saleem I threw something extra in there for him and to call me," responded Charlie, still holding on to Wakil's shoulder.

By the time he made it back to his car, Webb and Lil' Dizzy were easing up. And Charlie didn't see them coming Blah, Blah, Blah, Blah . . . Multiple shots were fired into the vehicle. A lady happen to be passing by with her son. She started screaming and dragging the child like he was a piece of garbage. Lil' Dizzy opened the driver door and to his surprise Charlie was still breathing, until Webb shot twice more in his head. All you saw was brains splattered all over the window. Webb grabbed the bag out of the back seat, after recognizing it was the same one Wakil carried earlier. Both ran back to the car, breathing heavy with their guns still out.

You could hear sirens wailing. Lil' Dizzy and Webb drove past the scene of the crime looking at the bullet holes that were in Charlie's car, admiring the work they had just put in. They continued straight down Arch until reaching 56th Street, taking it all the way up to Landsdown Avenue. Spotting Wakil standing outside his mom's house they parked right behind his car.

"You niggaz are crazy, but I like the sound of those guns going off. Is the chump dead?" asked Wakil, with his adrenalin pumping.

"As a door knob," responded Webb, passing Wakil the black book bag.

"Now keep this shit hush. It never happened," Wakil spoke, placing a zip lock bag full of cocaine into Webb's hand.

"No doubt old head. My lips are sealed, good looking out. How much is this worth?" asked Lil' Dizzy, smiling at what Wakil just gave to Webb. They thought they hit the lottery. It was a lot of drugs for them, being as though they sold packs for other people, if they weren't robbing somebody.

"It's something the corpse put in the bag. It looks like nine ounces or more," Wakil spoke. He also gave them a couple of thousand dollars a piece.

"Anytime you need us, you know where to find us on the block. Hey old head, what happened to Chris that got killed trying to rob a barber shop? He said he was meeting with you that same night," asked Webb, inquiring about someone who was part of the crew.

"Yeah he called me but I was busy, so I guess he just rolled out on some blind date shit," Wakil said, brushing the question to the side by not giving them a straight answer, when he really knew. He got rid of their weapons so there wouldn't be no evidence linking back to them. Wakil was smiling at the fact of being fifty thousand dollars richer with no plans of breaking Saleem off. He looked at it as another step to the top, which he was aiming for. The days of living in Saleem's shadow was slowly coming to an end.

✳ ✳ ✳ ✳ ✳

One day when I was riding on the train I heard these two kids talking about the Nubian rain has fallen. Saleem and Boog were in the zone coming back from North Philly, listening to Brand Nubian, a old school rap group. The syrup and pills hadn't kicked in yet, so they were smoking a blunt. it was fuel to boosting their high.

"Where Wakil at? He ain't call me yet to give me the status of that package, and to let me know he was alright," Saleem said, sounding worried about his friend.

"Wah probably scored and went to lay up with one of those broads," Boog responded, blowing smoke out his mouth from the weed he was smoking.

"Damn, I forgot he was suppose to holler at the chick, Jane," Saleem remembered, as the thought popped in his mind.

"Who the hell is Jane?" inquired Boog.

"This chick that works with Shay. She's half black, half Chinese with a body and walk that'll make a married man file for divorce," Leem said, picturing Jane in his mind.

"Shit my dick got hard when you said she was Chinese," Boog responded, hyped up about the female Saleem was informing him about.

"Family I'll cry to you before I lie to you. She a bad bitch," said Saleem, assuring Boog that she was a dime piece. He double parked in front of Mary's house on 56th and

64

Frazier, between Landsdown and media Street. As Saleem approached the door you could hear a dog barking. Being as though the row houses were so close, it was hard to tell where the barks were coming from. He rang the bell and a little baby opened the door with a diaper on. Saleem took it upon himself to walk in.

"Where's your mom at?" asked Saleem, speaking to J.T. one of Mary's sons. He had a little sugar in his tank, if you know what I mean.

"She's upstairs. Mom, Saleem's down here!" J.T. yelled at the top of his lungs, loud enough to wake the dead. In return, you heard her screaming that she would be right down.

"Hey Saleem, I been finished hours ago," Mary spoke, passing him a wad of mixed bills. She moved a lot of drugs out of her residence, making a transition from using them to selling it. A lot of her clientele came from those people she used to get high with.

"Did you call my phone?" asked Saleem.

"No, I told my son to beep you," Mary answered.

"I don't have nothing right now, so if you can wait until tomorrow I got something nice for you," Saleem responded. He always showed her love and no matter what, she remained loyal to him.

"Yeah I can wait," Mary said. She was old enough to be his mother.

"Where Kita at?" Saleem asked, changing the subject. His eyes kept closing and opening as he spoke.

"She's around the corner," spoke Mary, while changing her grandson's diaper. Kita lived on 56th and Media Street with her son's father, mother. Kita was Mary's oldest daughter. Saleem made his way to the door almost tripping on a baby's toy. Mary just shook her head. She knew he was high. Traffic was backed up and Boog was knocked out with his head leaning against the window. He didn't even hear the horns honking.

"Boog get up homey. Why you ain't move the car? You in here drooling all over yourself," Saleem said, shaking Boog back to consciousness.

"Naw, I'm good Leem," Boog responded, wiping the saliva dripping from his mouth. Saleem pulled around the corner outside Kita's apartment, right across from it, because there was a bunch of younger guys who hustle drugs in front of her door. From the outside it looked like a house, but it really was a two-story apartment and she stayed on the second floor. They both exited the vehicle.

"Well, I'ma slide up here real quick and holler at Kita, you coming up?" Saleem asked.

"No. I'ma chill out here with the youngins'," Boog said, standing against the wall, lighting up the half blunt he pulled out of his back pocket. They all spoke to Saleem as he walked past them. People ran in and out of the building on a regular basis. The bannister was falling apart but due to the state of mind Saleem was in, he had to hold on to it walking up the steps. The apartment was only a step away from being a trash dump. No one understood how a good looking girl like Kita would subject herself to that type of environment, even though her room was an exception to the circumstances. Her door was closed, so he entered without knocking. She was caught off guard, so she started yelling out.

"Hold up, Kita it's me," Saleem said, closing the door behind him. Recognizing the voice, she immediately became calm. It was dark in her room. The only light came from when the door opened.

"Oh shit boo, my bad. I thought you was one of those guys out front," Kita spoke, walking over to lock the door and turning on the night lamp.

"What you doing running around here naked for anyway?" Saleem responded, mesmerized by her body every time he saw her nudeness. She was gorgeous standing at 5'8", 160 pounds, bow-legged with emerald green eyes. At twenty-one years old, with three children, she was in good shape showing no signs of giving birth.

"I just got out of the tub a few minutes before you showed up," Kita said, removing her towel like she was giving him a striptease.

"Then I'm just in time," Saleem said, putting his jacket on the chair. The room was big enough to fit a queen size bed and dresser and a nineteen-inch color TV. Her clothes and shoes were neatly positioned in the closet by the tape deck stereo system.

"Check you out all high up again," Kita spoke, sitting on the edge of the bed watching him like a hawk.

"A little tipsy, nothing major," Saleem responded, easing his way over to her. He unlaced his boots and kicked them off to the side.

"I told you before I hate it when you're like that. You can't even keep your eyes open," Kita said, massaging his face with her soft hands. Kita was in love with Saleem. Even got pregnant by him before, but lost the baby. They always knew each other, but never spoke until Kita started coming over to her aunt's house, where Saleem cooked and packaged his drugs. She's been one of his girls ever since. Plus on top of him and her mom having business relations that made their bond tighter and she was well aware of Shay. But she didn't mind being second or third as long as she was in his life. Kita even got a tattoo with his name on her leg as a sign of loyalty to him.

"What you, my mother now? I'm cool, I told you," Saleem said, laying back on the bed.

"No, I'm not your mom, but I love you and care about you. Those drugs will kill you," she said, leaning over to kiss him seductively. Her lips were soft as silk. He became semi-hard as she continued to wiggle her tongue inside his mouth.

"Whoa, sexy momma," he spoke, grasping for air. She was trying to suck his tongue off. Even though he enjoyed the feeling, he would've rather had her mouth somewhere else on his body.

"Chill boo, let me take care of my man," she said, unbuttoning his pants and sliding them down to his ankles. His manhood was standing at attention. Kita climbed on top of him, teasing the head of his penis with her vagina. Then she slid down positioning her lower body on his legs. She took all of him in her mouth like she didn't have no tonsils.

All you heard was silent moans coming from Saleem. The pleasure he was receiving from Kita's mouth made his toes twitch. After moistening his penis with saliva, she straddled him, positioning her vagina around the shaft of his manhood.

"Oh yeah baby," Saleem mumbled, grabbing hold of her waist and helping her thrust harder on his penis. With her being a few years older than Saleem she was well experienced in the sexual department. Each time she moved her body down on him, her vagina muscles tightened up, causing her to have multiple orgasms. She remained speechless. He was still looking to reach his first one. The drugs allowed him to go for a long time. After a few more strokes, she felt his release come rapidly. Kita didn't lift up off of him until she was sure every drop of him was inside her, rolling over beside him with semen dripping down her legs. She grabbed a sheet to cover up their nakedness. Saleem was slowly dozing off. Startled by a loud knock on Kita's door.

"Who is it?" asked Kita, as they both leaped off the bed in a state of shock, bearing all.

"Mont, Boog said to tell Saleem to come on," he said, walking away without waiting for a response. Lamont was her baby's dad's little brother.

"Damn, I forgot Boog was out there," Saleem said, pulling his pants up.

"Why you didn't say Boog was with you. I thought you was spending the night," Kita spoke, sounding disappointed that he had to leave. Saleem got dressed in a flash.

"Look, stop acting like that. I'ma come through tomorrow and holler at you, plus I'm stop at your mom's crib. Do you need some money?" Saleem asked her, exposing a wad of money.

"Yeah, but that still doesn't get you off the hook," Kita responded, clicking on the light switch so Saleem could see what he was doing.

"I like being hooked to you," Saleem said. He gave her five one-hundred dollar bills, kissed her and rolled out as she locked the door behind him.

Wakil did his rounds collecting money from a few of the spots they had. There was no product to leave behind. Wakil had no plans of calling Saleem tonight to help cook and bag up the drugs. Riding around with ten-thousand dollars in his pocket, he didn't know what to do.

The Charlie incident still lingered in the back of his mind. Going down North Philly to get a drink was suicide. If somebody was seeking revenge for Charlie's death they wouldn't catch him slipping. With Saleem not aware of the fact his old head was dead, things were going to get a lot worse.

Damn I almost forgot about Jane, he just thought, as he fumbled through his pockets, finding her number. Wakil pulled into the Sunoco gas station on 52nd and Spruce across from Big George's Soul Food. It was a little after twelve o'clock, so people were still eating at the restaurant. He parked alongside the phone booth, not sure if she was asleep or not. Pulling out his cell phone, he took a chance and dialed her number. The phone rang twice before someone answered.

"Yes, who's calling?" the soft voice spoke.

"It's Wakil. Can I speak to Jane?" asked Wakil, sounding like he was calling from a club with the music playing in the background.

"Wakil, this is her," Jane responded, wondering when he was going to call.

"Saleem gave me your handle and told me you said to holler at you. Sorry for the delay," Wakil said.

"Better late than never, and where you calling from, a club or something?" she asked, hearing the loud music playing in the background.

"I'm at the Sunoco on 52nd and Spruce Street. That's my stereo system you're hearing," he responded, turning it down.

"For real! I live a few blocks from there on 54th and Addison, down the street from the police station," she said, excited about him being in her neighborhood.

"Are you giving me an invite?" asked Wakil, making it clear he was trying to come through.

"Why not? I never thought I would let the player himself in my house," she spoke.

"Don't believe everything you hear. A lot of people hate, it's a disease," was his response. Everybody knew he had girls at his service anytime he wanted and needed them.

"I don't care if you do or not, so come on. I'll be waiting," she said anxiously. After Wakil locked her address in, he drove straight there passing by the police station, not bothering to cut the radio back on. He had to drive past there with caution because if he got pulled over, the cops would have an early Christmas gift, with no job to account for the ten thousand dollars he was carrying around. He definitely didn't have a permit to carry a gun he stole. He parked right in front of the address she gave him. From the outside appearance the house looked to be in good shape. By the time he got out of his car, Jane was standing at the door waiting, draped in a red Victoria Secret nightgown that fit her curves to the maximum, not to mention the matching bedroom slippers that exposed her freshly pedicured toes. Jane wore her long hair in a ponytail.

"Long time no see stranger," she said, opening the door to let him in.

"I been around," he responded, allowing his eyes to deviate through her house. It was plush from the thick black carpet to the matching sofa and recliner, as well as the 52" floor model TV set, a few inches away from the china cabinet.

"You use to come past the shop with Saleem to pick up Shay," she said, sitting by Wakil on the loveseat.

"Yeah, I've been a little busy trying to get my finances in order," he said.

"Looks like you're doing fine to me. You can make yourself comfortable my heat work," she spoke, referring to Wakil still wearing his coat and hat.

"I see you're not doing bad yourself. This is a big house to live in by your lonesome," he said, loving the elegant taste she had in decorating, as he removed his hat and coat.

"My grandmom passed away, and left this house to me and my drunken ass uncle. She responded, watching Wakil's every move as though she was obsessed.

"Sorry to hear about your loss," he responded, searching his coat pocket for a blunt he stashed earlier.

"Thank you. She's been dead for over two years now. I still visit her gravesite every year, but enough of that. Do you want something to eat or drink?" she offered, standing up in front of him with her nightgown slightly open exposing her cleavage.

"A cold glass of water will do," he said.

"That's all you want? Don't come over here +9 with that shy shit Wakil," she spoke, holding her hands on her hips.

"I'm far from that. Maybe some other time. Do you mind if I spark this?" he asked, twisting the blunt in between his fingers. Food was the last thing on his mind.

"Yeah, let me grab your water. We can go upstairs to my room," she said, walking off, switching her butt. Wakil couldn't take his eyes off her. He enjoyed the view he had following her up the steps. She clicked her night lamp on to keep the room dim. Wakil had his money inside of his coat so he brung it with him.

"It's real cozy in here. I like this whole layout," he said, taking a seat on her queen size bed. Her room was decked out from top to bottom. Jane hit the button on the stereo. Power 99 FM was playing after dark hits. She then disrobed, leaving nothing on but her matching Victoria Secret bra and panties. Sliding her slippers off, she crawled across the bed next to Wakil.

"I like my room to be mellowed out. Let me hit that," she said, reaching for the blunt Wakil was smoking. Jane got high every once in a while. She wasn't addicted to the drug.

"Didn't know you smoked weed," he responded, taking two more puffs of the blunt before passing it to her.

"It's a lot of thing you don't know about me," she said, inhaling the blunt.

"Trust me, I'm ready to find out by all means," he responded, taking off his clothes like he lived there. Within a few seconds he was booty ball naked.

"Now you're talking honey," she said, lifting her body up to get a closer look at his manhood. She was astonished how well hung he was. She quickly took the rest of her clothes off, while still keeping her eyes on Wakil. He put the rest of the blunt out and they both climbed in bed facing each other.

"Your body feels so warm and soft," he spoke, massaging her breast with both hands.

"Since you didn't want me to cook you nothing to eat in the kitchen, how about some desert?" she said, laying back on the bed placing her legs behind her head. All Wakil seen was a clean shaved vagina looking at him.

"You're blunt and cocky I see, but I like that," he said, positioning his body so he could get in between her legs because eating girls out was his expertise.

"It'll definitely fill you up, and my pussy taste like strawberries," she said, bringing her two middle fingers to her mouth, licking them after removing them from her vagina. Wakil already had an instant hard on. He didn't waste no time diving in head first. He started to penetrate her clitoris with his tongue and using his two fingers. Jane couldn't stay still. It was driving her wild, even though she remained in the same position. The pleasure she was experiencing was too overwhelming and she didn't want him to stop. She continued to push his head deeper inside of her.

"OH! OH!. AH-AH!" she screamed out in ecstasy, reaching an orgasm one after the other, causing her to wrap her legs around him. He eased down and started sucking her toes. She was bringing the freak out of him. He climbed back up to the top of the bed, placing his hands behind his head. Jane couldn't help but look over and see his manhood standing straight up in the air. She immediately went down on him, not able to take all of him in her mouth. She went as far as she could go, licking and sucking all over it.

"Yeah! That's right, eat daddy," he cheered her on, encouraging her to do a good job. She was a pro at giving head. Jane took pride in using her mouth. The porno industry would've loved to have her in one of their movies. Her tongue was gentle and smooth. Jane wanted to feel all of Wakil inside of her, so her oral sex came to a halt.

"Babe you taste good. I can eat this dick all night, but I want to ride this pole," she said.

"Climb aboard," he said, in a playful manner and she did what she was told by easing her vagina down on his penis. It felt like a suction cup going down. She was tight in that area. He started fondling her breasts that were in perfect shape, as he squeezed both nipples causing her to go insane. Wakil didn't show no mercy. He pulled her down on him by grabbing her waist. She could feel him up in her stomach. The pain was overshadowed by the pleasure. They both came in unison. After both had reached multiple orgasms, Jane's face hit Wakil's chest. He rolled her over and they both dozed off in each other's arms.

CHAPTER 8

BACK TO BUSINESS

Saleem was tossing and turning on the couch, with no intention of getting up. After a long night of sex and drugs, Saleem's head was spinning like a merry-go-round. He tried to lean up, but fell back down due to him feeling a little sluggish. With a long day ahead, he didn't know where to begin.

"Leem, Leem," the little squeaky voice yelled out. It was his niece, Daisy, who was two-years old. She tried to get his full attention.

"Hey Daisy," Saleem spoke, holding his arms out for her to come to him. He picked her up and planted kisses all over her cheeks and forehead. It didn't take her long to wiggle loose from his grip. She ran off and climbed up the stairs. Saleem managed to make his way behind her. Entering the bathroom, he washed his face and brushed his teeth. Everyone who lived there was still sound asleep with the exception of him and his niece. Saleem put on a black dickey shirt and pants to match, along with his black Chukka Timberlands.

He was geared up to fit his hustle. Now all he had to do was contact Wakil, so they could take care of business. He picked up his phone and dialed Wakil's number. It rang three times before a male voice answered.

"Yo," a voice spoke, sounding drowsy.

"Wah what's the deal? It's time to make the donuts," stated Saleem, recognizing the familiar tone.

"Damn cuz, what time is it?" Wakil asked, looking over at Jane sleeping like a baby. Even in her sleep she was beautiful.

"You know the early bird gets the worm. I don't know what time it is, but it's early. Did you secure that situation last night?" inquired Saleem, making sure he handled business before pleasure.

"No doubt, that's covered," Wakil said, assuring him that the package was safe.

"I was waiting for your call. Me and Boog rode out last night," Saleem responded.

"It took me no longer than 10 minutes to grab that, then I got with Jane," Wakil answered.

"Okay player, you stayed out on Mimi last night," Saleem blurted out, knowing that Wakil never did, except on rare occasions.

"Man, I'm doing me. Where you want to meet at?" asked Wakil.

"I'ma walk around Sissy's crib, you know she's up fiening so meet me there," Saleem said. That's where they prepared and packaged their product.

"Alright, give me like a half hour to gather my thoughts," Wakil responded, as Jane was staring up at him, while he talked on the phone, not realizing she was awake.

"Cool, see you then," Saleem said, ending the conversation. He thought about calling Shay, but brushed it off, grabbed his coat and drove around to Sissy's house. Arriving at his destination he didn't bother knocking on Boog's door, who lived up the street from Sissy. It was too early and he knew Boog was probably asleep. So he rung Sissy's doorbell. Saleem peaked through the window of the enclosed porch to see if she was coming.

"Shit it's cold," Saleem mumbled, zipping his Wooldridge coat up. The wind chill was cutting through his dickeys. He seen her coming towards the door.

"Boy I was knocked out. I hope you got something to wake me up," Sissy said, as she turned to walk back in the house.

"Yeah as soon as Wakil gets here. I damn near froze my ass off outside. We gotta get to this table," Saleem stated, sitting down at the dining room table where they handle their business. Sissy was walking back and forth with her mouth twitching for a blast. Looking like she didn't sleep or eat in days. She was already naturally skinny. The drugs just added to her fragile frame. Sissy was 5'10", 120 pounds, brown skin with short hair.

Her lips were droopy red like she drank alcohol her whole life. The house was a Section Eight, provided by welfare. Sissy had two children who resided with her, in the house with three bedrooms. In her living room she had one sofa in mint condition and a 19-inch color TV that set on a broken nightstand. The only other furniture besides the beds was a dining room table and three chairs.

"Where is Wakil? Shit he's taking forever. Give me five dollars so I can run around the corner and grab one until he gets here," Sissy asked, getting impatient. She was pacing back and forth.

"Here, 'cause you're not going to bug me every five minutes," stated Saleem, passing her a ten dollar bill. Even though she had a drug habit, Sissy was loyal to Saleem and Wakil. So they made sure she was well taken care of. The door slammed right behind her. Sissy shot out the house like she was late for a smoker's meeting. Saleem set back flicking the clip on his beeper, patiently waiting for Wakil until his phone rang.

"Yo where you at nigga?" Saleem spoke.

"I'm home. A place you failed to show your face," a female voice spoke, on the other end of the phone.

"Shay, I got caught up last night. I was going to call but it was late," Saleem responded, recognizing who it was.

"Save your lies Saleem. I don't want to hear that shit," Shay spoke. She was angry. You could hear the fire in her voice.

76

"I'm not lying baby girl. I had to handle something and Wakil couldn't do it 'cause he was with Jane," responded Saleem, thinking by mentioning her girlfriend it would put him in the clear.

"And what's that suppose to mean? I called your phone and I paged you. You had me worried sick about you. I called your house. Ms. Cee said she hadn't heard from you all day," Shay responded.

"Look, I'm cool baby girl. When you get off from work? I'll be there laying on you," stated Saleem, pleading his case.

"Yeah, we'll see. Don't do that shit you did last night!" Shay blurted out, still rubbing it deep into his skin.

"I won't. Love ya," Saleem spoke, clicking her off. He wasn't trying to stay on the phone, arguing with her about nothing, even though he knew it wouldn't be the last time she brung up that conversation. But he had other things to do. Sissy came back and started cleaning her glass pipe at the dining room table.

"I'll be back on my job as soon as I blow this," Sissy stated, stuffing the pipe, with huge chunks of crack rock.

"Slow down before you bust your heart, and who did you buy that from?" asked Saleem, watching her light the tip of the glass pipe. She wasn't paying no attention to Saleem. Her mind was elsewhere. The doorbell rung, causing Sissy to jump back in her chair. Saleem started laughing. She was in a state of paranoia.

"What was that noise?" asked Sissy, looking around the room with her eyeballs ready to pop out. Some people were known to hallucinate off using this type of drug.

"It's only the door woman." He peaked through the peep hole. Wakil was standing there with a hood on his head. Saleem let him in.

"What's the deal Leem?" Wakil asked, shutting the door behind him.

"In here tripping off Sissy. She high as a kite," Saleem said, walking back to his seat. Wakil was right behind him.

Sissy was still in the same spot, looking down on the floor like she had lost something.

"Damn! She twisted already?" inquired Wakil, placing a black book bag on the table.

"Some shit she bought around the corner," explained Saleem, opening up the bag Wakil had just placed down on the table.

"Let's get this shit rolling cuz. We missing a lot of money out there. I just seen Turtle out there on the ave," stated Wakil.

"He out there early," Saleem said, pulling the digital scale out. Wakil took out two big Ziploc bags from the black bag. It was two kilos of cocaine. They started to break them down into four and a half ounces, which would've come out to sixteen of them. That was only done to make it easy to whip the cocaine using baking soda, putting only an ounce of it on four and a half ounces to stretch it to an extra ounce. Saleem turned the stove on and placed a coffee pot on there with a little water.

"Since we're only putting an ounce on each joint, the work should still be good," Saleem said, dumping the first quarter pound into the pot, followed by an ounce of baking soda. They did all of them like that. It took less than an hour, using two coffee pots. They both had their own pot. Now came the bagging up part. As soon as Saleem reached for the box of bags the doorbell rang.

"Who the fuck could that be?" Wakil snapped, placing the bags on the table, while he went to go answer the door. It was Boog.

"Yo Wah, you cool," Boog asked, entering the house. Wakil peeped out the door looking left and right before locking it back up. He was being cautious and still wondering why Saleem hadn't mentioned nothing about Charlie. Wakil walked back in observing Saleem and Boog already bagging up.

"A Wah what's to the chick Jane?" asked Boog, talking like he was still high.

"All man, you know I long dicked her and drop kicked her," Wakil responded, smiling as he flashed back to the session they shared last night.

"Did she give you a chewy and how's the shot?" inquired Saleem, with the razor still in his hand.

"Yeah she ate me up like a certified porno star. I tried to slam her in the ass, but she said my dick was too big," Wakil spoke, chopping the chunks of white substance into small pieces.

"Nigga please, like your 18 inches or something. Her ass was probably already ripped open. I'm trying party the chick," Boog said.

"Stop hating fat man. You couldn't pull that if you paid her," responded Wakil. They went back and forth for the next half-hour talking about Jane. Boog and Saleem were amazed by the story Wakil had told them, especially how flexible she was with her legs.

"Yo let Sissy try this shit out," Saleem said, breaking off the size of a dime piece from the yellowish substance that was on his plate. It was always good to give a taste test before putting the stuff out on the street.

"It looks good," Sissy spoke, examining the product before filling the tip of her glass pipe. She inhaled, then blew the smoke out, then she licked her lips. Not being able to talk was a clear sign that the stuff was good.

"Well we know we got the bomb 'cause she's tongue-tied," Wakil said.

"That stuff made my pussy tingle," said Sissy, finally coming out of the comatose state of mind she was in.

"Let's put this shit out on the streets fast," Saleem suggested, with all them bagging up. Using 5'8" Ziploc bags it wouldn't be long before they were done. The extras they brung back from whipping the coke was used for shopping and other miscellaneous things. One kilo was used for strictly weight sales, unless they ran out of everything that was bagged up. Their nick rocks were the size of pennies and the motive behind making the rocks that big was to shut down all competition.

"My hands are burning up bagging this shit. I need to get my break up front," Boog said, leaning back and stretching.

"Nigga, we always lookout! Whatever you need, you can get! We ain't your tight ass cousin String Bean," Wakil stated, staring at Sissy. Her eyes were glued in on all the cocaine that was spread out on the table.

"I'ma call old head, and let him know the work was love," Saleem said.

"Chill! Hold up. Let's finish this first," demanded Wakil, trying to discourage Saleem by any means. He didn't want him finding out about Charlie's death too soon.

"Man, I can do this shit—shower and shave at the same time," Saleem responded, dialing Charlie's phone. He let it ring four times, but no one answered. Wakil's heart was beating fast like he just ran a mile around the track. He felt a little relieved when Saleem didn't get through, especially the police. Wakil still needed time to perfect his story, so Saleem wouldn't think he played any part in Charlie's demise. The streets talk, so he knew it was only a matter of time before it hit the airwaves.

"Boog start putting them in five-hundred packs, so I can hurry up and drop these packs off," spoke Wakil.

It was a brown shopping bag filled with five-hundred packs. They were determined to flood the neighborhood. Saleem and Wakil weren't taking no prisoners and Boog was going to eat off their plate regardless. Even though other cats were getting their fair share, they were the youngest in charge. With only a little left on the plate, Saleem decided to break Sissy off something that would hold her halfway through the day.

"I'm hungry as shit. I can't remember the last thing I ate," Boog spoke, rubbing his stomach.

"Cuz be for real. You probably emptied the fridge out at your crib," Wakil said, laughing at the fact he couldn't picture Boog going without a meal. That was like a heroin addict going without a bag of dope the whole day.

"Dig, I'ma take Mary her package and Ms. Cook. Boog can ride with me and you can handle this. Hold it at your miz's crib," stated Saleem grabbing six, five-hundred packs.

"Alright. I got a few things to take care of anyway," Wakil responded, putting all the packs inside a brown shopping bag. Everybody else rolled out, leaving Sissy to scrape the residue off the plates. Saleem still had to make it up to Shay for not showing up at her house last night. As him and Boog drove down Allison Street, a black four-door Volvo was driving past Mom P's house. Saleem pumped the brakes at the stop sign, letting them go first. It was Ron Lee and McCann, two undercover police officers who were known for terrorizing the west Philly neighborhood.

"Shit, don't panic. There go Johnny law creeping on the low," Saleem said. They kept rolling, not looking over at Saleem and Boog.

"Damn that was a close call 'cause I can't run that fast," Boog joked, turning the sounds backs up. Saleem pushed the pedal to the floor trying to reach Ms. Mary's house in top speed, just in case the police decided to make a U-turn. Saleem parked outside her house in the vacant spot. He rang the bell and to his surprise Kita answered the door with a white T-shirt on and no bra, with some tight fitting blue jeans.

"Hey Saleem, you're up early," Kita said, moving to the side so he could slide past her.

"Gotta make the donuts and take care of you," Saleem shot back at her causing her to expose her pearly white teeth.

"You do look out for me and I love you for that, but you gotta stop getting high so much. You probably don't remember nothing that happened last night," responded Kita, flopping down on the couch.

"Yeah! Where your mom at? Give this to her. I'm out. I'ma holler at you later," Saleem spoke, not responding to her last remark about his drug use. He was going to continue using his drug of choice until he was ready to stop, and there was no one to tell him otherwise.

"Slow down boy. Darn, you don't got a respond to what I just said. Where's my kiss, hug or something?" Kita blurted, grabbing hold of his coat. He pulled her close, sticking his tongue down her throat, while palming her butt cheeks at the same time. It felt like she didn't have any panties on and her tongue moved around like a lizard in his mouth. Her lips were soft as silk.

"Whoa! You're trying get something started," stated Saleem, easing away from her.

"Boy, I wouldn't do that here, even though I'm tempted. But come through later so I can replay the episode from last night," Kita responded, with a look of seductiveness in her eyes.

"No doubt, plus I'm not getting high at all today," Saleem said, lying to her to keep her from worrying. But in all actuality a hot cup of tea would bring his high right back. Leaning out the door, he thought about being caught up between lust and love. He was in love with two women and making a choice wasn't on his agenda. Boog was bobbing to the music that was playing.

"So where to now?" asked Boog.

"Ms. Cook spot, then grab a bite to eat and some gank," Saleem spoke, driving off. He past Master Street and his youngbul Nell was out there with a bunch of other guys, shooting dice against the Jamaican store wall.

"Ain't that Nell over there?" Boog blurted out, pointing to the crowd. Saleem pulled up and beeped the horn. Nell walked over on the passenger side.

"Yo old head. I didn't have no work so I been chilling," Nell said.

"Here, take this, and be careful out here. Did my little brother come through here?" asked Saleem.

"Earlier, him and Baby James drove past here," responded Nell.

"Alright, I'm gone," Saleem said, pulling off, driving straight down 56th Street. He made a right at Wylusing to get on 57th Street. They drove past Headquarters where Shay and Jane worked.

"Don't Shay work at that salon you just passed?" Boog spoke, pointing at the sign over the top of the shop.

"Yeah, I ain't stopping there. I'ma catch her later. Plus I'm riding dirty right now," stated Saleem, with no plans of making a U-turn.

"Shit, I can't get Jane out of my mind. I gotta see what that broad looks like ASAP," Boog said, like he was infatuated with her without ever laying an eye on her.

"You're on some stalker shit. She'll want every dime you got and more," spoke Saleem, parking in front of Ms. Cook's door.

"If that's the case fifty bucks is right up my alley," responded Boog.

"You shot out," Saleem stated, exiting the vehicle. He knocked on Ms. Cook's door. She lived in the second house from the alleyway. Fifty-seventh and Appletree Street was a narrow one-way block, which was a perfect location for running a drug operation. She came to the door with her weave swinging from side-to-side.

"Saleem, I thought you was the police banging like that," Ms. Cook said, unlocking the black steel gate that separated her from the outside world.

"Naw, but it's a little brisk out here," responded Saleem, rubbing his hands together to heat them up as he walked in her house.

"People were coming through here all last night trying to buy something. I had to go across the street to those damn Projects," Ms. Cook stated, closing the gate but not locking it. She was in her early fifties, brown skin with poppy eyes, standing 5'8" and 130 pounds. You could tell the drugs were starting to take a toll on her body. Saleem never bothered to go upstairs. The house looked creepy. He went no further than the dining room. The house was in fair condition but still could use a little work.

"I know we had to reup. This stuff is the best. So if you run out call me. I'm grinding hard," Saleem spoke, placing one five-hundred pack in her hand. He had no choice but to leave it with her, being as though Smoke hasn't been seen in a week. That was strange because he never done a disappearing act before.

"Are these nicks or dimes? 'Cause they're huge," Ms. Cook asked, drooling over the size of the rocks.

"They big right? They're nicks. We stepped our game up," responded Saleem.

"Yes! Yaw did. Where's Wakil anyway?" Ms. Cook asked, still amazed by the size of the rocks, with plans of breaking them down. She knew she could get two or more from one of Saleems'.

"He busy right now, taking care of something. Let me go," said Saleem, making his way to the door. As soon as he opened it, a police car was driving down the block. Boog must've peeped them coming through the rear view mirror, 'cause he was slumped down in the seat with the car turned off.

"Fuck that. I ain't trying get knocked off," Boog stated, sliding himself back up in the seat. Saleem was laughing at him trying to hide.

"Nigga are you serious. Those cops seen your big ass trying to duck down," Saleem said.

"Whatever! Let's slide up Brook and catch some chicks," Boog suggested.

"You still high. It's only a little after 11:00. Overbrook don't get out until 2:30. We going to Micky D's," Saleem responded, making a right towards Market Street.

✳ ✳ ✳ ✳ ✳

Wakil had just pulled in front of his parent's house. He knew they were home because his father's brown pickup truck was parked outside, being as though it wasn't there earlier when he stopped by. Even though Wakil didn't reside at home with his parents, he still kept a set of keys that his mother gave him. His father was real strict about keeping the door locked, especially during the night, due to the neighborhood they lived in. When he walked in his mother was watching TV.

"Hey mom, what you doing?" asked Wakil.

"Nothing son. Me and your dad just came back from the supermarket," responded Ms. Sidney.

"Did Kenny call? I meant to go see him last week, but I was caught up," Wakil said, sitting down in the recliner, still holding on to the black duffle bag with the product in it.

"I spoke to Kenny yesterday. He always ask about you, but I don't know what to tell him. You don't come through as much. We see Saleem more than you," Ms. Sidney responded.

"Yeah, you right, but when I do come past you be at work. I see dad all the time," spoke Wakil.

Ms. Sidney was a certified nurse at the University Hospital on 34th and Spruce Street across from the Convention Center. And Mr. James, Wakil's father, was a construction worker and handyman on the side. Kenny was Wakil's fraternal brother and they were twins but not identical. But they were similar in looks and they had an older sister who was Muslim. She lived on the southwest side of Philadelphia with her two twin daughters who also were not identical.

"I just wish you would show your face more often to let us know you're alive. Kenny's appeal is coming up. The lawyer called," Ms. Sidney stated. She was trying her best to get Kenny home who was serving five to ten years for armed robbery.

"That lawyer better do his job. I gave him five thousand dollars on top of what you took him," Wakil said, running up the steps. He went to his old room where everything was still the same way he left it. Wakil pulled out a shoebox full of money from underneath his bed. After realizing what he had wouldn't fit with the money, he decided to leave everything in the bag, and slide it back under the bed. His parents knew what he did. Even though they didn't approve of the life he lived, they stayed out of his business.

"Yeah, I think he's going to do a good job of getting your brother home," suggested Ms. Sidney, sipping on a diet Pepsi, which she didn't need 'cause her weight wasn't an issue. Ms. Sidney and Wakil as well as her daughter, Gina, all looked alike. Kenny favored Mr. James, his father more. To be in her early forties she looked good. Some people would occasionally mistake her and Wakil as sister and brother.

"He'll be cool. He's up Graterford with my man, Fatta and his name rings bells in there," Wakil said, speaking about the state jail his brother was being housed. Graterford State Correctional Facility was one of the toughest maximum prisons in Pennsylvania.

"Where's that girlfriend of yours? Is she taking care of you?" inquired Ms. Sidney.

"Who Mimi? She's probably at the mall shopping with her girlfriends," explained Wakil, but in reality he really didn't know where she was. By the time he got home after staying out all night with Jane, he didn't have a strong alibi as to why he didn't call or come home.

"That's the one you live with, right?" asked Ms. Sidney.

"Yeah, mom. I'll make sure I check on you from now on. Tell dad I stopped by," Wakil said, kissing his mom on the cheek. By the time he reached the bottom of the steps, she yelled for him to be careful. Ms. Sidney constantly worried about Wakil, after losing his twin to the justice system. The streets had a lock on him that she found hard to break. Wakil still hadn't taken a shower. He only changed his shirt. Before he could close his car door, Saleem and Boog was driving up Hunter Street the wrong way. Wakil went over to holler at them.

"Wah you want some of these nuggets?" Boog asked, as he dipped one inside the barbecue sauce.

"Naw I'm cool," Wakil responded, walking behind him, entering Saleem's house. When they went inside, it was a house full of girls. Hazel, Margie, Mooky, Rasheeda, Karen, Roro and Wanda. Everyone was related to Saleem except Wanda, and Saleem was always whispering sweet nothings in her ear, but she would never bite the bait. Being as though Shay was over his house the majority of the time, Wanda knew he was trying to have his cake and eat it too. They were playing cards for money. Saleem slid right up on Wanda with a McDonald's bag in his hand and offered her some, but she declined.

"Wanda, what's up?" Saleem asked, sucking on a French fry.

"Nothing Saleem. I need a ride home though," Wanda responded, smiling. Little did she know that was right up his alley.

"Let's go. You know I'll drive you to the moon and back," Saleem shot back flirting. She could only laugh, but deep down she knew he meant every word. Saleem was attracted to her for many reasons. She was sexy and real hairy, but to top it off was the trimmed mustache above her lip that would've drove any man crazy.

"Boy you crazy, come on," Wanda said, walking towards the door. She said her goodbyes and they were on their way.

"Saleem, let me hold a couple dollars," Margie asked, sticking her hand out. She was Saleem's oldest sister. He passed her a fifty dollar bill, then him and Wanda and Boog rolled out. Wakil got inside his car and pulled off. Saleem made a right on Lansdown. Wanda only lived walking distance on 57th and Alden Street right off Landsdown Avenue.

"So Wanda when we going out? I think it's time we take things to another level," Saleem blurted out, looking over at her, patiently waiting for a response.

"You have a girlfriend, so don't try to play me. I'm nobody's second choice. Either I'm first or nothing," said Wanda, looking back over at him. Boog was in the back seat laughing at Saleem trying to be a player.

"For you sexy, I'll cut all these broads off, just to have you as my number one chick," Saleem spoke, turning down her block. She knew he was blowing smoke up her pants, but she loved his persistence.

"Saleem, you don't have to lie to me. Maybe one day it'll happen. Don't chase," Wanda said, exiting his car. She waved bye going up the steps and Saleem beeped the horn and drove off after Boog got back up front

＊ ＊ ＊ ＊ ＊

As Wakil was about to turn off of Hunter Street, a police car was coming in his direction. Wakil was frozen. He didn't know what to do until the officer beeped his horn, waving for Wakil to move to the side. He parked on the corner and the police car kept going, followed by an unmarked vehicle with two white males inside. Wakil got out of the car to see where they were going in such a hurry. To his surprise they drove down Saleem's block, but some cars still remained parked on Hunter Street.

But he still couldn't grasp as to what was going on. The chances of him going down there were slim to none. *What the fuck are they doing there*, Wakil thought to himself. He grabbed his cell phone and called his mother's house. She picked up on the first ring.

"Hey mom, look out your window and let me know where all those police cars went," Wakil asked, sitting on the trunk of his car. She went over and peeked through the blinds.

"Boy, they are all over the place. I think they're at Saleem's house because I see seven to eight men standing right in front of his house," Ms. Sidney said.

"Did they bring anybody out? If they are looking for Saleem he's not there," blurted Wakil.

88

"What yaw do? And where are you at?" Ms. Sidney asked, sounding worried.

"I'm up the street watching the cars in front of your house. Can you stay there for a minute and let me know if they bring somebody out?" Wakil asked.

"Sure, why not," Ms. Sidney said, pulling out a fold up chair. She sat there for about twenty minutes watching the police chat back and forth. Wakil continued to sit there, waiting for his mom to fill him in with each detail.

"Did they leave from Saleem's house?" asked Wakil.

"Well, a lot of them are pulling off from in front of their door. And two cops just came off the porch," Ms. Sidney said.

"So they all rolled out?" asked Wakil, driving towards his apartment. He got tired of waiting for the outcome of the police being present at Saleem's house.

"Yes Wakil. So be careful out there. And don't forget to call me," Ms. Sidney stated as a reminder.

"I will mom. Thanks for being a brief lookout," Wakil said.

"Anything for you son," Ms. Sidney responded. They hung up. Wakil continued to drive to his apartment to face the music with Mimi.

* * * * *

Shay was working on her third customer and it was only two o'clock in the afternoon. Even though she was still disappointed with Saleem, she wanted to hear about Jane's night out with her enemy. For some particular reason it was on her mind for the last couple of hours, ever since Jane called to inform her boss that she would be late. Shay knew she never came late, so she figured last night had to play a major role in her decision not to show up on time. Moments later, Jane came through the door sipping on her coffee.

"Damn slut. The day almost over and you came stumbling in here all late," Shay said.

"Girl, wait until I tell you about my night and morning," Jane responded, approaching her desk where another employee was filling in for her.

"Can't wait to hear it. It must be good to have you all roared up," Shay proclaimed, half-way finished with her last customer of the day, while Jane was just getting settled in.

"Let's just say it was a night to remember," blurted Jane, as she smiled thinking about Wakil. She couldn't get him out of her mind. It was like he was a drug and she was addicted.

"I bet it was," Shay said, sarcastically as she finished her last client.

"Yeah, Shay dude is packing and you know I've seen them all. But he takes the cake and I rocked his world," Jane spoke.

"So that's your man now? He ain't leaving his girlfriend for you," Shay suggested with a sly grin, but her facial expression showed a sign of jealousy.

"Now I don't expect him to. Shit I'll be his side joint with that monster dick he was packing in those boxers last night," Jane yelled out. People in the salon looked at her as though she was crazy.

"Are you done yet? Let's go in the back and get out all your dirty laundry," responded Shay, laughing.

"You're a trip. I knew you wanted to know. Bitch, trying act all nonchalant," Jane spoke, walking in the back. Everything was decked out, from the carpet to the floor model TV to the cream leather sofa and love seat as well as the matching stereo system.

"Spit it out! Detail by detail! I know it's killing you to tell me," Shay said.

"He called me around 12:00 or a little later than that, but shit, I was up. He just happened to be on 52nd and Spruce. So I invited him over. To make a long story short, he fucked and sucked my pussy like a human lizard," Jane responded, sounding real excited.

"Was he that good?" asked Shay, feeling a little moisture in her panties. The conversation was heated. She didn't look at Wakil from that perspective, as far as sexually, but she couldn't deny that he looked good.

"That's an understatement. It was like he went to school for pussy eating," said Jane.

Stop lying, okay! He might've been average like the rest and you're putting him on a higher pedestal, Shay thought, as Jane continued to ramble on.

"If I'm lying, I'm dying. Shit, you know I had to play my part putting these jaws to work. I couldn't even fit all of him in my mouth. Anymore and I would've died with a dick stuck in my throat," Jane responded. It was obvious that she was hooked and turned out after one night.

"Now you're exaggerating. I doubt if he was that big," said Shay.

"Girl, you ain't see it or feel it up in your stomach," spoke Jane, looking at Shay with a look of assurance that she was telling the truth.

"Alright girl. Shit, you make me horny. So Wakil's packing, who would've known," Shay responded.

"He made me a believer. I'ma call him later just to see if it was more than a one night stand." Jane was sprung, but she couldn't really accept the fact that he lived with his girlfriend. Her hopes were high. Shay felt sorry for her knowing how crooked and disloyal Wakil was to Mimi. She figured Jane would have to find out the hard way.

"Me and Saleem are going to Ribits, a food spot on 2nd and South," Shay spoke.

"Yeah, I heard about that place," Jane blurted out, getting up to stretch her legs.

"I'll be sure to let you know how the food taste, unless Wakil takes you there." Shay was being sarcastic on purpose, just to have something to throw back in her face.

"Damn Shay, you really sound like you want Wakil, with all your smart remarks," Jane said.

"Now why in the hell would I want him? Don't get it twisted. We both know my man runs the show," said Shay. Throwing heartfelt blows she was digging to the core.

"And you say that, to say what?" Jane jumped up and stood in front of Shay like she was ready to fight.

"Listen, I'm not arguing with you about no nigga, so back the fuck up out of my face, for you be on that floor." Shay was angry and Jane knew she couldn't beat her, but she wasn't showing no sign of backing down.

"If yaw don't cut it out, I can hear yaw fussing out front. Yaw been like sisters ever since I've known you. Whatever it is you two are arguing about, it ain't worth your friendship," the woman spoke, as she stood in between them so no punches would be thrown. You could feel the tension in the air. She was one of the older employees who worked at the shop. Once the peacemaker walked away, things remained calm.

"Dag, I know we wasn't that loud," Shay said, breaking the ice.

"Yeah we were in here about to kill each other about nothing," Jane spoke.

"Friends to the end. Give me a hug bitch," said Shay, laughing and spreading her arms out for Jane to embrace her.

"Always no matter what," responded Jane, squeezing Shay with all her might, like it was going to be the last time they saw each other. The shop was closing up later than usual. Shay was out at her regular time. She needed time to prepare for her night out with Saleem. Jane stayed to make up her hours for coming in late.

So Shay had to catch a ride with someone else. She decided to tag along with a known customer who frequented the salon on a regular basis. Shay had plans on purchasing a vehicle, once she moved out of her mother's house, being as though she drove her mother's car most of the time. So buying one was not her priority.

CHAPTER 9

ON THE RUN EATING

On the southwest side of Philly, Saleem and Boog were on 54th and Region Street over one of his other girl's house. Region Street was a small block in back of the Thriftway Supermarket on Chester Avenue.

"Yo Dee, come here for a minute," yelled Saleem.

"What's up Saleem?" asked Dee, coming down the stairs of her house. Everybody called her Dee, which was short for Donisha. They met at a strip club on Broad and Cumberland called "Foxy Valley." With plans of changing her place of dancing she was going to start at a new spot that was soon to open in a few months called "Cherekee" out west Philly.

She was light complexion with long hair and a well proportioned body. But later he found out she was related to Shay. That didn't stop them from having a private affair. Saleem looked out for her and her son, who was six months from a previous relationship.

"So when you going to stop popping your ass at the club and get a real job?" said Saleem, laying back in a comfortable position like he lived there.

"You know I only do it to provide for my son," Dee said, sitting beside Saleem with her legs stretched across his.

"That's no excuse. Do you know how many chicks have kids with nine to five gigs?" Saleem said, looking at her straight in the eyes.

"Well, I ain't those bitches. I'ma do what I have to do, when it comes to providing for mine," Dee responded.

"You're not getting any younger. You can't lap dance for the rest of your life," Saleem said, rubbing his hands up and down her right thigh.

"Nigga, you act like I'm eighty years old. I'm eighteen years old and my body is in tip top shape," responded Dee, lifting her shirt exposing her flat stomach so Saleem would see it. She had no signs to show that she had a baby.

"Okay, calm down! I'm on your side. Damn, I must've hit a nerve," Saleem assumed, slapping her on the butt as she was getting up from the couch.

"No, you didn't hit a nerve, but you getting on my last nerve talking that bullshit," Dee blurted out, rolling her eyes. She could be fiery at times.

"Stop tripping. I'm only joking. Hold on, let me get this," Saleem said being interrupted by his cell phone ringing.

"Hello, who this?" Saleem questioned.

"Yo Leem, where you at? The cops came to the house deep, looking for you," Malik asked, sounding like he was losing his breath.

"What they looking for me for?" asked Saleem, confused about the whole situation, as thoughts entered his mind, as if he did something last night while high.

"Man, they mentioned something about a murdered cop," Malik spit, not really going into detail.

"Nigga, are you crazy? What the fuck I look like, killing a cop? That's death row shit," Saleem blurted out, speaking in a aggressive tone. He was steaming hot like a radiator after hearing the accusation that was being put on him.

"Just chill for a while until I hear something from the streets," Malik spoke, trying to make sure his brother remained safe.

"How many cops came there and was Margie and them still there playing cards?" asked a nervous Saleem, pacing the floor back and forth. Dee couldn't say nothing. She was shocked from hearing the questions Saleem was asking. Boog was standing by the kitchen overhearing the whole conversation.

"Yeah, they were here when I came back in. The police searched for you, then left a number for you to call and turn yourself in," Malik spoke.

"Oh yeah picture that with Kodak. I'm not turning myself in. They gotta catch me like the gingerbread man," responded Saleem.

"A cop car rides passed every twenty minutes and one sits at the bottom of the block," Malik spoke.

"Damn! I gotta get my bread and a few outfits from there ASAP," Saleem said, sitting back down, holding his head like he had a splitting headache. After Malik said he would find a way to get everything he needed, he cut the call off so he could continue to contemplate on his next move. He didn't have a clue. Going on the run never entered his mind. Before he made any sudden moves he had to contact Wakil to help fill in the missing pieces to the puzzle.

"Saleem are you alright?" a concerned Dee asked.

"I'm cool. I just gotta gather my thoughts," Saleem stated, getting back up from the couch only to pace back and forth.

"So what's the deal on this killing cop bullshit?" Boog questioned, walking the floor with him.

"Cuz, it's drama. The law ran up in my spot, talking about I killed a cop." Saleem stopped pacing and stood to look at Boog as though he had the answer.

"You bullshitting," Boog said, not really believing it himself.

"Naw real rap homey," Saleem assured him. Dee came over to put her hand on his shoulder. She was trying to comfort him through such a difficult time.

Saleem wanted to go out to find the answers for himself, but Dee and Boog convinced him that he would be making a big mistake. So Boog took the car and went out to see what he could find out. Dee and Saleem stayed there and talked about his plans of going into hiding for a while, as they made passionate love in the process. Being as though Dee's mom was not home, they had the house to themselves. Saleem was prepared to do whatever it took to escape the clutches of the law because going to jail was not on his agenda.

✳ ✳ ✳ ✳ ✳

Meanwhile back at Shay's house was the normal hostile environment. Ms. Lacy was walking around with a bottle of liquor in one hand and a clear small Ziploc bag in the other with a white powder substance inside. She usually called it her nose candy. Her two sons were running around the house, wrestling and jumping on and off the couch. But she was too drunk and high to pay any attention to what they were doing. Shay was upstairs getting dressed.

This should do it, Shay mumbled to herself, looking in the mirror assessing her attire. She was laced in a black blouse, blue DKNY jeans, and some steel toe black Gucci boots. Shay was dressed to kill. Startled by the sound of the phone ringing, she jumped like she saw Jason from Friday the 13th. *Damn. I must be losing my mind*, she thought, as she picked up her cell phone.

"Yes, who's calling?" Shay said, sounding like a secretary at a law firm.

"Yo babygirl," the voice on the other end of the phone spoke.

"Who the hell is this?" asked Shay, not recognizing the voice.

"Calm down Shay. It's me, Wah," responded Wakil with a smirk on his face. He didn't have a clue as to what he was doing calling her, but he was willing to ride the wave to see how far she would allow him to go, even though he knew he was going overboard by calling his partner's girlfriend without his permission.

"Why you calling me, and I'm not your babygirl," Shay spoke.

"You know I ain't mean it like that," explained Wakil, still trying to keep the conversation alive.

"So are you going to answer my question or what?" asked Shay, getting frustrated with the games Wakil was playing.

"What you ask me?" Wakil questioned.

"Okay! I'm hanging up," responded Shay.

"Naw! Hold up. I was trying to catch Saleem, but he not answering his phone. So I figured he would be with you 'cause the police was at his crib," Wakil spoke, telling her half the truth and the other part was a lie.

"For what? I just talked to him earlier and he didn't mention nothing about the police," said Shay, not really comprehending what he was telling her.

"Because I doubt if he knows. It happened a few hours ago. Matter a fact as soon as him and Wanda and Boog pulled off, they came," Wakil said, throwing Shay a curve ball.

"Wanda! What the fuck is she doing in his car. That's why he's not answering," blurted out Shay, falling back on her bed.

"Beats me. I don't even know if she's still with them, but he probably knows from somebody in his house calling him." Wakil wasn't trying to find out, he didn't even bother calling Saleem. He had his own problems to solve.

"I'll give him some more time to come here or call before I start to panic," Shay suggested.

"Panic for what? I told you he's cool, plus I'm here for you." Wakil was on overkill. He didn't care that he was stepping out of bounds.

"Oh yeah, since when did I become a friend of yours?" Shay questioned, trying to figure out where all of this being nice to her was coming from, but she was enjoying it.

"Damn Shay we can't be enemies forever. Let's bury the hate," Wakil responded, hoping she would bite the bait.

"I hear you and Jane hit it off real good," Shay said.

"Chicks can't keep their mouth shut for nothing," Wakil said, acting as though he really cared if they spread his business out as to what went on in the bedroom. He was secure in that department.

"Boy please. Yaw the ones run off talking about how yaw be beating some girls pussy up," Shay shot back.

"Not me. Even though I do put dents in chicks, so I hope Jane didn't leave that part out," Wakil said, telling her what she wanted to hear. Saleem brought this on. he couldn't stop talking about Shay in front of him. About her wild sex drive. So he knew about the freak in her, which had him tempted to indulge.

"What do you think Saleem would say if he knew we were on the phone talking?" Shay asked, knowing Saleem would kill them both if he got the slightest idea that they were doing something sneaky behind his back. All he knew about them is that they hated each other.

"I'm my own man and I do what I want. So if you want to tell him I called your phone, be my guest," Wakil spoke, not caring if he found out or not.

"You got real defensive and I'm my own woman too. For the record, I didn't say I was going to tell him jack. Plus, he out with that bitch Wanda. He know I can't stand her ass," Shay snapped, letting Wakil know she made her own rules and could break 'em when she wanted to.

"Let's finish this conversation on a later date. My girl just walked in." Wakil pushed, trying to lock her in with no way out. He had no idea how far Shay was willing to take it, but if she had plans on bending over to touch her toes, he was going to stick her at her own expense.

"I don't care, that's up to you. Who just walked in Jane," Shay joked with a loud laugh.

"That's funny huh? I'ma find out why the police is looking for your man. So be easy and I'll be at you soon," responded Wakil.

"Is that a promise?" Shay asked, being flirtatious.

"No doubt, but I don't think you mean what you're asking. You might get yourself in too deep," said Wakil.

"Trust me, I know what I'm saying, plus I like deep situations." Shay was going for the gusto. She wasn't holding back.

"Look, we are definitely going to finish this talk. I gotta go," Wakil said, clicking her off. Shay stared up in the ceiling in a daze. She didn't know if she was getting way over her head, but crossing Saleem never entered her mind. Talking to Wakil for the first time in months opened up a can of worms that she never seen herself opening. The anger she once had for him suddenly turned to lust. Or was she just amazed by the story Jane had told her about his sexual performance.

At times throughout the conversation she could feel a wetness in her panties. *I'm tripping. I can't take it that far*, she thought, coming back to her senses. She also knew Jane had a fatal attraction to him after one night of sexual pleasure and desire. Drama at the workplace wasn't good for business.

* * * * *

Mimi had just walked in from shopping. While Wakil was in the bedroom finishing up his conversation with Shay, he had no clue to how she would respond to him not coming home last night, but had no plans of getting into a heated argument with her.

"What's up sexy?" asked Wakil, as Mimi entered the room with bags in her hand.

"Nothing, just tired. I been walking around King of Prussia mall all day," Mimi responded, throwing her bags by the closet door with no intentions of putting any of it away.

"Well, come here. Take a seat and let daddy go to work," suggested Wakil, waving Mimi towards him. As soon as she set on the opposite side of the bed, he reached down, removing her boots. Fixed on helping relax her, he grabbed both feet, placing them on the bed and slowly started to massage them. They were so pretty she could've won the world's best toes award.

"Oh Wakil, don't stop. That feels so good," said Mimi, enjoying every bit of the home health spa treatment she was receiving. She laid back relaxing, allowing everything to escape her mind. He took the blanket to cover her up and slid beside Mimi, placing his arms around her. She slowly dozed off in another world with Wakil right behind her. The topic of him not coming home the night before, never came up. It showed. She was too worn out to mention it.

CHAPTER 10

THE STREET IS TALKING

Boog had informed Saleem that a drug agent was killed on 60th and Arch Street last night. He was somebody named Charles Edney who went by the name Charlie, and had been working undercover for the last four years. Saleem was almost certain it wasn't the same Charlie he knew. But when Boog gave him the description, Saleem had a change of heart, especially when it came out two kilos of cocaine was missing.

"So Charlie was a cop, huh?" Saleem spoke, still trying to put everything together in his head.

"The only thing they found was a corpse and whoever hit cuz they made sure he was dead," responded Boog.

"Now I'm getting framed for some sucker shit by a faggot ass nigga," Saleem blurted out in anger.

Chill homey. First we gotta put you up safe, then scope things out to see who's behind this and who got that bread," said Boog, forming a plan to keep his best friend from going down for something he didn't do.

"Listen my uncle lives out in Coatsville, and he's eating crazy and he keeps telling my mom to send me out there. Well family that time has come," suggested Saleem.

"Yeah, that might be the best move to make. Me and Wah can hold things down and keep you updated on everything that's going on," Boog said, sharing some sincere advice.

"I know Shay going to be pissed, but this is where I'm really going to test her loyalty. Either she's with me or against me," stated Saleem, not really trying to leave her behind, but he couldn't drag her along with him. Extra company on the run was a hassle. Plus she had her own life to live.

"Man you can't worry about shorty. It's more fish in the sea. Nigga you're wanted dead or alive so remember that," Boog spoke, reminding him that his life was more important than a girl.

"Look, let me go. Get back when you can," Saleem said, clicking Boog off. Saleem had no clue to how Shay would react once he broke the news to her about him leaving town. He figured she would rather see him on the run alive and well instead of visiting him behind a jail cell. On top of all the drama he was laying up with Dee. But Saleem had no plans of conveying that information.

Just when things were looking promising everything took a turn for the worse. What him and Wakil had worked so hard to build was going down hill like a mack truck with no brakes. Saleem allowed the phone to ring three times before a soft spoken voice answered.

"Yes, who's calling?" the female on the other end asked.

"It's Saleem, can I speak to Shay?" Saleem asked.

"Hey Saleem. Haven't seen you around lately. I thought you and Shay broke up," Ms. Lacy responded, stretching out on the couch with nothing on but a nightgown.

"Naw you know that's my wife," Saleem spoke, smiling looking to see if Dee was watching him. She was glued into the conversation like she was going to make a two-way phone call a three-way.

"Well, hold on," Ms. Lacy said, as she yelled for Shay to pick up the phone.

"Hello," Shay spoke.

"What's up babygirl?" asked Saleem, with Dee still gawking down his throat.

"Nothing. I've been waiting for you to call all day. You had me worried about you once again. And what are you doing riding around with Wanda?" asked Shay, not mentioning the conversation she had with Wakil.

"My fault for not calling or coming through. Shit is crazy right now," Saleem said.

"How so? Hold up. Mom hang up the phone. Nosy ass," Shay said, after hearing a click.

"Mom duke be tripping. Look, somebody came up short and they trying to frame me," Saleem said.

"Who do you think set you up and who got killed?" questioned Shay, sounding like a private investigator.

"I have no idea who put the cross in on me, but the cat who got killed was a cop," Saleem responded.

"A cop? Are you kidding me? You can be put on death row with that Mumia guy! Saleem what are you doing?" asked Shay, sounding all hysterical.

"Damn, what you the Judge and Jury? Talking that death row shit." Saleem snapped at her like she had counted him out already. He quickly told her he would be leaving town for a minute and he would make sure she was well taken care of. He couldn't afford to let the law take him in because he was too young to die in jail. He knew he could trust her, but he wasn't taking any chances in case there was a reward out for his arrest.

After Saleem and Shay cleared the air on his situation, the conversation changed to a heated phone sex talk. That caused him to reach an instant hard on. Dee was turning red in the face and the jealousy was starting to set in.

"Tell mommy how you like it?" Shay asked, laid out on her bed, legs spread like an eagle wit her two middle fingers exiting and entering her vagina. She was all roused up.

"Look, I'll show you later," Saleem responded, not trying to continue to hurt Dee's feelings more than he already had.

"No Saleem now. I'm horny as shit, laying naked on my bed playing in my pussy." Shay demanded that he continue on talking nasty to her until she reached her climax.

"Stay like that until I find out how to get there without the police pulling me over," Saleem said, as he anticipated on making it to his destination.

"Oh, oh, oh, okay baby. I'll be here," said Shay, moaning as she began reaching an orgasm on her fingers. She was squirming around in her bed after enjoying a few moments of ecstasy.

Meanwhile, Saleem was in deep thought with the phone still in his hand. Dee kept her eyes on him even after the call ended. Startled by busy signal going off, Saleem jumped up. Once he realized it was the phone making the noise, he quickly relaxed and hung up. Dee lifted herself up and got close enough to Saleem where they could smell each others breath.

"Why your face frowned up like that?" asked Saleem, playing around in her head.

"You know why. I hate that bitch. She irks the shit out of me and you going sit there talking smut to her in front of my face," Dee spoke.

"She wanted to, but I told her no, 'cause you was right here. So stop tripping," Saleem said, unzipping his pants, allowing his manhood to be exposed. Dee was amazed by the cockiness of the man she was in love with. Without saying a word he pushed her head right down on his penis. She continued sucking him off until he filled her mouth with sperm. But he didn't become soft. She made sure of that. Dee pushed him on his back and rode him until they both went to sleep.

CHAPTER 11

NEW YEAR, NEW BEGINNINGS

A few weeks had passed bringing in the new year. Even though the ball dropped, Saleem was still underneath the radar. While Boog and Wakil partied every chance they got, things were still moving along as far as business was concerned. Wakil did all the purchasing of the drugs when it came time to re-up on the product. All three still bagged up together, they brought the package to him. They even found out the police were still looking for Saleem, but they had no plans of broadcasting it. It was a tight lid on the case, but Saleem wasn't buying it.

He wouldn't allow himself to get caught slipping. Especially with unmarked police cars still riding around. He felt it was a cheesy tactic to lure him out in the open. Saleem talked to his uncle and had plans of making his way out there shortly after the new year. He still saw Shay and his other female companions every once in a while with the money trail still coming in rapidly. Saleem had over fifty thousand saved up and his siblings as well, as his mom were well off. Boog made sure of that. Saleem would call and check in every now and then.

Saleem had found his hunch to be true. It didn't surprise him that Charlie was the cop who was murdered on 60th and Arch Street. The love he had for him had instantly vanished into thin air.

Saleem was staying in a one bedroom apartment right off of 52nd and Chester Avenue. It wasn't no luxury pad, but it worked, due to the present circumstances he was under. Living with Dee for those few days had turned into a nightmare. So he didn't see her as often as Kita and Shay. Saleem still hadn't put all the pieces together, as to who double-crossed him. Wakil remained mute about Charlie's demise.

As Wakil and Boog pulled up in front of Club Gotham, he felt out of place due to the luxury cars that were parked outside the young adult hot spot located on Delaware Avenue. *My turn is going to come soon,* he thought, placing his gun under the driver's seat. Only certain dudes got through with their pistol. As crowded as it was, you could've swore the party was outside. The door was being secured by two, three hundred pound bodyguards.

Wakil walked in making his presence known with Boog close by him. They both were dressed to kill. When they approached the bar all eyes were on them like they were celebrities. The majority being women. Both found two empty stools by the bar, and turned to face the girls who were in a group dancing while they sipped on their drinks. At the same time they couldn't help but notice some guys giving them the ice grill. Not paying any attention they continued to sip their Heineken's and proceeded to the back of the club to see if they recognized anyone familiar.

But this club had three levels to it. Boog and Wakil had no plans of going to the top. Slowly approaching their direction, there stood a light skinned female with attractive features and a body to be reckoned with.

"Hey Wakil," the woman occupant spoke in a seductive tone. Wakil stared at her trying to recollect his memory as to where he knew her from.

"Do I know shorty?" questioned Wakil, keeping his eyes on her. Due to the lights being dimmed, it was hard for him to get perfect vision.

"It's me, Tasha from 54th and Vine," Tasha said.

"Oh damn! My fault, long time no see," Wakil said, putting on a half grin, not really wanting to be bothered with her. She was old news to the entrée of women he had. After a few brief words, Wakil managed to escape the clutches of Tasha's seduction. Spotting one of his associates dancing with two females, he made his way over.

"Goddamn player, you doubled up tonight," said Wakil, breaking up the momentum.

"If it ain't the player, of all players Wah money," the guy, Eric said, as he shook Wakil's hand while giving him a half shoulder hug. They were High School buddies that never graduated.

"Naw not me man. I'm just out scouting for some new talent on the one night stand tip," responded Wakil, laying it on him thick.

"I hear you. Where's Leem at, your partner in crime? You dudes are always neck to neck," Eric inquired about Saleem's whereabouts.

"Oh Leem! He's out somewhere with his chick right now. I'll tell him you asked about him," said Wakil, giving him the full court brush.

After catching up on old times, Wakil continued to search for a girl he could take to the hotel. It was starting to get stuffy inside the club, so they decided to roll out. As soon as they reached the door of the exit sign, the same girl from earlier approached Wakil once again.

"Leaving so early?" asked Tasha, yelling over the loud music. Wakil started to ignore her comment, but decided against it, being as though she was so persistent to be in his company that night.

"Yeah, I guess I'll call it a night. Ain't nothing really popping in this camp," stated Wakil.

"Let's go to your crib and have our party," suggested Tasha, grabbing his hand.

"What about my man. I can't leave him stranded," responded Wakil pointing at Boog.

"Well, my girlfriend, she's down to take a ride on the wild side," Tasha spoke, looking over at her friend who in return gave a look of assurance that she was all for it. As they proceeded to walk through the front door, the night air hit them hard.

"So Wakil where's your Benz parked at? The streets talk, I heard you was eating," Tasha asked, looking around trying to spot it, like she knew for sure he had one.

"Benz huh? My Benz is parked right over there," Wakil responded, with a loud chuckle. Tasha looked as though she was embarrassed by the kind of car Wakil was driving. The rumors were false.

"Dag Wakil, I thought you was eating on these streets," Tasha blurted out digging to the core for some answers.

"Who told you that? I get my fair share. I'ma step my game up," Wakil said.

"Okay baller. I was just bullshitting with you. Where's the weed at? That shit gets me horny," Tasha responded, rubbing on Wakil's leg.

"A Boog pull that blunt out player and spark it up," said Wakil, meeting Tasha's request. Boog lit the blunt, took four puffs and passed it to the girl next to him.

"Here you go shorty. What's your name by the way?" Boog asked, halfway to the hotel.

"It's Lexus, but people call me Lex," Lex responded, with the weed and drinks running through her system. It wouldn't take Boog that long to get in her drawers. Boog put his arm around her. She fell right into his embrace.

"Look lovebirds, pass the gank," Wakil said, after he took a few drags of the weed and Tasha did her thing, as they pulled in the North America Hotel parking garage on City Line Avenue. Wakil and Saleem, along with those who were in his circle, took girls here to party one night stands.

"Wait right here. Let me go secure us a room for tonight," Boog said, exiting the car. He walked to the elevator and took it to the second floor lobby, where there set an elderly man who looked to be in his late fifties. Boog paid for one room with two beds, and ran off to the nearby gas station next to the hotel where he purchased two boxes of condoms and a variety of junk food.

Boog allowed his foot to hold the door between the elevator so it wouldn't close. As he yelled for them to come on, they got off on the third floor. Their room was right next to the ice machine. The North America Hotel wasn't seven star material, but it got the job done. As they walked in the room it was clean from top to bottom. It had a 19 inch color TV and two queen size beds. From the décor, you could tell the room was uncluttered but old fashion.

"Yaw some cheap ass niggaz going get one room," blurted out Tasha, putting her hands on her hips.

"Shit! Two rooms for what? I ain't shy about my work," responded Wakil, sliding his boots off, kicking them to the side.

"Me either," Lex said, as she started to undress down to her panties and bra. You could tell the liquor and drugs were taking their toll. Seconds later she was booty ball naked. Boog and Wakil were elated to see a striptease.

"Oh yeah! Two can play that game," spoke Tasha repeating the exact same thing her friend had done moments ago, until both were bare skinned. Boog looked at Wakil with a Kool-Aid smile. This was going to be a night to remember. They both had bodies like they went to the gym on a regular basis.

"Boog can you help me out in here?" Lex said, waving Boog towards the bathroom.

"Absolutely," said Boog, nodding his head. He took another look over at Tasha's body before going inside the bathroom with Lex.

"Fuck that bitch! Come over baby?" Tasha said, pulling Wakil by the hand, walking towards the bed by the window.

"Yaw tripping tonight acting like arm co-defendants fighting over some stolen merchandise," spoke Wakil, laying back on the bed.

"Picture that shit. I just ain't letting no slut outshine me," stated Tasha, as she began taking the rest of Wakil's clothes off. It was pitch black. The only light came from underneath the bathroom door. Tasha climbed on top of him, placing his manhood inside of her. Boog and Lex were still inside the bathroom with the shower running, but they weren't taking one. They were too busy occupying themselves in some sexual pleasures. Boog got naked and covered the toilet seat with a towel and sat down on it.

Lex positioned herself between his legs and started to perform oral sex on him. He allowed his head to flop back and focused his eyes on the ceiling, enjoying every bit of Lex's warm mouth. He pushed her head back and helped her stand up. She started to ride him backwards, moaning every time he pulled her body down on his manhood. You would've thought Boog was nine inches, how loud her moans got.

In the room, Tasha was riding Wakil like a rodeo show. She was more wet than a sprinkler. Every time she would lift up and slide back down on his manhood, it would sound like bubble gum popping. Wakil was trying to rip her insides out. He had no plans of making this into a love triangle, so he was giving her something to remember him by. Seconds later Boog and Lex emerged from the bathroom, which caught Tasha off guard, but it didn't stop her movement.

"I'll be damn," Boog said, grinning at Tasha going to work on Wakil's dick. Lex put her hands over his eyes and pulled Boog in the other bed with her. They set there and ate and drank, listening to Tasha moan out in ecstasy after reaching multiple orgasms.

✵ ✵ ✵ ✵ ✵

Saleem was at his room, debating on his next move, while Shay slept beside him. He woke up in a cold sweat after having a nightmare about the cops chasing him through a dark alley. As he moved his arm, he accidentally nudged Shay causing her to get up.

"What's wrong Boo? You're sweating like crazy," she said, reaching for the towel off the chair. She started to wipe his face and chest.

"I'm cool Shay. These nightmares are getting to me," he responded, stopping her from wiping his body.

"When did it start? This is the first time I ever saw you wake up sweating that bad," she asked, sounding concerned about his wellbeing.

"I think a little while after that barber shop incident. But this on the run shit has me on tilt. I can't do shit in Philly. It's time I roll out. Coatsville here I come," Saleem stated, with his mind made up.

"So you're leaving me just like that huh?" asked Shay.

"Shay I love you, but I have to go or I'ma be behind a door locked in for twenty-three hours a day," Saleem responded, rubbing his hands through her hair, not trying to see the inside of a jail cell.

"I know Boo. It's just I'm going to miss you like shit," explained Shay, while in the back of her mind she wasn't certain if their relationship could last long distance, even though Coatsville wasn't that far of a ride. She was used to having Saleem close by. So only time would tell. With Wakil still lurking around in her head things could only get worser than they already were.

"Don't worry. I'll be back for you, so keep the lames at bay," Saleem spoke, turning the shower on.

"Trust me, these niggaz know I'm spoken for. They been trying to get at me," Shay said, smiling at the thought of her being unfaithful to Saleem.

"I'm glad to hear that, but I know shit happens when needs aren't fulfilled," responded Saleem, giving her a look of seriousness.

"Now you don't trust me? I never cheated on you before, and a few hours or less away won't make me now. So don't worry," Shay stated, assuring him that her loyalty was to him, even though people were saying she slept with one of his cousins. Being as though he never had solid proof, he brushed it off.

"I'm not worried, and I do trust you. It's your hormones I don't trust," Saleem said, knowing how devilish a girl could get outside of your presence. As much as he loved Shay, he knew she could be vindictive if she wanted to. Shay was on the phone arguing with her mom for not returning her car.

"Bitch hung up on me. She gets on my nerves thinking everybody is suppose to jump when she says so," Shay said, pulling the sheet off, unveiling her nakedness. She started dressing quickly to get home before her mom had a nervous breakdown.

"Slow down baby girl before you break your neck. My bad for not getting you out of that spot," said Saleem, feeling as though he was part the blame for her still living with her mom.

"Saleem it's not your fault. My dizzy mom is coked up so bad she forgot I had her car," Shay responded. After she was dressed, she placed her arms around Saleem and tongue kissed him like she knew it would be the last time they ever saw each other.

He watched her walk out the door. Then he reached for his phone and called his uncle to let him know he was coming. His uncle was looking forward to his arrival. After he got all the information the call went dead. It was affirmed. Coatsville was the spot Saleem would hibernate for awhile until he could figure things out. He was counting on Wakil and Boog to see to it that the real gunman behind Charlie's murder got what they deserved. In the process of all that, clear his name. *Now I got to call Wakil to drop me off,* Saleem mumbled to himself. He allowed the phone to ring six times before a woman answered.

"Yeah! Let me speak to Wakil," asked Saleem, not sure as to who he was talking to on his partner's phone.

"Hold on," Tasha said. You could hear her calling his name as she nudged him to consciousness.

"Yo! Who this?," Wakil said, wiping the cold from his eyes.

"It's daddy," Saleem spoke, in a joking manner.

"What's the deal cuz? I had a long night player," responded Wakil, knowing off the top who it was. He sat up on the bed and looked around, examining the room noticing the empty chip bags, cookie wrappers on the floor, and the unused condoms on the table by the lamp. Boog and Lex were still asleep.

"I see you got chicks picking up your horn. What you high?" asked Saleem.

"Naw, me and Boog didn't even drink last night. I'm slipping dog. This bitch knows not to answer my phone," Wakil responded, giving Tasha the ice grill. She put her head down like a dog being disciplined by his master. He couldn't afford for her to pick up the phone if Mimi had called.

"Well look, I only called to tell you I'm on the move. So scoop me and drop me off. I just spoke to my Uncle Slim. He said it's a go," spoke Saleem.

"Oh yeah cuz! Damn homey it ain't suppose to be like this. Look, let me get my shit together and I'll be right there," Wakil said, feeling a little down about Saleem leaving town. But at the same time, he knew this was the break he needed. Nobody would slow him down or try to stop him. It was skies the limit and the only one he trusted was Boog, being as though Saleem wouldn't be in the picture. So there was no doubt about making Boog second in command.

The streets of Philly were about to witness a dynasty like no other. Money was coming in at a fast pace, even though the product they were purchasing from different people wasn't top quality. So he knew New York was definitely in the plans. But Wuwu was Saleem's man for the New York connect. Wakil knew him by seeing him outside the three two center and they only spoke on several occasions, but that was about it. So Saleem would only have to co-sign Wakil's name for the trip.

✳ ✳ ✳ ✳ ✳

Shay had just gotten home after stopping to get a bite to eat at a nearby breakfast spot, only to find her mother stretched out on the couch, mouth wide open and legs open enough to see her prize possession. Awakened by Shay slamming the front door, Ms. Lacy hopped up like she heard a gunshot. After realizing it was her daughter who caused the loud bang, she quickly became at ease.

"Hell girl, slamming that door like you lost your goddamn mind. I hope you put gas in my car," Ms. Lacy said, as she sat back on the couch, pulling her nightgown over her knees.

"Mom you are bugging out laying around half-naked with boys running all through here," Shay responded, flopping down next to her.

"Shit, I ain't got nothing they ain't never seen before. I only dozed off for a few seconds," Ms. Lacy stated, reaching over and grabbing a piece of Shay's sandwich.

"Dag mom, if you was hungry you should've told me when you called me," Shay blurted out, quickly leaping from the couch and headed towards the kitchen, while Ms. Lacy set there licking her hands and picking up the crumbs she dropped on herself.

"Keep it up smartass," Ms. Lacy yelled at Shay, walking towards the kitchen, while Shay sat at the dining room table still eating.

"You probably won't be seeing Saleem around for a while. He's leaving town for a while. Somebody's trying to frame him for murder," Shay spoke.

"Yeah right, and I was born yesterday. I knew he had a hidden agenda. He did that shit." Ms. Lacy speaking as though she witnessed him pulling the trigger.

"You're a mess. He ain't have hidden agendas when he was bringing your drug addict ass those pills," Shay mumbled low enough so her mom couldn't hear her.

"What was that?" asked Ms. Lacy.

"Nothing mom. I was just thinking out loud," Shay spoke, lying to prevent a heated argument. Even though it was still early in the morning, Ms. Lacy was obviously high off something, from the way she was acting, like she had bipolar. Most of the time it was normal for her to act out. Shay had only been in the house for a little over an hour and her little brothers were nowhere in sight. Ms. Lacy had informed her they were asleep. Shay went to lay down and kicked her shoes. off.

Ms. Lacy took no time undressing to enter the hot shower. Moments later Shay's so-called cat nap was disturbed by her cell phone ringing. She was real hesitant about answering it, but decided against it.

"Yes! Who's calling?" asked Shay, with her eyes still closed.

"It's me slut, long night I see," the woman's voice spoke.

"Jane go to hell with your whore ass," Shay spoke, recognizing the familiar voice.

"Girl shut up. What's going on? Fill me in with the latest," asked Jane, eager to get updated on the gossip.

"Trick ain't shit to tell you. I was at my man's house all night getting fucked," Shay spoke sarcastically.

"Your man. Who, the cop killer? Shit I thought he was playing hide and go seek," Jane responded, to add fuel to the fire. The news had traveled fast. If Jane knew the whole world knew.

"Damn you love holding on to false rumors. He ain't hiding nowhere! And don't nobody know nothing about a murder," Shay shot back, not feeding into her trap. Even though they were close friends, they occasionally would get into heated arguments over the smallest things.

"You know I was only joking," Jane said, bowing out gracefully.

"Bitch you know I don't play like that," Shay responded, knowing for a fact Jane wasn't just jerking her chain.

Somebody had leaked the information about Saleem's current situation and that wasn't good. So leaving town was the best move to make.

"Look Shay I'll holler at you later 'cause you're not yourself," Jane complained, hanging up in her ear. As soon as Shay hung up, the phone rang again. *Damn who the hell is this now*, Shay mumbled.

"Hello, what now?" spoke Shay, not wanting to be bothered.

"Hey baby girl just called to make sure you got home safe and to let you know I'm on the move as we speak," said Saleem.

"Hi boo. Didn't mean to yell in your ear like that," responded Shay.

"And know that me forgetting you is like me forgetting myself so don't panic. My two road dogs will hold you down," stated Saleem, assuring her she will be taken care of no matter what. Shay started to sniffle on the phone. She was crying, watching the man she was in love with slip away right before her eyes. They blew kisses to each other. Saleem felt like he was going to cry, but he didn't want to seem soft in front of his boys. The phone call ended on a sad note. But on a new beginning.

CHAPTER 12

COATSVILLE

"Goddamn lover boy ease up with the Love Jones," Wakil blurted out.

"Naw homey, you know that's wifey. I'ma need you and big fellow to hold her down for me," spoke Saleem.

"Don't worry, she's in good hands," Boog confirmed.

"Man I'm on it dog. We're still going to be on top. Boog gotta bigger part to play," spoke Wakil, letting Saleem know they were going to represent in his absence.

"I need you to be my eyes and ears and stay on point about who laid that fag cop," stated Saleem, as they were passing King of Prussia Mall. They were only fifteen minutes away from Coatsville, pulling up outside the Elk's Bar. Saleem called his uncle.

"Yeah! Who this?" a male voice asked.

"It's Saleem, Big Slim's nephew," Saleem responded to the male occupant on the other end of the phone.

"Oh! Damn youngin', he right here. I heard a lot about you. Call me D-roc. I'm your uncle's right hand man," D-roc stated, passing the phone to his uncle. D-roc sounding like he was from the country with a deep southern voice.

"Nephew, what's to you?" asked Big Slim.

"I'm in your area, right outside Elk's Bar on 7th and Marchant Street," responded Saleem.

"You're in the heart of the hood youngin', so I'm sending my man to pick you up now," Big Slim spoke.

"Alright," Saleem said hanging up.

"So what did he say?" asked Boog.

"He's on his way to snatch me up. So yaw can roll out. Listen I'ma be out here laying low. But hopefully I start something out here. I'm only a phone call away," Saleem said.

"Give me WUW's number?" asked Wakil.

"No doubt get with him. He knows the way out there and I hear the price is all love," Saleem stated, passing him the phone number.

"Look love ya boy. I'ma ride for you until the end," said Boog, giving Saleem a bear hug wrapping both of his arms around him. He looked a little depressed and Saleem knew from his facial expression.

"Cheer up nigga. I ain't dead. Shit will get greater later, believe that," Saleem said, breaking away from Boog's embrace. Wakil gave the same farewells and drove off.

While Saleem stood there, seconds later a black Mazda MVP with dark tint, pulled right in front of Saleem. Remembering what his uncle said about this neighborhood he didn't know who was in the van. So he put his hand inside his coat pocket to look as though he was carrying a gun.

Trying to bluff whoever was behind the wheel, the window rolled down and someone hand gestured for Saleem to come to the van. With his clothes in one bag and fifty thousand dollars in the other, he wasn't taking no chances.

"Come on little nigga," the man demanded with a southern accent. Recognizing the voice, he walked over and got in. It was D-roc, his uncle's right hand man.

"What's up D-roc?" asked Saleem, not sure if he was the same person who answered his uncle's phone. Plus he didn't like the fact this guy was calling him little when they were almost the same size.

"Same shit youngin', getting paid. You looked a little scary over there for a minute," D-roc suggested, judging by Saleem being hesitant about walking over to the van. D-roc could easily intimidate someone. He was dark skinned with a bald head, around three hundred pounds solid, six feet four inches and always wore dark shades, no matter if it was winter or summer. People gave him the title of Big Slim's bodyguard. He wasn't, but he could easily have portrayed the role.

"Naw old head, I'm just cautious. I'm new in town and I don't know these cats out here," responded Saleem, sliding his bag between his legs.

"What kind of gun are you carrying? Because around here these young bucks get stupid. But you'll be cool. Out here your uncle's reputation holds high standards. You can't underestimate these slimy mother fuckers. The first time you sleep on the smallest dude around here, consider yourself a dead nigga," said D-roc, giving Saleem the rules of how to survive out Coatsville. Occasionally, he would look over at him to see if he was paying attention.

"I don't have a gun on me. Sometimes bluffing works when your back is against the wall," Saleem responded.

"Man are you crazy? You got a lot to learn youngin'. That bluffing bullshit don't work out. These youngins' will try you. It's life or death," D-roc said. It was bad out there, but D-roc was putting a lot of extra sauce on the dish he was trying to serve Saleem, to see if he was cut for the task that was ahead of him.

"I'm no bitch old timer. I dig you for trying to school me to the rules of the Ville. But I was born in, not sworn in," spoke Saleem, talking slick with his Philly slang coming out. D-roc looked over at him and laughed. He was digging Saleem.

"You're alright youngin'. I think we're going get along just fine," D-roc stated, still trying to reach his destination to where Big Slim lived.

It was a little after twelve o'clock on Saturday with a slight wind chill. Saleem was looking forward to meeting his uncle who he had heard so much about during his years of growing up. Pulling up outside a building that looked like a project, but smaller than the ones in Philly, D-roc and Saleem exited the van and walked up the flight of steps reaching the third floor of the building. They were greeted by Big Slim opening the door, as if he timed their presence.

"Well, I'll be damned! Looking like your mother. Give me a hug nephew," spoke Big Slim wrapping his arms around Saleem. He was six foot three inches with over three hundred pounds of fat. But he dressed in the best attire. His weight didn't bother him. My uncle and D-roc favored each other and they both sported a bald head.

"Yo unc, it's been a long time coming for us to meet," blurted out Saleem, excited about being in his presence.

"You got that right. Haven't seen you since you was yeh high," Big Slim responded, placing his hands to the top of his knees to demonstrate the actual size Saleem was the last time he saw him.

"Nice spot unc. You got taste," Saleem said, admiring his uncle's apartment, but couldn't understand why he didn't have a house with all the money he was getting. Besides from that, the apartment was decked out from top to bottom with black fluffy carpet and a matching living room and dining room set. A black sofa long enough to be broken into a recliner as well.

"Well, you'll be staying here in this room. I call it the guest suite," Big Slim spoke, opening the door, exposing Saleem to the plush small room that had everything you needed for a room to be complete.

"This will do unc, no doubt," Saleem responded, flopping down on the bed.

"Get settled in. Then we can chat about how the ville is ran," Big Slim stated, walking off. It didn't take long for Saleem to put away his few outfits and hide his money. D-roc had rolled out. It was business as usual with him, so it left Saleem and his uncle time to catch up. They talked for hours, laughing and joking. Saleem informed him of the trouble he was in back home. Big Slim let him know the accusation was serious and as long as he stayed out here, he was in good hands. Big Slim didn't show his face around as much. So he had plans of letting his number one youngbul show Saleem around. Saleem listened to everything his uncle told him. But all the talking was making him tired.

"Damn unc. I'm beat. I gotta get me some rest," Saleem spoke, covering his mouth as he yawned.

"Yeah nephew get your rest. Tomorrow is another venture," Big Slim stated. Saleem shook his hand and went straight to bed. Only removing his boots, he laid there for a half-hour tossing and turning. He couldn't get Shay out of his mind. He thought about his mom and siblings who would look after them. Of course Malik would have to step up to the plate, but Saleem felt his presence was most needed. Minutes later he dozed off into another world.

CHAPTER 13

GAME OVER

Wakil didn't waste no time putting things back into perspective, without the help of his sidekick. Boog was ready to take his position even though he knew he couldn't fill Saleem's shoes. Everyone knew things would be different without his presence. Boog wasn't sure if Wakil could hold on to the empire Saleem helped build. But disloyalty wasn't in him so he was prepared to ride the wave with Wakil, even if it meant risking his own life.

Knowing that Wakil was unpredictable, the heat was at a minimum, as far as the police circling the neighborhood searching for Saleem. So business continued as usual. The little product that Wakil had left he distributed it amongst the major spots that brought in the most money.

Hooking up with Wuwu was mandatory to get back to some good product. Going back out, Coatsville wasn't in Wakil's plan, even though it was only a half-hour away. Parked outside the ranch which people called Boog's house, Wakil and Boog kicked it about their next move.

"So what we going to do now?" asked Boog, letting his seat drop back like a recliner.

"We going take over the world cuz. Eat hardy and drive Maserati," said Wakil, with a loud laugh as he pictured himself behind a wheel of such a luxury car.

"Well let's do it," Boog spoke.

"You got Appletree Street and Mary with the Packs Saleem use to give her. I'ma hold everything else down," Wakil responded, laying out the blueprint to continue to run their illegal drug operation.

"Yeah, I can handle that with no problem. I'm beat. I'ma go jump in the shower and get a few hours of sleep. So what you going do?" asked Boog, now leaning on the passenger side door.

"Check on Mimi, then try to track that nigga Wuwu down and try to lock that connect down," responded Wakil.

"Hit me later," said Boog.

"No doubt," Wakil assured him driving off. He popped on 'Ready to Die,' by Biggy Smalls and drove straight to his apartment. He had a lot going through his mind, but the most important part was getting rich, and being able to buy the things he always wanted. He hadn't eaten or changed his clothes. They were the last things on his agenda.

When he walked in, Mimi was stretched out on the couch with little to nothing on. His entry failed to wake her. It wasn't until he kissed her on the cheek, that brought her back to consciousness, looking up with a smile on her face.

"Hi baby. Where have you been all night? I missed you," Mimi spoke.

"I know Mimi. I been trying to secure Saleem's safety. You know the police are looking for him," Wakil stated, thinking of the first thing that came to mind.

"Oh, I forgot about that. As long as you're safe and here now," said Mimi, getting up so she could slide closer to him. Wakil was surprised by her response and wasn't quite sure if he told her about Saleem's situation or she heard it from somebody else, so he just brushed it off.

"Did you eat, are you hungry?" asked Wakil, massaging her shoulders.

"No, I'm fine. I ate a turkey salad earlier. Wakil does anything look different about me?" she asked, standing up so he could get a better view of her figure.

"Not really, but turn around so I can check that ass out," he said, motioning with his hand, to do exactly what he asked of her. She had no problem baring it all by lifting her long T-shirt up, exposing the black thong she wore.

"You still don't notice anything?" she asked, wanting him to guess before she dropped the news on him.

"What babe? Tell me and stop playing these wheel of fortune games." He was getting impatient and didn't feel like playing mind games with her.

"Alright! I'm pregnant," she said, rubbing her stomach.

"Stop playing Mimi," he responded, shocked by the sudden news, but elated at the same time.

"Boo, I'm serious. You're going to be a daddy," she said, flopping down on his lap.

"That's a wonderful thing. I can see a little me running around here," Wakil stated, rubbing her belly.

"I know. A little Mimi. It'll be a pretty girl with long silky hair," Mimi spoke, picturing how the baby would look in her mind.

"Girl? You better try a little Wakil, Jr. You know he's going to be stuntin' like his daddy."

"More like frontin' like his daddy. Plus, Boo it doesn't matter as long as you're around to see the baby born."

"Why wouldn't I be there? I ain't no dead beat dad," Wakil asked defending his honor. He didn't know where Mimi was taking the conversation, but he was prepared to hold his own.

"You know the life you live anything can happen and I don't see me raising my child on my own," Mimi spoke.

"Don't think like that. Trust me, I don't see me doing this the rest of my life. With Saleem on the run I gotta hold shit down, because I see these lames trying me sooner or later. As soon as I'm where I want to be, I'm out," Wakil said, but was he in too deep to pull out now or even after he reached his goal?

"Do you mean it? Because I know how hard it is to leave those streets alone," Mimi asked.

"I love you and my unborn seed, not the streets. No doubt the game has been all love to a nigga, but sometimes you gotta know when to fold your hand," responded Wakil, saying anything to make her happy.

"Ooww . . . Wakil," she said, wrapping her arms around him while kissing him on the mouth. She was astounded by everything he told her. It didn't take long for the foreplay to turn into passionate lovemaking. They enjoyed every bit of it for almost a half-hour. Wakil didn't even care if she smelled sex on him from last night or tasted it from performing oral sex on him. After they both took a shower together, washing each other up, Mimi dried off and got back in bed naked. Wakil pulled the covers over her wanting her to rest, being pregnant and all. He couldn't help hearing his beeper vibrating on the table next to the bed. He picked it up and placed it back down, being as though he recognized the number. Mimi was glued in on him.

"Who's that Boo?" asked Mimi.

"No one, just business as usual. Go to sleep. You and the baby need rest," he responded, kissing her on the forehead. He grabbed his coat and exited the apartment. It was a little after eight o'clock. He cruised down Landsdown Avenue and couldn't help but notice the crap game going on beside Stacy's Bar. But he ignored it. Instead he pulled on the side of Nick's Bar on 56th and Landsdown Avenue to holler at his man Turtle, who was out there hustling.

"Yo Turt," Wakil said, walking up on him.

"What's the deal Wah? I heard about Saleem. That's crazy. It's like I just seen him," Turtle spoke, shaking Wakil's hand.

"Yeah, tell me about it. He's cool though. He just chilling until the heat dies down," Wakil told him, not mentioning where Saleem was hiding out at.

"I know these niggaz want yaw out the way, the streets talking. Plus, I'm tired of these jakes around cutting my bread short," Turtle said, serving three customers that were lined up to buy his product.

"It's whatever old head. I'm with you. Call me to let me know, 'cause I'm sick of those dirty motherfuckers too," Wakil responded, prepared to ride all out with Turtle against whoever.

"I'ma let you know," Turtle responded, counting all his money standing by the phone booth in front of the bar. Wakil shook his hand and hopped back in his car and drove off. Wakil rode around to pick Boog up. He rung the bell three times. While he waited, he couldn't help to notice a black van kept circling the block. Wakil pulled out his 357 magnum and held it in his hand. He wasn't taking no chances. He didn't know if he was just being paranoid or bad karma was catching up to him.

"Damn Wah, don't break the bell. I ain't flash Gordon," said Boog, shutting the door behind him.

"Man, shit I ain't Scarface, but my mind is playing tricks on me," Wakil said, looking up and down the street. Sissy was heading right towards him.

"Nigga what happen? Put that gun up!" Boog asked, watching Wakil like he lost his mind.

"Wakil, let me get a couple bucks and where's Saleem?" Sissy asked, sticking her hand out. She was dressed like she was going trick or treating with a bunch of make-up and her hair halfway done.

"I don't know where he is. Here, take this and keep moving," stated Wakil, passing her a ten dollar bill.

"You cheap as shit," Sissy said, snatching the money and walking away. Wakil just flagged her and laughed.

"Did you call Wuwu?" Boog asked, standing next to Wakil on the same side he was holding the gun.

"Man, I'ma call dude right now," Wakil said, giving Boog his gun to hold, while he dialed the number. Wuwu picked up on the second ring. Wakil informed him that they needed to talk, so the meeting was to happen on Hunter Street,

Wakil's mom's block. Boog and Wakil drove around there and parked by the garages across from the abandoned buildings.

As they were getting out of the car a white Maxima station wagon was driving through the block and it parked behind Wakil's pop's truck. A short, dark skinned man got out of the passenger's side and the car was still running. Wakil figured it had to be Wuwu, so he walked in the direction and the guy yelled out.

"Yo Wah. It's me Wu," Wuwu spoke, identifying himself.

"What's the deal player? You got here fast," Wakil said, shaking his hand, but still keeping his focus on the tinted car Wuwu was in.

"I told you I was close. Damn, you make me look like a midget," expressed Wuwu looking up at Wakil.

"So what's the NY price and is it butter?" Wakil asked, getting straight to the essence of their meeting.

"Well, I got a Dominican connect on 149th and Broadway. They sell weight, but they go by grams, which I pay no more than five-hundred dollars an ounce for cooked up coke. Fuck that gram shit," Wuwu explained, giving him detail by detail, letting him know the uncooked would be more. Wakil agreed to ride out in the morning, stating he wanted to buy two kilos, but Boog decided against it on the first trip. It was Wakil's call to make. He had to meet Wuwu at 13th and Filbert at seven o'clock sharp.

"I'll be there like clockwork," stated Wakil, shaking his hand before they parted ways. Boog and Wakil jumped back in the car.

"That's one ugly nigga," Boog spoke, laughing as he expressed his opinion of Wuwu.

"You ain't never lied homey," responded Wakil, agreeing with Boog on Wuwu's looks. He was five feet five inches tall, 225 pounds, cross-eyed with a chipped front tooth.

"He paying those bitches for sex, 'cause he ain't peeling them on his looks alone," Boog said.

"Cuz you crazy," Wakil said, laughing at Boog's remarks. They continued to go back and forth. Grinding Wuwu up they headed down North Philly to drink, cutting through Fairmount Park.

✳ ✳ ✳ ✳ ✳

Jane and Shay were at the shop finishing up the last few customers they had left. Being as though this particular night it was more crowded than usual, they haven't spoken to each other all day. Shay still had Saleem in her mind and she thought about how life would be without his presence. It was time for Shay to break the ice.

Jane have you heard from Wakil?" Shay asked.

"Not in a few days, but I expect to soon. I called his phone but no one answered," Jane responded, looking at Shay, trying to see where she was taking her line of questioning.

"That's how they treat you when you give it up on the first night," Shay responded, throwing darts at Jane.

"Look at the kettle calling the pot black. For your info, it wasn't the first night," Jane shot back, even though she knew Shay was right. Letting her win out on an argument wasn't going to fly in front of other customers as well as employees.

"I'm just saying we all know what men want. Plus I warned you he wouldn't leave his girl for you," responded Shay.

"Enough about my man. Where's Saleem at? The cop murderer," Jane asked, hitting Shay where it hurt. Shay's face turned red. All the customers and employees looked around, like they had heard something they wasn't suppose to hear.

"Bitch! Don't go there." Shay leaped from behind her workstation, plunging at Jane and grabbing her hair. Shay punched her like three or four times in the face, causing a cut on top of her right eye. The customers and co-workers had to pull Shay off of Jane or Shay might've killed her and been on the run with Saleem. The modern day Bonnie and Clyde. After they broke them up, Jane still wanted to fight.

"No! Don't hold her back. Let that bitch go. She can dish shit out, but can't take it," blurted out Jane, positioning herself in a fighting stance.

"Yaw been friends as long as I been working here and you continue to fight about these men who probably don't give a damn about either one of you," one of the co-workers said, who repeatedly stepped in every time they fought or argued. Her words never changed.

"This nosey broad speaking about stuff she has no clue about," Shay stated, with rage in her eyes.

"You know it's true," said Jane, still adding salt to the wounds.

"Whatever whore. I'ma catch you at a later date and this time won't nobody stop me from beating your ass," Shay said, walking back over to finish up her client.

"Whatever!" responded Jane, brushing Shay's last remark off. It's been tension between them ever since Jane found out Wakil called her phone. She knew how Shay could be.

Jane regretted telling her about what her and Wakil did, even though she knew they both hated each other. But some how that brick of ice that was between them was suddenly melting. Shay finished her client, cleaned her area up and left, like she was late for a corporate business meeting.

Shit it's cold out here, Shay mumbled under her breath, opening up the car door. She was still driving her mom's car. Saleem never got around to buying her one. Not in the mood to party, so she drove home, pausing at the stop sign on 56th and Master. She went into a daze thinking about Saleem, as she watched the younger guys run up and down the street hustling. The sound of the car horn behind her quickly snapped her out of it. As she pulled off, her cell phone rang.

"Hello," answered Shay.

"Hey stranger," the caller spoke.

"Hi Wakil. It took you long enough to call me back," Shay said, like she was anticipating him calling.

"Shorty, I've been busy taking care of business. It's a lot on my shoulders right now," responded Wakil, not mentioning Shay's name in front of Boog. He was playing it safe, while walking on deadly grounds, knowing how much Saleem loved her.

"Too busy for me?" Shay asked.

"Never," Wakil said.

"Well, I'm on my way home. I just beat your girl's ass," Shay stated.

"Who?" asked Wakil, not sure if she ran into Mimi and said something stupid.

"Damn! How many you got?" asked Shay, trying to get him to spill the beans.

"One," spoke Wakil being blunt.

"Whatever liar. Jane's whore ass," Shay responded, ignoring his last response. She knew he was a player, but he never really was interested in her until now.

"Oh yeah! I thought yaw were friends," assume Wakil, catching a breath of relief that it was Jane and not Mimi.

"Well that's over. Bitch got a smart mouth," Shay said.

"I haven't really spoken to her lately. So I wouldn't consider her my chick, more like a one-night stand," stated Wakil, trying to act like he wasn't really attracted to Jane. But he was. Shay wouldn't know if it was up to him. He was trying to play his cards right.

"I could've swore yaw were married with children," Shay said, parking in the empty space in front of her house.

"Let's just say I have that affect on people," Wakil said, as they talked for a few more minutes. Shay invited Wakil over. He agreed to stop through, but he informed her it would be late. She didn't care. She had the house to herself. She rushed to take her clothes off and ran her bath water putting shampoo in there to spark up the bubbles. She allowed her body to soak in there for a half-hour. After she got out, she dried off and put on a red Victoria Secret nightgown and laid across her bed flicking the channels, patiently awaiting Wakil's arrival.

* * * * *

Meanwhile hours had lapsed and Wakil and Boog were going inside the new go-go club, that had just opened on Wylusing Avenue between 52nd and 53rd, called the Cherekee, a two-story building right next to the townhouses.

When they went up to the door a fat bouncer searched and checked them for guns. But Wakil figured they would do that, so he left his gun in the car. After reaching the top of the steps, to the left was a guy taking pictures of the dancers and some dude. Boog and Wakil were a little tipsy but still alert and able to function.

The place was dark. The only light came from the stage where the strippers were taking everything off for the money people were throwing at them. Boog walked towards all the action, while Wakil eased through the crowd heading to the back of the club where the bar was at. He purchased a Heineken with Grenadine. As he turned around, he couldn't help but notice Dee coming in his direction.

"Hey Wakil, didn't expect to see you in here," Dee yelled over the loud music. She was standing there in a two-piece bikini that her butt-cheeks swallowed. If it wasn't for the front covering her private area, you would've thought she was naked, judging from the back.

"What's up Dee? Long time no see," Wakil responded, using his eyes to inventor her body.

"Yeah, it has been some time now. Is Saleem alright? I haven't seen him or spoke to him since that stuff happened," Dee spoke, not getting into the details of Saleem's situation.

"He's chilling right now until the smoke clears," stated Wakil, cutting her off, as he ran up the front where an altercation had broken out. He knew Boog was up there, so he had to make sure he was cool. To his surprise, Boog was arguing with another person about dancing with a girl, that the guy was claiming as his personal stripper.

Boog wasn't having it, plus the girl was standing next to Boog. It was three o'clock in the morning and the club didn't close until six o'clock. Wakil seen the guy Boog was having the dispute with turn his back to talk to one of his homeys.

Wakil whispered in Boog's ear to lure the guy out front and he would meet him out there. Boog called the man out, even though he looked to be older than Boog. Backing down wasn't in his blood. Wakil had already went to the car and grabbed his pistol. He stood on the side of the club in the small parking lot. He didn't even care about all the people who was out there smoking their weed and talking.

Boog came down the steps. Wakil called him and threw the car keys at him and told him to start the car. The man was walking down the steps as Boog got into the car and he seen him get in. He started yelling profanity at Boog, but didn't spot Wakil walking by him. Blah, Blah. All you heard was shots ring out. Wakil ran and jumped in the car and pulled off. Boog couldn't believe Wakil just blew the guy's brains out in front of all those people.

"Wah you crazy," Boog said.

"Naw dude was crazy for fucking with anybody in my circle," Wakil responded, looking out the rear view mirror to see if any cops were coming, being as though the sirens sounded like they were close by. Wakil ain't feel no remorse about killing the guy, and him being high only added to the heart he already had.

"So what we going to do now?" asked Boog.

"I'ma go grab this money from my mom's crib, and get you to drop me off up Shay's crib, so I can get with Wuwu in like three hours," Wakil explained to Boog hoping he wouldn't ask why he was going up Shay's house.

"Alright," Boog said, looking back making sure they weren't followed. Wakil ran in the house and grabbed a bag full of money, then ran up the steps to the house next door to his parents and hid the gun he had just used in a brutal murder. He pulled off, driving towards Parkside. He called

Shay. She was still awake waiting for him. It didn't take him long to get there. Boog hopped in the driver's seat and pulled off. Wakil rung the bell. Shay came to the door with panties and a long T-shirt, no bra. She left the door open so he could enter.

"Took you long enough. You said late, but not this late," Shay said rolling her eyes.

"I had gotten tied up handling some business," Wakil stated, following her up the steps.

"It's me and you here," Shay spoke dimming the lights.

"That's cool with me, but where can I put this at?" he asked, pulling the money out of the bag. Shay's eyes lit up like a Christmas tree.

"Where are you going with all that money?" she asked, like it was the first time seeing a large sum of money.

"I'm taking a trip in a few hours, so I gotta be out of here by at least seven," he told her, putting the money in her drawer with the panties and bras.

"What a vacation? Or business?" she asked, searching for an answer.

"The second question is more like it. I have to, if I'ma take care of you and my family," Wakil assured her.

"Look out for me huh? I'm grown. I can take care of myself," Shay responded.

"Believe me, I know you can. And all this shit you got didn't come from doing hair," Wakil said, speaking on the closet full of clothes and shoes she had piled up.

"Are you going to continue to talk or fuck me?" asked Shay, removing her panties and T-shirt.

"NO," responded Wakil stripping down to his socks. Shay crawled on the bed and stuck her butt in the air giving Wakil an easy entrance to her vagina. He slid his penis inside her, then grabbed her waist and continued thrusting his manhood in her. She moaned and screamed loud enough to wake a dead man. After a few more strokes, he pulled out and slid right in her asshole. She leaped forward like he hit a nerve.

"You're not sticking that monster in my ass," Shay said, in between deep breaths.

"Chill Shay. Let me do me, he won't hurt you," Wakil spoke, as though his penis had a brain of his own.

"Shit no," Shay repeated, remembering the episode with Saleem. Wakil quickly stuck it back in her pussy before he went soft. He didn't show her no mercy, trying to rip her insides out.

After a few more pumps, he exploded all up in her, and rolled over on his back. Shay was on her stomach, exhausted like she did all the work. The phone rang. It must've rang about four or five times before one of them even attempted to answer it.

"You going answer your phone?" asked Wakil.

"That's yours. Mine is turned off," Shay responded, grabbing his phone off the table.

"Yo, who this?" asked Wakil.

"Old head it's Nell. Me and KB were chilling with Boog and a car turned the corner and started shooting at your car. Boog was sitting on the passenger side. He got hit bad. They rushed him to the hospital," Nell said, giving Wakil the unpleasant news about his friend. Nell was another youngbul who hustled for Saleem and Wakil. He was only sixteen.

"Nigga who shot Boog? What the fuck you talking about? I was just with Boog!" Wakil snapped. He was on tilt about what he just heard.

"Old head I don't know. Being as though me and KB was on the driver's side of the car, we were able to dodge the bullets." explained Nell, trying to fill Wakil in as much as possible.

"Whoever it was, them motherfuckers going to pay!" Wakil responded.

"He was rushed to Misercordia Hospital," Nell spoke.

"Where you at?" Wakil asked, putting his clothes on faster than when he took them off.

"I'm on the Avenue," Nell responded.

"Are you strapped? I don't have no gun on me," asked Wakil, not taking any chances of riding around butt naked. He figured somebody from the club remembered what kind of car they drove off in, and were retaliating. Wakil wasn't even sure if the guy was dead or not, but two shots to the head should've gotten the job done.

"I got my 38 pistol in the alley," said Nell, motioning his hand, directing KB to go get it.

"That'll work. Get it and meet me at the hospital. I should be there in less than an hour," stated Wakil. He knew he was racing through morning traffic, people trying to get to work.

"No doubt old head," Nell said, hanging the phone up. Wakil must've forgot that Nell and KB didn't have a car. So they waited to see if a fiend would come through and they would pay 'em to drive them to the hospital.

"Let's go. I need you to take me there, and let me drive," Wakil spoke, throwing Shay a pair of jeans and a sweater he picked up off the chair. She was still laying there asshole naked with cum dripping out of her.

"I'm coming. Shit! This is crazy. I hope he's alright," stated Shay, putting her hair in a pony tail. She slid on her Timberland boots, grabbed her coat and they were out.

Wakil ran every stop sign, making every green light. Shay was holding on to the door handle and looking at Wakil like they were being chased by the police. He drove straight down 55th Street. Misercordia Hospital was on Cedar Avenue between 54th and 55th. Wakil parked in an empty spot right outside the emergency room. Shay tried to keep up, but trailed way behind. Wakil ran up on the first doctor he saw.

"Excuse me doctor. I'm looking for my brother William Briggs who was just brought in here for a gunshot wound," explained Wakil, trying to get some information on Boog's condition. Shay was right there with him, waiting to hear what the doctor had to say.

"Well sir you're not the only one because more of Mr. Brigg's family are over there in the waiting room," the doctor said, speaking with an Arabian accent. Wakil looked towards where the doctor had just pointed.

"How is he doc?" asked Wakil, still trying to get some information out of him.

"He's in the operating room right now. I must say his injuries look serious," the doctor answered.

"Thanks doc," responded Wakil, parting ways with the doctor. They headed towards the waiting room to join the rest of Boog's family. Everybody was there from aunts, uncles and cousins to his mother. Nell and KB were sitting there like they were lost and high off something. Wakil went over to embrace Boog's mom.

"Hi, Ms. Val. How are you holding up?" asked Wakil, giving her a hug. You could tell she had been crying the way her eyes were puffy and the dried up tear marks on her face.

"They hurt my baby," she cried out, squeezing Wakil tighter, not trying to let him go. Shay stood by and looked as though she was about to cry. She knew Boog from Saleem, even though they weren't close.

"I know Ms. Val. I'm here for you. I promise you it won't end like this," Wakil whispered in her ear. She was the spitting image of Boog. Moments later the doctor entered the room.

"Is there a Ms. or Mr. Briggs here?" the doctor asked, searching for Boog's parents. Alongside the doctor was a man dressed in all black. Looked to be a pastor or preacher.

"Yes, I'm Ms. Briggs, William's mother," she responded, walking closer to the doctor and the gentleman standing by him.

"Ms. Briggs," the doctor said pausing, "I'm sorry, we did all we could to revive your son. The bullet to the head was so severe, that it was impossible to stop the bleeding in the brain," explained the doctor, as he continued to give them the sad news. Ms. Val was in shambles. Wakil had to hold her up to keep her from passing out. Tears started to flow down Shay's face. She didn't even know why she was crying. Watching Ms. Val fall to pieces over losing her only child had overwhelmed Shay, causing her to break down.

"Can we see him doc?" Wakil inquired.

"Sure, and if anyone needs to speak to Mr. Wilcox here, he's our pastor at Misercordia," the doctor said, pointing to the man beside him. The doctor led the way to the room where Boog's body was.

When they entered, on the table laid Boog's naked, lifeless body. Even though he looked as though he was sleeping, the reality of it was, he was dead. Ms. Val ran over and jumped on top of him, kissing him all over his face. They had to pull her off of him.

Wakil viewed the body and made his exit. It was too much for him to bare. He stepped past the waiting area and grabbed KB and Nell who remained in the same position Wakil had left them in.

"Yo! Come on, we out," Wakil said, shaking them.

"Dag old head, what time is it?" asked KB, as he got up from the chair, stretching his arms out.

"Time to take your ass home," Wakil responded, backing out the emergency exit with Shay right beside him and KB and Nell lingering behind them. They got in the car and drove off. Shay looked out the window the whole ride. She had a few tears coming down her cheeks as she thought about Saleem and how much he loved Boog.

Shay was also having mixed emotions about sleeping with Wakil.

Saleem wasn't gone for twenty-four hours, and she had slept with one of his best friends, on top of losing a best friend. Thing's couldn't get any worse.

"Aye old head. Who that in the front seat? She look familiar," asked Nell, leaning in between Wakil and Shay.

"None ya," yelled Wakil, over the loud music.

"None ya, what's that?" Nell inquired, speaking with his eyes closed.

"None of your fucking business! Now fall back with your high ass," said Wakil, using his right hand to push him back into his seat. Now wasn't the time for Nell to be acting stupid. Wakil was still feeling a little tipsy from the drugs he had in his system. The death of Boog had his high wearing off, slowly but surely.

"Are you still taking that trip?" asked Shay, turning the music down.

"Shay, the show must go on. Now don't get it twisted. That was my fucking man and somebody's gonna pay for that," Wakil proclaimed, with business still on his mind.

"Now I don't need you getting locked up or killed," responded Shay, with her eyes glued on him. He never turned to face her, pulling in front of the deli on 56th and Master.

"Okay get yaw little asses out," said Wakil, holding his seat forward to allow Nell and KB to slide out, with Nell almost falling flat on his face, until Wakil held him up.

"Good looking old head, I'm tired as shit," Nell spoke, fixing his clothes. KB was standing on the steps waiting.

"Yaw better stop getting so high. How much money you got on you?" Wakil asked.

"I think it's like $1,200 or close to it," Nell responded, passing him the lump sum of money he pulled from his inside jacket pocket.

"Did Boog give yaw enough to hold you until we scored some more product?" Wakil asked, sticking the money in his pocket.

"He gave us five grand worth, so that should hold us for a minute," responded Nell.

"Cool, I'ma get at yaw later on tonight. Keep yaw ears to the street. We gotta find out who did that to Boog," Wakil said, driving off.

Shay stayed quiet the remainder of the ride home and Wakil didn't bother to break the silence. He had so much going through his mind, he had nothing really to say. But New York was still part of the plan.

He would seek revenge later for Boog's death, but business was first and nobody would stand in the way of that. Once inside the house they went straight to Shay's room. Wakil went inside the dresser drawer and grabbed his money, stuffing it inside his coat pocket. He sat down on the chair as Shay laid across her bed kicking her boots off.

"Damn Shay! What you mad at, me? I didn't mean to snap like that on you," Wakil said, finally breaking the ice.

"No Wakil, I'm not mad. I'm just confused and tired as hell," Shay said, rolling over on her back.

"Confused about what?" asked Wakil.

"About us! I'm still in love with your best friend, but at the same time I'm sleeping with you. And who's going to tell him about Boog?" Shay asked.

"As you should. But Leem wanted me to look after you and I'm doing just that. He don't have to know about us. I'll tell him about Boog," Wakil said, laying beside her, speaking as though he had everything figured out.

"If you say so. If this is a dream please don't wake me," Shay said, turning to kiss Wakil. It didn't take them long to start making passionate love. Afterwards, Shay dropped Wakil off at 13th and Filbert Street. On her way back she stopped by 30th Street station. She went inside to the McDonalds, where she purchased some breakfast and hopped back on the expressway.

CHAPTER 14

BIG CITY OF DREAMS

On 13th and Filbert Street, underneath the parking garage was a bus terminal, with a sign that read 'Peter Pan Trailways.' It was so small one bus at a time had to park on the street right in front of the place.

Greyhound Bus Terminal was right behind Peter Pan, but they didn't have televisions on their bus. Wakil walked in looking around to see if he could spot Wuwu, before he purchased a ticket. Heading in the direction of the pay phones, he saw Wuwu coming out of the bathroom.

"Damn cuz, you look like you had a long night," spoke Wuwu sipping his coffee.

"Man you don't know the half of it," responded Wakil, looking over his attire. His pants were wrinkled as well as his shirt, so he zipped up his jacket to hide what he could.

"You cool. Go grab a one-way ticket to New York. I'll give you the game on that later, why you never buy a two-way ticket," Wuwu told him as he continued to sip his beverage. Wakil paid for his ticket while other people were boarding the bus. Him and Wuwu weren't that far behind them. They walked straight to the back of the bus, and sat in the three-man seat by the bathroom. It wasn't crowded so that was a good thing. Wakil decided to unzip his coat since nobody would be able to see his shirt, unless they were up close on him.

"Yeah, you might as well get comfy. We should be there, in like an hour and a half, no more than two at the most," Wuwu said, removing his jacket and throwing it over top of him, covering his upper body.

"No doubt, wake me up when we arrive. I'ma catch up on my z's," spoke Wakil, turning over on his left side, facing the window and pulling the jacket hood over his head. He got in a comfortable position to doze off. Wakil never mentioned Boog's death to Wuwu. He didn't feel it was his concern.

"I'm trying to see what movie they going to play," responded Wuwu, pulling a bag of chips and a cake out of a brown paper bag he was carrying. Wakil didn't bother responding. He was already asleep.

The bus pulled off. Wuwu leaned back like he was on a lounge chair and started to eat his snacks. *Damn this nigga snore*, Wuwu mumbled with chips coming out his mouth. They still didn't play the movie, so Wuwu ate all his junk food and decided to join Wakil in a deep slumber. The bus made one stop at a Jersey hotel, about an hour away from Camden, New Jersey.

Just as they were driving through the Lincoln Tunnel, Wakil was wiping the cold out of his eyes. You could tell he had a rough night from the bags starting to appear below his eyes. He looked over at Wuwu, who was knocked out with his mouth wide open.

"Yo! Let's roll. The bus is pulling in," said Wakil, shaking Wuwu back to consciousness.

"Shit, I was under like that?" asked Wuwu, brushing the crumbs off his jacket.

"I was comatose and I woke up hungry as shit," stated Wakil, checking his pockets, making sure his money was secured.

"We can grab a bite to eat on the way to the spot," Wuwu responded, licking his dirty hands, then wiping in between the corners of his eyes. When the bus finally completed its stop everybody got off.

"Now which way? It's a million people down here including a bunch of cops," Wakil spoke, not use to being in a big city like New York. The Port Authority was a busy place to be, no matter what time of the day it was.

"Chill player, just follow me and don't look so suspicious," Wuwu said, leading the way. They took the escalator to the street level and walked towards the turnstile. Wuwu was looking for the sign that read Uptown. Both of them rode the A-train up to 145th and Saint Nichols.

"This makes Philly look like a small village," spoke Wakil, admiring how big New York was compared to where he was used to living.

"And their chicks are bad," blurted out Wuwu.

"So we're gonna walk to 149th and Broadway?" asked Wakil.

"Naw we're going to jump into one of those cabs," responded Wuwu, pointing at the black Lincoln Continental riding by.

"I heard the cops be driving these cars, working undercover," spoke Wakil.

"Yeah some of them, but we ain't gotta worry about that right now 'cause we don't have no drugs on us," Wuwu said, flagging one of the cabs down. It stopped on the dime.

The driver took them to 148th and Broadway. They walked one block over. Wuwu looked around to see if he could spot his connect. It had to be six or eight people standing outside the pizza store on 149th and Broadway. They were all Dominicans and neither Wuwu or Wakil spoke Spanish. Wuwu quickly located the person he was looking for.

"Papi what's up? Wuwu yelled, walking over to shake his hand.

"Long time me friend," the Dominican man spoke with a Spanish accent.

"Yeah, I been grinding to get my money right," said Wuwu.

"I hear you Papi. Who you friend?" asked the Dominican, inquiring about Wakil.

"This is my man Slim. He's good peoples," responded Wuwu introducing Wakil to the Dominican Papi, without disclosing his real name.

"What's up Papi? Call me Yamega," Yamega stated, shaking his hand.

"I'm cool, just starving like Marvin," Wakil said, rubbing his stomach. With so much going on in the last twenty-four hours, he hadn't taken time out to eat.

"No need to worry me friend. We do you good here. Come follow me," Yamega said, waving Wakil and Wuwu to come with him. Wakil knew this was part of the game to make you feel comfortable when you're spending money. They walked down the hill and went to one of the many high rise apartment buildings that was located between Riverside and Broadway.

Taking the elevator up to the sixth floor, as they were getting off, you couldn't help but notice the female standing by the door in the direction they were walking. She had reddish brown hair and was either Spanish or Dominican. Yamega walked right up to her, entering the door that she was in front of.

"Make yourself at home. My name is Rita," Rita spoke, revealing that she spoke English well. You could tell the place was only used to conduct business. It was barely furnished with only a tore down sofa, a dining room table with three chairs and a black nineteen inch color television.

"So Papi, what can I do for you and your friend?" asked Yamega, getting down to business.

"I got thirty grand. I need two kilos of that cooked butter," Wuwu asked.

"Two for thirty grand. I can make that happen," responded Yamega, with a smile on his face.

"Yeah," said Wuwu, moving his head up and down.

"No probably. Only do for you," Yamega stated, trying to speak English as best as possible. He pulled his cell phone out and started talking to somebody in Spanish. No more than ten minutes later somebody was knocking on the door. Wakil was looking around trying to keep his eyes on everything moving, especially Rita.

Rita was thick in the waist and her reddish hair made her dark brown complexion stand out more. But he was too far from home to try to cross enemy lines thinking with his manhood. Two men came through the door. One had a pizza box in his hand, the other was carrying a plastic shopping bag. They went right over to Wakil and gave him the pizza.

"Good looking Papi," Wakil thanked him, taking the box that Papi just gave him, with a head nod.

"Do you need some napkins?" asked Rita, winking her eye at Wakil.

"Yeah, thank you," responded Wakil, never losing eye contact.

"Okay business now," Yamega said rubbing his hands together. Wuwu tapped Wakil on his shoulder letting him know it was cool to give up the money. Wakil reached in every pocket, pulling out chunks of money, passing every bit of it to Yamega. Rita came right behind him and put her hand out to collect the money to make sure the count was thirty thousand.

Inside the plastic bag, Yamega pulled out two zip lock bags full of cocaine. He started cooking up one of them in a pot, two sizes bigger than a coffee pot. It took him less than an hour to finish cooking the drugs and weighing it on a triple beam scale.

"Good stuff Papi," Yamega said to Wakil and Wuwu pointing to the cocaine on the scale.

"I see it. That's some creamy yellow shit," Wakil responded, with his eyes zoomed in on the product.

"You better believe it cuz. I told you they got nothing but the best," stated Wuwu, agreeing with Wakil. They put all the pancake shape cocaine pieces inside two separate zip lock bags and wrapped them in a brown bag.

"Come check me anytine," Yamega told, Wakil extending his hand out.

"No doubt I'll be back," Wakil assured him.

"We have a cab outside waiting for you," spoke Rita, as she walked them down to the elevator. Another man rode down to the first floor with them making sure they reached the car safely. Outside was a gray Lincoln Continental parked in front of the building. As they hopped in, Wakil kept looking behind him making sure it wasn't a set up, and the police didn't jump out on them.

"Nigga you paranoid. I told you we cool. I ain't tryna get knocked out here with two bricks of hard," Wuwu stated, lighting up a Newport.

"Naw, I'm chilling. Just being cautious with this shit," responded Wakil, shuffling the bag around that was tucked in between his waist, as he tried to sit comfortable.

The driver pulled up in front of the bus terminal. Wakil gave the driver a twenty dollar bill and they both jumped out of the car. They made it just in time to catch the next bus back to Philly that was scheduled to leave at 12:15 sharp. As the bus was loading up, the movie was already starting to play.

"Now they want to start the movie on time," Wuwu spoke, sitting in the seat right in front of the small ceiling television.

"That's 'Lean On Me,' a classic. Dig Wuwu, give me the game on why you don't buy a two-way ticket," Wakil inquired, leaning over the seat.

"Aw, man that's being smart, 'cause you don't want to get pulled over with a two-way ticket back to Philly. The first thing the cops going assume, looking at us, is that we're drug dealers coming to buy drugs," Wuwu explained, breaking it down so Wakil would understand where he was coming from.

"I hear you dog," Wakil assured him. They set apart going back to keep the tension down, so they wouldn't look suspicious.

It seems like a long ride back. Wuwu told Wakil to get back at him when he was ready to take that trip again, and everything he did was on the strength of Saleem. They shook hands and went their separate ways. Wuwu disappeared down Market Street and Wakil walked towards the subway. He wasn't taking any chances of riding in a yellow cab.

CHAPTER 15

BACK OUT THE VILLE

A week had passed since Saleem left Philadelphia. He was learning how to survive out Coatsville. It didn't take long. His uncle gave him the game. The dos and don'ts of staying on top and safe in the Ville. He was living proof of that.

Saleem had already set up shop inside Elk's and Gillie's Bar, selling weight from eight balls up to ounces. He was making a hundred dollars off of each gram. But he would look out for certain individuals, allowing them to make extra money by selling his product to them for a cheaper price.

He gave them eight balls for a hundred dollars so they would make a profit. His ounces sold for fourteen hundred. The price in Philly was a lot cheaper. Saleem had moved out from his uncle's apartment and rented his own place out Rock Run, a ducky spot. His Uncle Slim wasn't doing so well, after he found out he was diagnosed with lung cancer, so he wasn't able to move around like he used to. He introduced Saleem to his connect, where as though Saleem was only paying eighteen grand a piece for each kilo. The profit was overwhelming. Philly couldn't match what he was accumulating out of Coatsville.

"Yo Monk you're up. I just beat dude two straight games," Saleem said, screwing chalk around the tip of his pool stick. He learned how to play back home at the Capri Bar, one of his many hangouts.

"I'ma bust your ass Leem," Monk responded, grabbing his pool stick. Monk was Saleem's right-hand man out the Ville. He was a big youngbul, 6'3, 260 pounds solid. He looked like a human gorilla. So nobody rubbed him the wrong way, plus he was from Oak Street Projects. That Project was like Sagon in Philly.

"Is that my phone or yours?" asked Saleem, not sure if his phone was ringing or Monk's.

"Yours," responded Monk, looking at his that was hooked to his belt.

"Hello," Saleem answered.

"Nephew, I been trying to get in touch with you for a few days now. I got some bad news from back home," Big Slim spoke.

"Hold on unc. Let me go outside. It's too loud in here. Yeah, what were you saying?" asked Saleem, as he left the sports bar, more like a mini club. You could do anything in there from shooting pool, dancing and video games as well as drink.

"I got a call from your mom a few days ago. She said a close friend of yours was gunned down outside his house. Boog? I think she said," Big Slim stated, filling Saleem in with each detail.

"Boog, are you sure?" asked Saleem, not trying to hear that his best friend was dead.

"That's what she said," Big Slim spoke.

"Why! Wakil ain't holler at me? This shit can't be happening!" Saleem blurted out with tears starting to roll down his eyes. He was hurt and angry that he couldn't do nothing.

"Now hold firm, don't go doing nothing stupid. You'll get the chance to put the pieces to the puzzle together in due time," Big Slim said, coughing. He was getting worse, but he never let Saleem know. He didn't want him worrying.

"Unc, I gotta handle my business. I feel like a bitch playing hide and go seek," responded Saleem, with nothing but revenge on his mind. Running from the police wasn't on his mind no more. He was determined to find out who killed Boog and why.

"Nephew, I hear you, but think about your situation. You gotta make your first move, your best move 'cause you can't afford to miss," Big Slim explained, reminding him he was still being accused for a crime that could land him in prison for the rest of his life.

"That's my fucking man unc! I'ma kill whoever had something to do with it," stated Saleem, wiping the tears from his face as people were staring at him as they walked past, going inside the sports bar.

"You're not thinking right now, talking reckless on this phone. This is the game son, and you can't ride on emotions. Emotions will have you six feet under or in jail and broke," Big Slim spoke, trying to get his point across.

They continued to talk for a few more minutes and Big Slim managed to calm Saleem down. Big Slim also informed him the chemotherapy wasn't working, but he was doing alright. Saleem didn't believe him, but decided not to comment on his situation, being as though Big Slim wasn't the type to let something small or big keep him from living his life.

"Did my mom mention anything about Wakil?" asked Saleem.

"No, she didn't. But I almost forgot. Some girl named Tiffany came past your house, left her number for you to call her and said that it was important," responded Big Slim.

"Tiffany? The only Tiffany I know is a black scarface chick," Saleem said, trying to figure out, was it the girl he knew or someone else.

"Well, that might be her. Do you have a pen to write it down?" asked Big Slim, giving Saleem the number. Saleem wrote the number down and ended the call. It was so much on his mind he didn't know what to do first. Monk was walking up behind Saleem.

"Dag Leem you was out here for a minute, so I slid out to check on you," said Monk.

"Yeah, my man got slumped out Philly. I need to find out who did it and why 'cause he wasn't the type to get caught up in dumb shit," responded Saleem.

"Do you have any idea as to who would want him dead?" asked Monk, holding his hand on his gun inside the pocket of his coat.

"Naw, but I'm gonna find out, even if I gotta sneak back to Philly. He was like my brother," Saleem spoke, zipping his jacket up as he started to feel the cool breeze cutting through his dickie shirt.

"I'm with you. I' been trying put this to use," Monk stated, lifting up his shirt, exposing the black nine shot glock that was tucked in between his waist. He was strapped for warfare.

"Then I haven't heard from Wakil in a week. I tried his cell. That shit is disconnected," responded Saleem.

"You know how cats get when you're not around, out of sight, out of mind," Monk spoke, as he finished up the last drop of his drink.

"But me and dude is tight like spandex. He wouldn't cross me. Especially, since we been grinding together for most of our lives," stated Saleem.

"Man, I thought the same thing until I did that five to ten upstate. Me and cuz, we grew up from kids, robbing and hustling together. But when the cuffs went on, he shitted on me hard!" Monk said. You could hear it in his voice that this was a touchy subject to discuss.

"Me and Wakil are close like that. I would hope he wouldn't cross over on me that way," Saleem said, starting to second guess Wakil's loyalty to him. It never crossed his mind, that Wakil would stab him in the back.

"He got killed a year after I came home and I didn't even attend his funeral," Monk spoke.

"Damn that's some cold shit. Why not pay your last respects to the dead?" asked Saleem, really trying to grasp the whole concept of Monk having that much hatred for someone he considered a close friend.

"Once a cross, always a cross. Try doing five years, no letters, no money and no flicks. But that's not the bad part. He ain't take my mom shit!" Monk responded, with anger in his speech.

"I hear you champ," Saleem spoke, getting inside Monk's blue Ford Taurus station wagon. After talking outside the club for twenty minutes, they were heading back up to Oak to chill. You really had to be somebody or know someone to chill in Oak Projects. Just anybody wasn't allowed. Niggaz stayed getting kicked out of Oak. It was like that for real. It started to get heated with police when some cats threw a cop off the ramp. Half-way there Saleem's phone rang.

"Yeah! Who this?" asked Saleem.

"It's Tara baby," she spoke, in a seductive tone.

"Hey shorty. I was just thinking about you," Saleem said, lying to make her feel good. She was the furthest thing from his mind after hearing that bad news.

"You were? I'm sitting here waiting for you in the tub," responded Tara.

"At my spot?" Saleem asked.

"Yes, I told you I would be here early," Tara explained. She was a girl he met through his uncle's girlfriend. She wasn't really into the street life. So that caught his attention, on top of her being attractive. She was 5'4, 145 pounds, thick hips and pretty in the face, with light skinned complexion.

"I forgot Tara. I just received some bad news from back home, so I haven't been thinking right," stated Saleem.

"All baby come home, so mommy can cheer you up," Tara said, splashing the bubbles around in the tub.

"I'm on my way, so keep that pussy warm," responded Saleem. She had a way of making him feel energetic and knew how to lift his spirits. She wasn't no Shay, but she filled the gap of love he was missing from not being able to get to the woman he was to make his wife one day.

"Don't worry baby, it's hot and all yours, so hurry," said Tara.

"I'll be there. Keep the door locked," Saleem told her, even though he was located in an area where a lot of drugs weren't sold. He stuck to the street code. It was better to be safe, than sorry.

"I took care of that already," responded Tara.

"See you soon." Saleem clicked her off.

"Look at you, already in love," Monk blurted out.

"Not at all. My chick is back home waiting my return," Saleem stated. He liked Tara, but he was in love with Shay and they had just met. So far it was just good sex.

"You straight homey? Hold your head, we gonna handle that problem back home, so don't worry," Monk said.

"No doubt champ. I'ma hit you tomorrow to swing past and snatch me up," responded Saleem, shaking his hand. Monk waited for Saleem to get inside before he pulled off. Monk and Saleem became close in the short period of time. And Monk never showed nothing but love and loyalty from day one.

Saleem yelled for Tara and she didn't respond. So he walked straight to the back room. This was his first apartment and it was plushed from top to bottom. Tara played a major role in helping him decorate the two bedroom apartment. He had a 52 inch floor model television, a matching black leather sofa and loveseat, as well as a dining room set and a three thousand dollar hard wood bedroom set. When he entered the room it was dark, with a little light coming from the night lamp.

"Hey baby. Don't turn on the light. You'll ruin the moment," Tara said in a sexy tone that had Saleem shivering. Every time she spoke, her voice was so soft and seductive, she could've had a career in phone sex.

"Trust me, I'm not," responded Saleem, starting to undress.

"Come here," Tara demanded and Saleem did as he was told and laid beside her. He was harder than a brick house. He knew she could feel his manhood poking her thighs.

"Your skin is soft as silk, sexy," Saleem stated, causing her to blush. She kissed him and moved her body on top of his, as she mounted his penis and motioned herself up and down, so she could feel every inch of him inside her. Just as he was about to cum she slid off of him, placing his dick in her mouth and as he released everything he had, she swallowed it. Saleem laid there shaking from the uncontrollable orgasm she just gave him.

Tara climbed back up to the top of the bed and pulled the sheets over them. He wrapped her in his arms and they dozed off into the night.

The following morning, as Saleem was turning over, he caught the attention of Tara standing naked in front of him, like her vagina was his breakfast.

"What's wrong sweet thing?" asked Saleem, wiping the cold out of his eyes.

"Don't sweet thing me. Who the hell is Tiffany?" Tara asked, flashing the piece of paper in his face.

"All baby come on. Do you think I would leave that laying around if it was a girl I was seeing?" Saleem asked.

"Why do you have it then?" Tara inquired, sitting on the bed beside Saleem.

"Remember that news I told you about? Well that was my best friend who was murdered out in Philly. My mom called my uncle and told him about my man and this girl Tiffany left her number for me to call. She had some important information, so I plan on calling her today." Saleem explained everything to Tara bringing her temperature back down to normal.

"Boy I was about to snap. Don't be playing with my emotions like that," Tara said.

"Trust me, hurting you is the last thing on my mind," responded Saleem.

"I'm glad to hear that 'cause I'm really feeling you and I haven't let my guard down like this for a man in a long time," Tara spoke, kissing him as they got back into it again. This time Saleem didn't pull out. He came inside her.

They took a shower together and washed each other up. Tara got dressed and went home to change her clothes so she could go to work. She only lived twenty minutes away with her dad and little sister. Saleem sat on the sofa contemplating on rather to call Tiffany now or wait a few more days. But he was hoping she had some news on Boog, so he dialed her number. It was still early in the morning and he wasn't sure if he had her cell number or her house number. The phone rang six times before someone picked up.

"Hello," a female voice spoke.

"Can I speak to Tiffany?" asked Saleem.

"This her," Tiffany spoke, in a drowsy cracked tone of voice from the phone waking her up.

"Tiff, what's up? It's Leem," responded Saleem.

"Awww shit. Leem how you been? I assume you got my message," Tiffany spoke, sounding as though she was happy to hear from him, even though they weren't close.

"I'm good. Just trying to stay above sea level, you know," stated Saleem.

"You know Boog's funeral is today. It's sad what happened to him," spoke Tiffany like she knew the people behind his murder.

"Yeah, I've been in the dark about that situation and that news broke my heart. That was my brother," Saleem expressed, sharing his view on what Boog meant to him.

"Well, word on the street is he was set up," said Tiffany, ready to spill all the beans. She got around enough, in and out of other men's beds.

"By who?" asked Saleem, eager to know.

"You wouldn't believe me if I told you," she answered, not mentioning any names.

"Look, I don't have time for the guess who games. This shit is serious," Saleem blurted out, getting angry.

"Well, your ace Wakil's name is mixed up in a lot of sheisty shit and he wanted you out of the way. He's the one they said killed that undercover drug agent up the street from my house and let you take the fall," she said, only releasing part of what she knew.

"That's bullshit. Who told you that?" Saleem snapped, not believing her story.

"I knew you wouldn't believe me. I don't have no reason to lie to you. Yeah, I don't like Wakil from the way he treats me, but I can't make all that up from nowhere," she responded, still maintaining her composure.

"What else did you hear?" asked Saleem, searching for evidence to convince him she wasn't lying.

"He's sleeping with your girl. I think her name is Shay or something? It begins with an S," Tiffany said, laying it on him thick. This time she didn't hold back.

"Bitch, if you're lying, I'll kill you," Saleem blurted out. He was boiling with anger at the thought of mentioning Shay's name. If he could've jumped through the phone and strangled her he would've, after she dropped that bomb on him.

"Darn Leem, I know you're hurt, but don't shoot the messenger," Tiffany responded.

"It's hard to believe because he don't like Shay and he wouldn't do Boog dirty like that," Saleem suggested, not accepting the fact that someone he loved and trusted would betray him like that.

"First of all Wakil only thinks with his dick. I know that firsthand and I don't even know your girl," Tiffany said, making her story sound more believable.

"Damn Tiff, that nigga crossed me like that? I showed him love and loyalty from day one, and we got a history," spoke Saleem, revealing hurt in his voice. His eyes were becoming watery. He had mixed emotions.

"That's not the last of the information. I think a few months back you were at Bob Turner's barber shop getting your hair cut and one of the youngbuls got killed by a gun you had with you," Tiffany said.

"Yeah, what about it? Some cats tried to rob the barber shop. I just happened to be there at the time, me and my youngbul KB," responded Saleem.

"Saleem they knew you were going to be there. The plan was to kill you, until your youngbul squeezed his gun and everything went wrong. The youngbul who got killed was Wakil's youngbul from 52nd and Girard," spoke Tiffany.

"Are you sure?" asked Saleem.

"I haven't lied to you yet. This is all fact," stated Tiffany.

"Who else knows about everything you just told me?" Saleem inquired.

"I don't know but the streets are talking. He has a lot of youngbuls riding with him," Tiffany stated.

"Well look, you didn't talk to me and keep me updated because the element of surprise is a motherfucker," Saleem said, with revenge on his mind.

"You can trust me. I don't fuck with too many people," Tiffany responded.

"Write my number down and if you need anything at all, dial my phone and where's the funeral going to be?" asked Saleem.

"Woods Funeral Home on 56th and Girard across from Lebel's Pizza Shop," spoke Tiffany, giving Saleem the location to Boog's funeral.

"I know where it's at. I need you to tell Boog I love him and I won't let it end like this. He'll be able to hear you so don't forget," said Saleem, asking her to give his friend his farewells, being as though he wouldn't be able to do it.

"Don't worry, I can handle that for you. Whatever you do Saleem, be careful. I think the police are still looking for you," responded Tiffany, sounding as though she cared about him.

"Look I'm cool Tiff and I appreciate all your help. You won't be forgotten, so stay in touch and don't give anybody my number." Saleem gave her the number and clicked her off.

He sat there in a daze, trying to take everything in. He had no idea why Wakil would put the cross in on him, but he was determined to find out. A flash popped in his head from what his uncle told him, so it all was starting to register in his mind. So jumping out of the jet without a parachute was out of the question. The ringing of his cell phone broke him outta the daze.

"Hello," spoke Saleem.

"Yo cuz, I was waiting on your call," Monk spoke.

"Yeah, I know. I was just hollering at the broad Tiffany," Saleem said.

"What's to that chick?" asked Monk.

"I'll give you the game over some steak and eggs," said Saleem.

"I hear you. I'm on my way," Monk responded, hanging up. Saleem waited for Monk so they could go eat at the breakfast spot out Oak. He would tell him everything Tiffany just informed him of.

CHAPTER 16

WOOD'S FUNERAL HOME

A lot of people was showing up for Boog's funeral. The cars were jammed pack in the middle of the street. The trolley was blocked off until the police car showed up and ordered the people to park on the side streets, so they wouldn't block traffic. Boog's mom, Ms. Val was sitting in the front row alongside his uncles, aunts and cousins. He had a big family. Shay was attending with one of her girlfriend's to pay her respects. Her and Jane has yet to make amends.

There was still no sign of Wakil. The line was long for all those who were coming through to view the body before the service started. Reverend Willis B. Townes was in charge of the final viewing and he was leading the service that was scheduled to start at eleven o'clock.

A couple minutes before the service was about to begin, Wakil came walking through the door with Mimi in his arms. You could tell she was pregnant, even though she was only a couple of months. Wakil had dressed down a pair of Guess jeans, Polo button up shirt and black Chukkas, and his waist length mink.

Mimi wore a black Donna Karen pants suit with matching shoes and a three-quarter length black mink. They dressed for a disco ball, not a funeral. Reverend Willis B. Townes started the ceremony. He spoke about Boog like he was a certified saint. People screamed and cried in grief.

The sermon lasted thirty minutes. A few of his relatives got up and said their farewells. Everybody started exiting, to drive to the burial site. After that, Ms. Val was having a get together at the ranch. Wakil spoke to Ms. Val and kissed her on the cheek and passed her a card with a thousand dollars inside. She inquired about Saleem and Wakil informed her that he couldn't attend, but he sent his regards and will contact her at a later date. Tiffany had walked right past, catching Wakil off guard. He just flagged her off after she rolled her eyes at him.

"Hey Wakil," Shay spoke, with a smile on her face. She told Ms. Val she was sorry for her loss and Boog was a good person. Ms. Val thanked her and departed from the church.

"What's up Shay?" asked Wakil. They were talking like they haven't seen each other in years.

"Did you read the obituary? They put Saleem down as Boog's best friend," responded Shay.

"Naw, not yet. That's what's up though. They were like brothers," Wakil said, turning his back to see what Mimi was doing. To his surprise, she was being occupied by an elderly lady.

"I see you ain't come alone and it looks like somebody has something in the oven cooking," Shay commented, looking Mimi up and down. Shay couldn't hate, she was dressed to impress.

"Yeah, nothing that we should have to discuss," Wakil said, cutting her speech short before she tried to cause a scene.

"You're right. Do you think Saleem found out about Boog?" Shay asked, switching the topic of the conversation to something else.

"Yeah he knows. I spoke to him a few days ago," Wakil responded.

"You did. How did he take the news and did he ask about me?" Shay asked, sounding real excited.

"He was hurt, but he knows I'm taking care of business. Yeah, he asked how you were doing."

"What did you tell him?" asked Shay, looking at him, hoping he didn't say nothing stupid. Webb was coming towards them.

"Old head you cool? I'm out. I got something to take care of," Webb said, dressed in an all black Dickie pants and shirt set.

"Yeah, I'll hit you later," responded Wakil, shaking his hand.

"Alright," Webb spoke, walking towards the exit of the church. Shay just stood there waiting for him to finish.

"Back to you. I didn't tell him nothing, but you were in good hands," Wakil stated, focusing his attention on the two white men who had just walked in like they were fresh off Wall Street, suited and booted.

"I hope so. He doesn't need to know nothing. Let me go get ready for work," Shay said, walking off, passing the two gentlemen coming in the opposite direction. Everybody had left the church except for a few stragglers. The men had stopped dead in their tracks in front of Wakil.

"Are you Wakil Davis? I'm Detective Todd Bradly and this is my partner, Mr. Roger Mills," Detective Bradly spoke, holding a brown folder under his armpit.

"That depends on why you're looking for him," Wakil responded, showing them that he wasn't intimidated by the flashy Brooks Brother suits.

"No need to be sarcastic young man. You're not under arrest. We would like to ask you a few questions down at the station," Detective Mills said.

"I don't have no answers to your questions," Wakil stated, not trying to give in to the pressure they were trying to apply. Plus, he knew how crooked they could be down at the police station inside the interrogation room without a lawyer present.

"I wouldn't be too sure of that. The car your friend William Briggs was shot in was registered to you," Detective Bradly responded, with aggressiveness in his tone. They were determined to walk out of the church with Wakil, rather by force or choice.

Shay hadn't left yet. She was standing by the entrance. Her and her girlfriend zoned in on the two men talking to Wakil. Mimi was making her way over.

"Wakil are you ready?" asked Mimi, interrupting the conversation.

"Yeah babe, but look, I have to go answer some questions for these gentlemen. So I'll meet you home," Wakil spoke, passing her the keys to the car as he kissed her in the mouth. He wanted to make the situation less stressful as possible for her, being as though she was pregnant.

"Why you gotta go with them? Well, I'm coming with you," Mimi asked, letting it be known she was riding for her man.

"No, go home! I told you I'll be there shortly. So stop it!" Wakil stated, giving her a look, as though this wasn't a good time to stand here and argue. She sucked her teeth and strutted down the aisle. Wakil and the detectives were two steps behind her. He walked freely, as they had no intentions of putting the handcuffs on him. Shay was still stuck in the same spot as she watched Wakil walk past her followed by the detectives. He winked his eye at her.

They took him to the Eighteenth District of 55th and Pine, second floor homicide division. Wakil was led into a room with a table and three chairs and a large tinted mirror that was impossible to see out of. He was asked about Boog's murder, the whereabouts of Saleem, as well as the homicide outside the Cherekee go-go club that happened nights ago. They even tried to trick Wakil into believing that they had an eye witness that seen his car at the crime scene, where the undercover cop was murdered.

But he didn't bite the bait. He just laughed. After two and a half hours of questioning, they had to release him. There was no evidence to charge him with a crime, only speculations. With no transportation to get back home, he thought about calling Mimi to come pick him up.

The detectives had his phone the whole time, so he knew Mimi probably called a million times. He decided not to call her.

Jane rung a bell in his head. She was trying to get at him for the longest, but Wakil was ignoring her. So he had no idea how she would act, by him just popping up unannounced. Her car was parked outside. He walked up and rang the bell. Jane opened the door while she was talking on the phone and waved her hand for Wakil to come in. She quickly ended her call.

"So who do I owe this unexpected visit to?" asked Jane, taking a seat beside Wakil on the couch. She was elated to see him.

"Stop playing. I was thinking about you so I decided to come through and surprise you," responded Wakil, looking Jane up and down from head to toe. She was still in tip top shape, wearing a pink cut off wife beater that exposed her flat stomach and some black daisy dukes that could've gave her a yeast infection.

"And my head screws on and off? I haven't heard from you in weeks, but you call Shay to check up on her and I hear yaw been spending a lot of quality time together," spoke Jane.

"Not hardly! I only called to check up on her, on the strength of my man. So don't sweat the small stuff," Wakil said, rubbing his hands up and down her legs.

"Small stuff. That bitch couldn't wait to rub that shit in my face," Jane snapped, as she got up and walked towards the kitchen. Wakil followed right behind her, as she inventoried the refrigerator. He wrapped his arms around her. She was pissed.

"Baby you know I missed you," Wakil claimed, kissing on her neck. Jane gave in and decided to go along with Wakil's so-called foreplay. She turned around and French kissed him hard in the mouth. He slid his mink off and threw it on the chair. Things were starting to escalate. The temperature was heating up between them. Jane slipped off her shorts. She had no panties on. Wakil caught an instant hard on, so he lifted her up on the counter. She hopped in his arms faster than a speeding bullet.

"Oh shit," Jane screamed.

"What?" asked Wakil, like he had done something wrong.

"The counter is cold," Jane responded. So he carried her to the couch and bent her over and started to drill her from the back like a construction worker. He only pulled his pants to his ankles but removed his shirt. Every stroke caused her to moan out in ecstasy.

He held back from releasing and turned her around, making her spread in an eagle position. He dove in head first licking and sucking her clitoris, causing Jane's body to squirm. He could taste her juices dripping down his lips. Wakil couldn't hold back no longer, so he entered her in the same position. After three strokes he released inside her and rolled over beside Jane.

"I wish I could have that every night," Jane said, standing up, using a beach towel to wipe herself.

"Shit that's a Bally's Gym workout. I wouldn't have enough energy in my body to perform like that every night the way I run the streets," Wakil spoke, taking the same towel and wiping his mouth and private part. Her scent was all over him. He got dressed and sat back down.

"For real Wakil, why were you down here on this side of town?" asked Jane, searching for the truth behind his unexpected visit.

"I was at my man's funeral and these detectives came and took me to the station for questioning about a whole bunch of bullshit," stated Wakil, only providing her with half the story. He didn't feel he really owed her an explanation to why he showed up.

"Somebody told me about your friend Boog. I'm sorry for your loss," Jane said.

"Yeah, he was a good dude and I'm still trying to find out who did it," Wakil spoke, watching Jane drink her fruit beverage.

"You know, I'm going away for a while. My aunt on my dad's side of the family wants me to come stay with her," Jane announced, staring at Wakil to see what his reaction would be and would he try to stop her from leaving.

"Oh yeah? So you're skipping town on me?" asked Wakil in a joking manner.

"Like you wanted me to stay so I can continue to be your fuck buddy?" Jane blurted out.

"Not at all. I love your company and you're flat out, a bad bitch," Wakil stated, causing Jane to showcase a cool aid smile from the unfortunate compliment.

"You're crazy," said Jane, slapping him across the leg.

"Yeah, crazy about you." Wakil had her blushing from ear to ear.

"I have to go, but I promise I won't forget about us and what we could've had together, even though we never got to spend any real time together. Even the sex will be memorable." Jane was getting sentimental.

"Where does your aunt live?" asked Wakil.

"Out in Virginia," spoke Jane.

"You'll be straight out there and here's something to take with you to help you open up your own shop," Wakil responded, reaching in his pocket, pulling out a wad of money. He peeled off ten one hundred dollar bills and gave them to her.

"I don't need your money," Jane said, forcing it back to him.

"Just take it! I don't care what you need. Just stay in touch with me and call if you need anything else," Wakil responded, kissing her in the mouth.

"Alright, if you insist and you know I'ma call your cheating ass," Jane said, folding the money and stuffing it inside the pocket of her shorts.

"Now drop me off on 56th and Master Street," Wakil said, walking to the kitchen to get his jacket. Jane ran upstairs to put on some more clothes and they rolled out.

CHAPTER 17

HOT OUT THE VILLE

A few months had passed and the weather had changed. Summer was here and it showed from the men walking around shirtless, to the women wearing their mini skirts and flip flops.

The task force was running up in all known drug spots. Saleem and Monk had opened up more locations to push their product, including the Stage Bar. It was doing more than Elk's local bar down the east end. Gillies Sports Bar on Second Avenue was still bringing in a nice piece of change.

Saleem and Monk started branching off to weed and wet, but crack is where they accumulated the majority of their wealth. They were seeing more money than they ever saw in their lifetime.

Tara had moved in with Saleem and he was expecting his first child. He told her to quit her job, but she still did hair for close friends like Big Lex and Taheerah who only got their hair done by Tara. Monk moved in an apartment around the corner from Saleem with a white girl who he was starting to take seriously.

But Saleem didn't have to depend on Monk for a ride anymore, unless they were out handling business or just partying on guys night out. He had just purchased Tara a black 94 Acura Legend sedan.

He tried his hardest to block Shay out of his mind ever since Tiffany started informing him of the events that were taking place back home. Even with her cheating on him with Wakil, deep down inside he still loved her. But he hated Wakil for the disloyalty he showed and all the double crossing that he was involved in to get him out of the way. Not understanding Wakil's agenda was really eating him up on the inside. After all, he treated him like his brother.

"Tara come here for a minute," Saleem called out.

"What's up Boo? I'm fixing breakfast—turkey bacon, eggs, and grits, your favorite," Tara claimed, entering the room with a piece of bacon in her hand.

"I know babe I smell it. Look at your stomach getting big. I have to speak to you about a few things," spoke Saleem, rubbing her stomach as she stood there in the bedroom in front of him.

"What's wrong?" Tara asked, as though she was concerned.

"Nothing's wrong. Everything's good. I gotta go out of town on a business trip," Saleem explained.

"Where at out of town and why can't I come with you?" Tara asked.

"Baby, I have some unfinished business to handle back home and taking you in this condition will complicate things," Saleem stated.

"With your old girl Shay?" asked Tara, now sitting beside him waiting for an answer.

"Tara, it's more to the story than what I've told you in the past," Saleem stated. He never informed her about the police officer he was being accused of killing, but she knew about Shay and how much he cared for her.

"So our relationship has been based on a lie?" Tara asked, trying to get to the moral of the story.

"I'm a real dude Tara. If I would've told you I was out here with my uncle because Philly had a warrant for my arrest for killing a cop, would you have went out with me?" asked Saleem, staring straight into her eyes. She was puzzled by what he just told her.

"Saleem you killed a police officer?" Tara spoke, being surprised, with tears starting to run down her cheeks.

"I'm a hustler. I would only kill somebody if they threatened me or somebody in my family. I just found out that someone close to me, framed me and tried to kill me," responded Saleem, wiping her tears away.

"Why would they do that to you if he was close to you?" asked Tara moving his hand away from her face.

"It's a long story baby," Saleem said.

"I'm listening. Hold on for one second," Tara said, walking to the kitchen to cut the stove off. When she returned, Saleem told her everything. He didn't leave nothing out. He spoke about how him and Boog were and Wakil. Even speaking about the women who were in his life before he came out there. From Dee, Kiya and Shay who she already knew about. And how Tiffany was just his eyes and ears. Tara laughed when Saleem spoke about Tiffany being the neighborhood smut.

"Now it all makes sense, because when I used to ask my aunt about you she wouldn't say much. Plus, she was in love with your uncle, so she would never betray his trust," responded Tara.

"I told you my whole life story. So if you're leaving me, there's the door," Saleem said jokingly, pointing in the direction of the door.

"Oh no you don't. You can't get rid of me that easy. Plus, I'm not raising this baby by myself," spoke Tara rubbing her stomach.

"I wasn't going to let you go anyway. I need you to hold on to this just in case something happens to me," Saleem stated, passing her a trash bag full of money that he took from the closet.

"Saleem, what's all this? It's a lot of money in here," Tara said. When she looked in the bag her eyes were about to pop out.

"It's a little something I've been saving up since I came out here. There's seven-hundred fifty dollars there. I put it in ten thousand stacks," Saleem said.

"What," Tara blurted out, shocked by the amount of money she was holding in her possession.

"You heard me. So take it to your mom's house and put it somewhere safe. I trust you with my life and I want you to be secure no matter what," spoke Saleem.

"I'll hold it until you come back," Tara told him, placing the bag back where Saleem had retrieved it from.

"When I leave in a few, you have to take that out of here. Nobody knows I have that kind of money. They know me and Monk took over unc's business, but the money we got they have no clue," Saleem stated, trying to get his point across.

"I know Boo. I'ma handle it. Are you going to see Shay while you're out there?" asked Tara crossing her arms, waiting patiently for his reply.

"You don't have to worry about her. You're the one I love good and plenty," Saleem said referring to her tattoo on her lower back.

"Is that because I'm having your baby and you didn't get that chance with her?" Tara inquired.

"No doubt. Shay and I wanted to have kids together, but anybody who crosses me loses me. Simple as that! So she's no longer my concern," responded Saleem, meaning every word of what he said.

"I'm gonna be your wife one day, not just your baby mom. I love you Saleem and I won't never cross you. I promise you that," Tara said, leaning over to kiss him in the mouth.

"You know people make promises and they break them," Saleem shot back, just to see her reaction.

"I'm a loyal girl and there's not a man on earth I would rather be with than you. So remember that on your trip," responded Tara, letting him know she was there until the end of the ride.

"Best believe I feel the same way. That's why I'm trusting you with my life's savings," Saleem spoke.

"Money isn't everything. I'm gonna still be here when all of that is gone," Tara responded. She wasn't turned on by the material things, even though Saleem kept her laced in the latest fashion. Saleem didn't have a chance to respond, due to his phone ringing.

"Hello," Saleem spoke, placing one finger up to tell Tara to hold up while he answered his phone.

"Yo playboy, you ready? I left Ty with enough to hold the spots down and he made a move on his own out Hillside by C.A.S.H.," Monk stated. Ty was one of their most trusted workers who worked his way up to boss status.

"That's good. Where you at?" asked Saleem.

"I'm home," responded Monk.

"Oak, are around the corner?" Saleem asked, unsure as to where he was laying his head, being as though he had two spots.

"Near you and we gotta slide past and snatch up my other youngbul, Spider. He's going along for the ride," Monk said.

"Cool, come scoop me," said Saleem.

"Give me twenty minutes," responded Monk. The phone clicked off. Tara sat there and ear hustled the whole conversation, but remained non-judgemental.

"That was Monk. He's coming to pick me up," Saleem said.

"You have to be careful Boo. I wouldn't know what to do if something happened to you," Tara spoke, wrapping her arms around him. She was trying to squeeze the life out of him.

"Don't worry, you just take care of my baby so we can live as one big family," Saleem responded, kissing her lips. He was only wearing his boxers, so he slid them off.

"What you doing? Monk is on his way," Tara stated backing away. She knew he was trying to get a quickie. She only had on a long T-shirt and some panties.

"Come on, just let me get some for the road," Saleem pleaded, stripping Tara of all her clothes. She didn't resist. He bent her over the bed and entered her, taking it easy on her because she was pregnant. He knew she wouldn't be able to stand the pressure, so he stroked in a slow rhythm. Tara was wetter than a water hydrant, causing Saleem to cum instantly. The doorbell rang at the same time he reached his climax. He wasn't concerned with Tara reaching her orgasm.

"It's probably Monk. Let me jump in the shower real quick," Saleem said, snatching a towel off the chair and a pair of drawers off the pile that was stacked on the floor.

"Damn Boo," Tara blurted out, lifting herself from the bed. He didn't bother to help her up. She slid on some sweatpants and a T-shirt, no bra or panties and went to answer the door. It was Monk.

He was dressed in a short sleeve dickies suit, with some black Chukka Timberland boots and a black skully hat. As he sat down on the couch, him and Tara spoke briefly, then she went back to the room. Seconds later Saleem emerged.

"Nigga! Where you going dressed like a bank robber?" asked Saleem, laughing at Monk's attire that wasn't fit for the hot weather.

"Man, this shit is cool. Plus, it's short sleeve," responded Monk, getting up to do a full evaluation of his appearance.

"I'm dressed to fit that hot ass heat out there and I ain't trying to draw the tip carrying this toaster," Saleem stated, flashing a Clint Eastwood silver, six shot 357. It looked like something from a western movie.

"You tripping, but them Nikes are hot though. What they ACG's?" asked Monk, admiring Saleem's footwear.

"No doubt. I still put that shit on cuz," responded Saleem. He had some purple and gray ACG Nikes, a purple Polo shirt and some black Polo swim trunks.

"Nigga, you think you a pretty boy. I'm a gorilla thug ville for life nigga," Monk confessed, like he was a gang member repping his set.

"Whatever man, let's roll," Saleem said, waving off Monk's last remark. Saleem gave Tara a long kiss goodnight. Her facial expression reminded him that she didn't want him to go, but his mind was made up. He was sticking to the script. They stopped past Willie's Breakfast spot by Lincoln Highway. Spider was to meet them there, so they could drive straight to Philadelphia.

"I'ma show you Philadelphia. At least some of the chicks I was laying pipe to," Saleem said.

"I look forward to slaying one of those sluts," responded Monk, with a sly grin on his face.

"Them hoes will turn you out. I'ma call Tiffany. You might want to hammer that? She ain't no looker, but that ass makes up for the face mask," Saleem said, laughing at Monk's facial expression.

"Shit, who didn't fuck an ugly broad before? I don't have no picks when it comes to my dick," Monk blurted out.

"Dirty dick nigga," shouted Saleem.

"Them hoes love me. There go Spider right there," spoke Monk, pointing at the dark skinned, stocky guy standing outside Willies, as they were pulling up. Monk got out of the car and greeted Spider. Turning, they both walked inside the breakfast joint. Five minutes later they were out. It didn't take long since Monk had pre-ordered on the way there.

"What's up Leem?" spoke Spider.

"Ain't shit youngin," responded Saleem, reaching back to shake his hand. They knew each other from Monk, so he showed him love on the strength of Monk.

"Let's ride cuz and go get these suckers who crossed my man," said Monk, cracking open the bag of food. You could smell the aroma from the freshly cooked food.

"Yeah, I gotta release some stress," Spider blurted out, showing Monk and Saleem he was packing.

"Keep that tucked. We riding three deep and dirty," Saleem said, pulling in the gas station. He filled the tank up and hopped on the expressway.

CHAPTER 18

BAKER'S PLAYGROUND

The playground was jumping. Disco Dave was blasting the music loud enough that people two blocks away could hear it. The swimming pool was jammed packed. They were running a full court basketball game. Mr. Cruise's water ice shed had a line as long as Broad Street. It was a crap game on the side of the recreation hut. The whole city was out partying and enjoying the summer heat. Wakil wasn't touching nothing, unless he was going over New York to purchase more product.

His twin brother had just came home after getting a sentence reduction, so Kenny was put right in position. Wakil couldn't stand to get caught red handed, because the streets had his name mixed in a lot of crooked stuff. But that didn't stop him from flossing his success.

He bought a 300 CE Coupe and painted it candy apple red with MoMo rims, with the red lining between them. Mimi was driving a black GS 300 Lexus bubble. Even Shay had a new blue Q45 Infiniti all at the expense of Wakil.

Kenny was driving an up-to-date squatter 'cause he was still on parole. Jane moved to Virginia. She constantly stayed in contact with Wakil. She opened up her own shop down there called All About Perfection. Her and Shay still hadn't reconciled their differences.

Mimi was showing more, now being five months pregnant. Shay gave in to being Wakil's main side piece and after not hearing from Saleem since he skipped town, she considered their relationship over. Wakil was her man now.

Wuwu never came around no more after taking Wakil back over to New York a few more times. Yamega and Wakil established their own relationship, where he was buying five bricks every two weeks. He would ride the bus over and have a girl bring the drugs back on the train the following day.

Apple Tree Street was still bringing in major money, as well as Master Street. Kenny had opened up Hunter Street on top of the weight sales. He was doing good for himself after spending years behind bars. Fifty sixth and Jefferson slowly dried up, so that was left to the Jamaicans and the stragglers. Lansdown Avenue was still doing numbers. Wakil's homeboys had that. It was hot around there after him and Turtle killed the Jamaican coming out of Hi-Lad's Cleaners, but nobody knew it was them 'cause they were wearing ski masks. The Three-two Center was Saleem's stomping grounds, so he left that alone altogether. Wakil was giving Malik nine ounces for five thousand dollars a piece. He had a team of his own hustling on 56th and master and Media Street.

Wakil didn't drop off none of Saleem's cut to his mother. He felt like by looking out for his little brother he was doing enough. With all Wakil's popularity steadily on the rise, he felt the hate and tension in the air. They were accusing him of crossing Saleem and being behind Boog's death. Being as though he was riding with some reckless youngbuls, cats thought twice about coming at him. Webb and Dizzy kept in close contact with him. He was even supplying them with coke. Everything they purchased, he matched it.

Wakil pulled up next to the garages near his mom's house. He had just got the top chopped, so the roof was down. This would be the first time driving since he changed the color and hooked everything else up on it. Ms. Cee and

Malik were sitting on the steps and couldn't help but notice the bright colored car that just pulled up. Wakil waved Ms. Cee didn't pay him any attention. Malik was walking over to him.

"Damn Wah, this shit crazy. You did your thing to this Benz," Malik spoke, mesmerized by the uniqueness of the car that was before him.

"This ain't shit lil' homey. A small thing to a giant. If your bro was here he would have a hot whip too," responded Wakil.

"Yeah, I know. I haven't heard from him since he left. How about you?" asked Malik, still admiring Wakil's Benz.

"I tried to call him, but I think he changed his number," Wakil said, watching his brother, Kenny, running towards them, sweating like he just ran a race at a track meet.

"I should be ready for you later on today," Malik spoke.

"No problem. I just got some butter. It's that yellow shit that'll have those fiends at your doorstep looking for you," Wakil responded.

"What yaw talking about?" asked Kenny, sounding like he was out of breath. He still thought he was locked up, running three times a week and going to the gym to work out.

"Wakil was giving me the heads up on the new package he has," Malik stated.

"Yeah that stuff is the bomb. You see those smokers lined up like a church, giving out free cheese," Kenny responded, wiping his face with the already sweaty T-shirt he was wearing. Hunter Street was bringing in five thousand a day or more. Kenny used five to eight inch bags. The rocks inside were the size of a dime. He had Darnell, an old head who resided on the block, hustling for him. A lot of people called him Bumpy Nell. He had more bumps on his face than rocky road ice cream.

"I see Bumpy doing his thing up there," Malik said, witnessing the crowded sidewalk of fiends. A black car backed up and parked right in front of Wakil's car. When the occupants got out they realized it was Mimi and her girlfriend Tasha who was the spitten image of Toni Braxton, but with longer hair and voluptuous figure.

"Here comes wifey," Kenny said, watching Mimi wobble up the street.

"That's Mimi pushing that GS bubble? Wah you eating like Escobar," Malik spoke, fascinated by all the luxury cars he was seeing, pull up on Hunter Street even though he had an Acura Legend of his own.

"Shit I wish I had tons of that coke like Esocbar. Maybe in a few years?" Wakil was trying to be modest and cocky at the same time. He wasn't the same person everybody once knew. He was hypnotized by his new found success and he didn't care how he achieved it and was prepared to die to keep it.

"Hey Boo," Mimi said, walking up and kissing him in the mouth. She had on a Chanel sun dress with matching Chanel sandals.

"Chilling with my boys," responded Wakil, embracing her with a hug.

"What's up Kenny? This is my girlfriend, Tasha and that's Malik, Saleem's little brother," Mimi stated, officially introducing everyone to her girlfriend, who stood there in a white and purple Nike mini skirt set with some Air-Max Nikes, no socks to match, wearing her hair in a bun.

"Tasha?" responded Kenny, raping her body with his eyes.

"Yeah! You like my name?" Tasha asked smiling.

"That's not the only thing I like," Kenny spit back, being blunt. He was loving all the back and forth flirting they were doing.

"I was always curious about dating a twin," said Tasha.

"Well, today is your lucky day." Kenny was putting the seal on his package he had just wrapped with Tasha, and she was loving it as much as he was.

"Okay lovebirds. Malik get with me later," spoke Wakil, as Malik made his way back across the street. Mimi went inside to speak with Wakil's mom. Kenny sat on the steps and continued his conversation with Tasha. Wakil hopped in his car and sped off.

* * * * *

"It's scorching out here. Let's go get some water ice. The Marones Truck hasn't been past here all day," Shay said. When she got up off the steps the booty cut shorts were glued to her ass cheeks. Her girlfriend, Peanut, was sitting beside her, wearing a one piece DKNY dress that hugged her buttocks.

"Let's go, 'cause I'm catching a tan out here," responded Peanut. She was light skinned with dimples and an ass that you could put a glass on. They got in Shay's new car and rolled the windows down until the air kicked in. Even the seats were hot.

"My mom be trying to drive my car now, but I be like not at all. Shit, ain't nothing wrong with her car," said Shay.

"Girl you need to cut it out the way you dogged your mom's car," Peanut said, shuffling through the bag of cassette tapes.

"Every time I drove it, she would piss a fit, so I'ma do me," Shay spoke, being more conceited than ever now that she had a man who gave her gifts and money rapidly. Working at the hair salon was optional.

"I know just the place to get a soft pretzel and a good water ice," said Peanut.

"Where?" inquired Shay, like there was a new spot that she wasn't aware of.

"Right behind the playground. The red and blue shack on Wakil's mom's block," responded Peanut.

"On Hunter Street? That's Mr. Cruise. He does have good water ice. I haven't been around there in months." Shay stopped going around there after Saleem left town.

"Well, do you want to go around there?" asked Peanut.

"Yeah why not?" asked Shay, making a U-turn in the middle of the street, and driving straight down Lancaster Avenue. She didn't know what to expect going around there, and hoped not to run into any of Saleem's family, being as though she had remained absent for so long, especially after Ms. Cee had taking a liking to her.

"Look at all these people out here. What they having a block party?" Peanut asked, not aware the block was known for heavy drug traffic.

"Girl you stupid. Do you really think those nappy hair, dirty men are out there with a BBQ grill?" asked Shay, laughing at Peanut for confusing smokers for people, who were having a block party due to the over crowdedness of the block.

"Shit! I ain't used to seeing them deep like that," Peanut responded.

"Damn there's Wakil's brother sitting on the steps talking to that girl and I think that's Mimi's Lexus right there," Shay said, pointing her finger, like she was an eyewitness to a murder.

"Well we can go elsewhere," suggested Peanut, never taking her eyes off Wakil's twin brother.

"Hell no, we're here now. I ain't playing duck baby momma games. If they can't control their man, put a leash on him," Shay said.

"Ain't that the truth," agreed Peanut, slapping Shay's hand. The line outside the shack had decreased so Shay and Peanut were like number seven or eight in line. They were still partying in the playground like rock stars.

"They are doing it in there. Let's check that out," Shay said.

"I don't care. It ain't like we gotta work," responded Peanut. She didn't have a job. The men she slept with paid what they weighed. She was like Tommy on the Martin Lawrence Show, always claiming she had a job.

"You don't work anyway," said Shay laughing.

"My men don't complain when I'm performing in the bed. That's a lot of work moving these jaws and opening and closing these legs." Peanut was a certified gold digger and she had guys eating out of the palm of her hand. Her theory was . . . why give sex away for free when you can get paid for it.

"Don't no man complain when you're sucking their dick or giving them some good pussy," said Shay, looking up and down the street to see if she spotted Wakil. But she didn't see his car, so that assured her he was nowhere in sight.

"I wanted to know what tricks did you pull out in that bedroom to make Wakil go out and buy you that new car," said Peanut. They got their water ice and pretzel and walked inside the playground and stood near the wall watching the fellows play ball. Shay and Peanut's presence couldn't be ignored. All the guys stared at them like a bunch of hungry lions eyeing their prey. Even though there were other women hanging around, competition didn't exist.

"I can't help it if I'm the bomb," Shay responded, placing her water ice down, putting her hands on her hips and looking over her body. She was infatuated by what she saw.

"You had two best friends chasing you. I can't hate girl," Peanut said.

"Saleem had his chance. Life goes on. I got needs and wants and he didn't bother to call me since he left," Shay spoke.

"So you go to Wakil for comfort? Look, you're my girl, but I feel I have to tell you the real," Peanut responded, jumping backwards to prevent the melting water ice from getting on her clothes.

"I hear where you're coming from. To be honest the shit just happened. I didn't plan it like this." Shay was starting to feel guilty by the things Peanut was bringing up.

So overwhelmed by the good sex, money and cars, she never thought about it like that and being as though she was so far gone it was too late to turn back. Little did she know Malik was coming up the street and heading in her direction. He looked over to see if he recognized any familiar faces out of the two of them. Shay turned around locking her eyes with his. She was paralyzed by his presence. Malik yelled out her name to see if it was her.

"Shay, that's you?" asked Malik, coming closer.

"Hey Malik," Shay spoke, not really knowing how to handle the awkward situation.

"Well, I be damned. That is you. Long time no see. I see why my brother was in love with you," Malik said, allowing his eyes to wander over Shay and Peanut's body like he worked at a warehouse and they were the inventory.

"Cut it out. It hasn't been that long. I just saw you at Boog's funeral," said Shay, smiling.

"Yeah I know, but I'm talking about around my crib. My mom asks about you all the time. I meant to say something to you at the funeral, but it slipped my mind," Malik responded, leaning against the fence getting into a comfortable stance like he was going to interrogate her.

"Oh yeah, how is she doing? I just didn't want to stress her out with everything that's going on." Shay spoke the first words that rattled off her tongue.

"Leem is straight. He's laid up with my uncle, so don't let that keep you from showing your face more often, and who's this fine cherry?" Malik said, lusting off Peanut and he wasn't hiding it. He had no idea Wakil was messing with Shay, and that he was the one behind setting Saleem up, to get locked up, as well as plotting to kill him during a robbery gone bad.

"Boy you better stop. She's too old for you. Have you talked to your brother?" Shay asked, trying to lick the blueberry off her lips, that didn't seem to be going anywhere due to her continuous eating the water ice.

"Naw, I haven't talked to him, but you know how he is. He'll stay low and put his thing down wherever he's at," Malik said.

"I just hope he's alright," spoke Shay.

"Don't panic. He's alright. So what's up with your girlfriend?" Malik asked again, being persistent.

"I can talk and the name is Peanut with a capital P," she spoke, tired of Malik speaking about her as though she was invisible.

"Well Ms. I can speak. We going out or what?" Malik asked, being sarcastic.

"I have a boyfriend," said Peanut, trying to let him down easy. Even though Malik was seventeen, he looked older.

"Check you out you been hanging around your brother too long," Shay said.

"Do your boyfriend get bread like this?" asked Malik, pulling a knot of money out of each pocket. Peanut's eyes lit up like a Christmas tree.

"If they didn't have money, trust me I wouldn't call them my boyfriend and like Shay said you're too young," said Peanut.

"Age is only a number and I'm hung like a grown man, so that makes me a double threat. Big dick and long cheddar." Malik wasn't easing up on her. He was determined to prove that he was more man than she thought he was. Believe it or not, Peanut was smiling like she was loving his young cocky swag. Shay just shook her head.

"It won't hurt Shay, if me and him go out?" Peanut responded, like she was looking for Shay to give her the okay.

"Do you honey child," said Shay.

"Give me your number and I'll call you tonight to come pick me up Mr. Hunglow," said Peanut, throwing a dart back at him. Malik didn't hesitate giving her his cell number.

"I'll be waiting for your call," Malik said.

"Look forward to it," Peanut stated. Her and Shay walked towards the car. Malik slid off to his house. A couple minutes later a black Acura Legend Coupe pulled up beside Shay as she was about to get in her car. The dark tint made it hard for them to see who was driving it until the window came down.

"Shay that's yours? And I thought I was stuntin'?" Malik asked.

"Yeah and who's car you driving?" asked Shay.

"Who do you see behind the wheel?" Malik said his Acura was only a ninety square box, but it was in good shape. Shay was driving a ninety four Q45.

"My girlfriend said 'she'll see you later,' " Shay said.

"She can bet on it and don't be no stranger. You're family, so call me if you need anything. But from the looks of it, you look like you're doing fine to me," spoke Malik.

"I'm alright, thanks though," responded Shay, getting inside her car. Malik sped off and beeped the horn. Shay looked through her rearview mirror to see if Mimi was still up there, but she was long gone.

CHAPTER 19

MONEY, LOVE OR REVENGE

The sun was just starting to set while Saleem, Monk and Spider were chilling at Dee's house on Regin Street. She was happy to see him. Her appearance hadn't changed much and she was still go-go dancing at the Cherekee, better known as the neighborhood smut spot. She informed Saleem of the event that happened at the Cherekee, the same night Boog got killed and how Wakil shot some guy twice in the head, but it only grazed him. Saleem introduced her to Monk and Spider. They were psyched about the strip club and wanted to go. After seeing Dee they assumed it had to be more girls that looked as good as her.

So Saleem let them know, in due time they will get their chance to play, but business first. He couldn't lose sight that he was still a wanted man. He had no intention on calling his mother, even though he wanted to hear her voice and see her face, but couldn't risk knowing how worried she would be if she knew he was back in Philly.

"So Saleem you never told me why you came back. I would assume the police are still looking for you," Dee said, sitting by Saleem on the couch while Monk and Spider were at the dining room table eating pizza from a local pizzeria.

"Dee a lot has been going on these last few months. I met someone and she's three months pregnant," Saleem responded, looking at her to see what her response was going to be.

"I'm glad you're being honest with me, but we did our thing in the past. It is what it is. I will always love you and no matter what happens in your situation, I'm here." Dee meant every word she said and Saleem felt the realness coming out of her mouth.

"That's some real shit and I dig you for that," Saleem said.

"I'm here like I said, so if you need me to do anything, name it." Dee was persistent in trying to convince Saleem that she was prepared to ride or die for him.

"I hear you, but what I'm about to do is dangerous and I don't need you getting hurt. Me and Wakil are no longer friends, more like foes now," said Saleem.

"He's your enemy, why? What did he do? Yaw were close," Dee asked, caught off guard by Saleem's sudden change of heart towards Wakil.

"Too much to let slide. I got word that he put a hit out on me, framed me to take the fall for the cop getting killed and I think he might be behind Boog's death," Saleem responded. Dee put her hand over her mouth. She was in a state of shock by what she just heard.

"You're kidding, right?" asked Dee.

"I wish I was, but it's the real deal and I'ma handle that shit tonight! I promised Boog I wouldn't let it end like this." Saleem's mind was made up and no one would stand in his way.

"That's crazy," Dee said, still not believing it.

"And he's smashing Shay," Saleem stated, grabbing his phone.

"Damn friends ain't shit nowadays. That's fucked up Saleem. Shay doesn't deserve you anyway," Dee responded.

"I gotta call this girl who's been keeping me updated, so be quiet for one minute." Saleem called Tiffany. The answering machine picked up on the first ring so he tried right back and somebody answered.

"Hello, stop playing on my phone," the woman's voice spoke.

"I'm not playing on your phone. I'm looking for Tiffany," said Saleem.

"Hey Saleem. My bad, somebody keeps calling and hanging up," Tiffany said, detecting his voice.

"Yeah they stalking you huh? You got that snapper," Saleem responded.

"Boy, cut it out. Where you at?" asked Tiffany.

"I'm out North Philly," Saleem said, not revealing his location. He didn't care who it was.

"Well, are you ready for the latest?" Tiffany inquired.

"Better believe it and don't leave nothing out," Saleem said.

"First, your man Wakil is splurging around in a red Benz Coupe and the top is convertible. His baby mom, Mimi is driving a black GS 300, and from what I'm hearing, he paid for Shay's blue Q45. After Tiffany ran down everything to Saleem, he fell silent, taking everything in.

"Let me ask you something. Who's been telling you all this? Not saying I don't believe you, just making sure all the screws fit," asked Saleem.

"You know Chante that lives across the street from the playground? The same side as Wakil's mom house? Well, she mess with Webb and he tells her all his business," Tiffany said, informing Saleem where all her information was coming from.

"Webb from 52nd and Girard, they call Smiley?" Saleem asked.

"That's him and he's the one who killed the cop along with some other youngbul named Lil Dizzy. He suppose to be Webb's partner in crime." Tiffany was like the daily news. She knew everything that was going on in the neighborhood.

"Okay, I got all I need. You still got my number, so don't be afraid to use it. And I got a gift for you as soon as I handle this business." Saleem hung up after Tiffany told him to be careful.

He called Monk and Spider into the room where he was at. He informed them of the plan and how he was going to ride down on Webb on Girard Avenue first. Then Wakil, being as though Monk and Spider didn't know their way around, he had to stick by them like magnets.

He let them know everything down to what kind of cars Wakil and Mimi drove. He had no idea she was pregnant and Kenny was home. He decided to use Dee after all. Two cars were better than one. He wanted to get Wakil's stash, because he felt half belonged to him. They thought of all the ways to catch Wakil slipping or his girlfriend, Mimi and hold her hostage for a ransom.

"I knew you could use me Boo," Dee said, happy to be able to assist her man. Saleem had no idea if she was cut out for what was about to go down. Due to the circumstances he had no choice but to put her to the test.

"Your job is to drive. That's it! So don't get excited. This is not a game. I just hope you can stomach the shit that's about to take place." Saleem had made himself clear. They rolled out. Saleem and Dee drove together while Monk and Spider followed, as they drove towards Girard Avenue to find Webb. It was a little after ten o'clock so that meant good timing and the weather was beautiful with a night breeze.

It didn't take them long to reach 52nd and Girard Avenue. There were people standing all around there on every corner, so it would be hard to pick Webb out of the crowd. Saleem told Dee to park on the corner of Stiles Street, the block where Webb's grandmom lived and hopefully he would come there. An hour had lapsed and Saleem got tired of sitting there, especially with the police cars riding back and forth. He decided to knock on Webb's grandmom's door.

Being as though the house was on the corner, he told Monk and Spider to stand on the side of the house.

The lights were on, so that meant someone was home. Saleem rung the bell and seconds later a young girl answered, who looked to be in her early twenties.

"Yes," she said, smiling with little to nothing on but a long black T-shirt and some white panties, as though Saleem had come at the wrong time.

"I'm looking for Webb. Is he home?" asked Saleem, looking past her to see if somebody else was lurking around in there.

"Yeah, he's here. What's your name?" the girl asked.

"Wakil," Saleem responded, giving her the wrong name.

"Hold on. Let me get him. You can come in," she said. Saleem hand signaled Monk and Spider to come in. She ran up the stairs calling his name. Saleem locked the door behind them and walked towards the kitchen to make sure nobody was in there. Webb came down the steps, talking to himself, trying to figure out what Wakil wanted, when he usually would call before he came through.

As he lifted his head up, all he saw was a gun in his face. He was thinking his girl set him up, 'cause he didn't recognize any of the faces who were standing in front of him, until Saleem emerged from the kitchen.

"Damn Leem what's this about?" Webb asked, confused about the awkward situation they had him in. He was trembling, standing at the bottom of the steps with a T-shirt and boxers on.

"You tell me cuz. I hear you been busy lately putting in a lot of work with Wakil," Saleem shot back, getting straight to the point.

"A few jobs here and there. Nothing major," Webb claimed as they pushed him to sit on the couch.

"So you rode with Wakil on a sting for two kilos on 60th and Arch Street?" asked Saleem.

"I don't know what you're talking about. I wasn't there for that one," Webb stated, looking back and forth at Monk and Spider. He looked like a piece of meat stuck between two pieces of bread ready to be demolished.

"Now you give me everything you know about that caper and that barber shop heist that went wrong, as well as who killed Boog and I'll let you live to play another day," responded Saleem, looking Webb straight in the eye.

"Man you're fooling Leem. I don't know nothing about that. You got the wrong dude. Wakil used other guys to help him," Webb said, still holding firm, showing no sign of folding. Saleem shook his head and Monk smacked Webb across the face with his gun, causing blood to burst out all over the place. He screamed loud enough so the neighbors could hear him, as a tooth dropped to the floor and his nose looked to be broken.

"Nigga, I'm not playing with you. What's the girl's name who answered your door?" asked Saleem, raising up from the couch.

"Lisa," Webb said, wiping the blood from his mouth.

"Well, unless you start talking, Lisa is going to be cleaning up blood and body parts off this couch," Saleem stated. The girl came running down the steps after hearing a scream. She couldn't believe what she saw. How these three men had their guns out and her man stuck in between them with blood leaking from him. Saleem heard her footsteps and quickly grabbed her by the hair.

"Yo, let her go. She doesn't know anything," Webb said, like he was running the show.

"You're in no position to be dictating my friend," Saleem said.

"Look man. Let's blow both their brains out and roll 'cause this faggot ain't budging," Monk spoke, becoming frustrated with all the prolonging going on. Lisa was screaming at Webb to tell them whatever they wanted to know.

"Leem, I'ma tell you all that I know, because this shit is getting out of hand," Webb said. Looking at Monk and Spider he knew they meant business. And looking at Lisa he could tell she was frightened.

"I'm listening," Saleem said.

"Wakil called me and lil' Dizzy to ride with him on the 60th and Arch heist. He told us to start shooting when he got back to his car and grab the black bag with the money in it," Webb explained, only telling him half of what he knew.

"And the barber shop?" asked Saleem.

"Man I told Wakil don't do it, but he be high off snorting that powder. He knew you was going to be there so he told us to take everything from you and everybody else we held hostage, then to kill you. He said he was tired of living in your shadow," Webb explained, still holding back from all he knew.

"Snorting since when! That's news to me. Wakil on coke on top of drinking syrup," Saleem said, unaware of Wakil's new drug of choice.

"Shit! He snort heavy but the syrup covers that up, so he looks like he's on a down high," Webb spoke, like Saleem needed him to explain how drugs worked.

"Okay. About my man Boog," Saleem said, getting back on the topic of discussion.

"Now Wakil wanted Boog out of the way, 'cause he knew he was more loyal to you than to him. So he let us know that Boog would be driving his car, but he knew they would never assume Wakil had something to do with it. The finger would point to the dude Boog got into an argument with at the strip club. Wakil shot him in the head," Webb continued to explain, causing tears to roll down Saleem's cheeks at the mention of Boog's name.

"So you fired those shots into that car killing Boog?" Saleem asked, wiping his tears away. Monk and Spider looked as though they felt his pain.

"Yeah, but Wakil ordered me to," Webb said. Before he could speak another word, all you heard was shots ring out, causing Webb's brains to splatter all over his couch from Monk's gun.

Lisa tried to scream but Spider grabbed her mouth and squeezed two off in her head. They knew the neighbors might've heard the shots so they eased out the house leaving the two lifeless bodies laying there in a puddle of blood.

Dee was asking, what had happened. But Saleem didn't respond. All he had on his mind was Wakil. So they headed towards his apartment, to try and catch him leaving or coming. Saleem wanted that chick who played a part in the barber shop heist. He figured lil' Dizzy was the one KB killed.

* * * * *

Wakil was on 56th and Master Street gambling. Even though it was midnight, they had a big crap game going on. Nothing but bosses and a few workers. He was knee deep after losing his first three grand. At first he didn't have to run home for money, because he would take whatever Nell and KB had on them.

Eventually, Wakil drained them out of cash, causing him to take a ride home again. "Damn, I lost six thousand," he mumbled under his breath, walking to his car with Nell following behind him.

"Damn old head, you sweating like crazy," Nell said.

"Shit. I just lost six grand out there to those flee tick ass niggaz," Wakil complained, wiping his face on his crispy, white T-shirt. Wakil didn't want to run home to get some more cash, thinking that these suckers ass niggas would take his money and run.

Halfway down the block he stopped in front of Cann's Hoagie Spot at the corner of 56th and Media Street and decided to call Kenny to bring him some money. So he dialed his cell.

"Yo, how much bread you got on you?" asked Wakil.

"Not much, a couple of hundred. Why?" Kenny asked, trying to figure out why Wakil is asking him for money.

"I'm in a heated crap game and I don't want to leave these flee ass niggas out here with my cash," Wakil explained.

"How much did you lose?" Kenny inquired.

"Six g's," said Wakil, reluctantly.

"Damn. That's a lot to be blowing," Kenny responded.

"It's my money nigga. Don't question what I do with mine!" Wakil said, wiping his nose, that kept dripping due to the amount of cocaine he was snorting on a regular basis. "Where you at?"

"I'm at the apartment."

"Bring me like a couple of stacks," Wakil demanded.

"I can't," said Kenny.

"What you mean you can't?" asked Wakil, sounding frustrated.

"I got a smut over and I don't have any clothes on," Kenny explained.

"So!" Wakil blurted out, getting more frustrated.

"So, it will take me at least twenty to thirty minutes to get to you," said Kenny, not wanting to come out this late, being comfortable.

"I'll come get it myself," Wakil said, banging the phone shut. He jumped in his car, adjusting the steering wheel, hoping to make it to the crib, get money from his safe and make it back to the crap game. Before he pulled off, Nell slid into the passenger seat.

Wakil put the top down to get some air, being as though it was a warm night. They drove past Nick's Bar on the corner of 56th and Lansdown Avenue, where there was a crowd of people standing outside. As Wakil and Nell drove by Nick's, everyone stared at Wakil stunting, leaning hard enough to fall through the door, with the music pumping through the six by nine factory speakers.

Saleem was parked on the opposite side of the street and Monk and Spider were on the other side, a little distance from Wakil's apartment, but facing that direction. Little did they know, Wakil and Nell were heading their way. Wakil pulled his Benz right up in front of his apartment building, double parking and ran inside. Saleem leaned out the car window, giving a hand signal to let them know that was him.

"That's a pretty motherfucking car. I didn't think he had it in him, to step out like that," Saleem said, surprised by the car Wakil was riding around in, which was a big jump from the Caprice station wagon.

"Why you say that Boo?" asked Dee, being confused by Saleem's statement.

"Dude was riding on my coattail for years. I didn't think he had the street smarts to hold a boss position," Saleem responded, as Wakil ran into the apartment building.

"He spent a lot of money at the club on the other girls. We would see each other and speak, but I really didn't pay any attention to him," Dee said, rattling off at the mouth.

Saleem picked up his phone and dialed Monk's phone, not paying Dee no mind. "Yo that's dude right there who just ran into the building. There's someone else in the car," Saleem spoke.

"When you want us to move, I'll put both of them to bed early, right now, without no blanket," Monk said, ready to move.

"I want his stash first before he takes a nap," responded Saleem.

"Fuck the money Leem. You don't need it. This nigga crossed you and broke the G-code. Death before dishonor. So let us have a little fun with this mark and make things right." Monk was pissed off. He figured loyalty to a comrade was far more important than money.

"You're right champ," Saleem said, hesitating, "do you," he said, giving the okay to kill Wakil, a longtime friend, who quickly became his enemy. As Monk and Spider were exiting the vehicle, a police patrol car came cruising past, so they played it off by walking up the steps to a house next to where they were parked.

Once the police car turned off, they reversed back in the direction of the Benz. Nell was laying back in the seat, bobbing his head to the music.

As soon as the front door to the apartment building opened and he stepped out, the pistol was placed to the side of his head.

"Surprise bitch. You think you can shit on my man Leem and get away with it," Monk said. At the same time, Spider climbed in on the driver's side of the car and turned down the music which startled Nell. When he looked up, he was staring down the barrel of a gun.

"Yo M, this nigga look like he saw Casper, the not so friendly ghost," Spider said, not mentioning Monk's whole name, while still holding Nell at gunpoint. Nell looked like he was about to cry.

"We ain't got time to play. Check that nigga's pockets and then take whatever that bitch has," Monk said, looking around to see if anyone was coming down or up the street. He wasn't worrying about the cars riding back and forth, unless it was a police car.

Look M, this little nigga is carrying a little ass six shot 22 revolver and a few hundred," Spider said, flashing the loot so Monk could see it.

"Put that shit in your pocket," Monk said, searching his victim's pocket. He pulled out two wads of money from separate pockets. "This lame riding around with stacks of cash and a hot whip," Monk said, grabbing the back of his victim's white T-shirt and pushing him to the side of the Benz, close to the trunk.

"Say good night lame," Monk said, squeezing off two shots in the front of his victim's head, causing brains and blood to splatter all the way up to the hood and trunk of the car. Blood sprayed on Monk and Spider, as well as Nell, from peeping up when he heard the gunshots. All Nell could see was the side of his face and his white T-shirt. He was in a state of shock, having never witnessed such a tragic event.

"What about him M?" asked Spider, pointing the gun at Nell.

"The way he looks, leave him, he can't even stop shaking," Monk said, as him and Spider ran back to the car. Dee was already positioned to drive off. They drove down the hill towards Lancaster Avenue.

You could hear police sirens coming in their direction. Dee kept looking out her rearview mirror. She was nervous and her heart was beating at a fast pace, after witnessing somebody getting murdered. But Saleem was applauding her for holding firm through the whole ordeal. Saleem had one more mission to accomplish. As soon as they reached one Crazy Greek Pizzeria on the corner of Wynnfield, Saleem's cell phone rang.

"Yeah," spoke Saleem.

"Hey baby, are you alright?" the woman's voice spoke. It was Tara calling from Coatsville. He knew it had to be something important for her to call.

"What's wrong babe?" asked Saleem, sounding concerned about her wellbeing.

"I'm okay. Somebody named D-roc called and said your uncle was rushed back to Brandywine Hospital." Tara spoke as though she was holding back some valuable information.

"Is my uncle cool? And why D-roc ain't call my phone?" Saleem asked.

"Saleem your uncle didn't make it. They said the chemotherapy wasn't helping," responded Tara. The phone was silent for a few seconds. Saleem put his head down. He was trying his best to hold back his tears, but that didn't stop his eyes from becoming watery.

"Yeah, he ain't make it huh?" Saleem asked, as though he failed to listen to what Tara just said.

"No baby, he didn't," repeated Tara.

"Look, I'll be home soon okay. I love you," Saleem stated. He was hurting deeply inside for the loss of two people who were close to him. He figured he owed his uncle so much, for him allowing Saleem to be safe out Coatsville and helping him accomplish so much while on the run.

"Love you too. Stay strong baby," Tara said and the phone disconnected. Dee looked over at Saleem and she could tell he had just gotten some bad news.

"Dee, get in the car with Monk and Spider. I'ma go visit Shay by myself," Saleem spoke.

"Are you sure? 'Cause I'll go with you and stomp a mud hole in her ass," asked Dee, punching her fist into the palm of her hand.

"I need you with them just in case shit don't go right. I'ma let Monk know now." Saleem called Monk and told him about his uncle's death which had him messed up a little due to the relationship he shared with Saleem's uncle. He told Monk he loved all the loyalty he showed since they met, and he had to confront Shay on his own, and Dee would make sure they were straight if anything went wrong. Saleem got behind the wheel and Dee French kissed him hard in the mouth and told him she loved him.

He drove down Shay's block, spotting her Q45 parked in front of her house and there were like three women sitting on the steps. Dee, Monk and Spider still had Saleem in eyesight. They had no plans of leaving him. Saleem double parked right in front of the residence. As he exited, making his presence known, Shay jumped up, not believing what she was seeing. He walked on to the pavement and stood there and stared at Shay.

"Long time baby girl," Saleem said with his hands inside his pockets. Shay didn't know whether to run and hop into his arms or go in the house and avoid him altogether.

"Didn't think I would ever see you again," Shay said, coming down her steps and leaned against the railing.

"No hug, no kiss? I missed you and I always told you I would come back for you." Saleem's mind was running rampant. He thought about Wakil being dead and his uncle passing away, as well as the police still looking for him.

"A lot has changed Saleem. I'm seeing somebody else now. I hope you can understand," Shay spoke, as her girlfriends looked on as though they were watching a soap opera.

"Yeah, I know. Why Wakil, of all people? Don't you know he's the reason for me going on the run and why my man Boog is dead?" Saleem responded. Shay stood there in total disbelief.

"Now you blame him for your problems? He was there for Boog, at the funeral and everything else. So stop it!" Shay said, defending Wakil in his absence.

"Well, he's visiting Boog now for good, so you can go to his funeral," Saleem said, with a sly grin. He felt good about rubbing that in her face.

"What are you talking about? I know you ain't hurt Wakil," Shay said, walking up on Saleem like she was going to punch him in the face. No one could've predicted what was about to take place.

"Feisty little bitch huh? Shut the fuck up whore bitch before I kill you too," Saleem snapped. He went overboard, putting the gun to her head. Shay had just witnessed the dark side of Saleem. Her girlfriends ran in the house, yelling for help.

"Saleem, why are you doing this? You said you loved me. We can talk about it. I know how you feel," Shay pleaded. Her whole demeanor changed. She had no idea what Saleem was capable of. She felt she was too young to die.

"That love is gone. You only get one time to cross me," Saleem said, kissing her all over her face. She didn't resist his boldness, being as though the gun was still aimed at her.

"Somebody called the police. Saleem go get out of here. I hear the sirens getting closer," Shay said, trying to save herself and keep him from getting locked up. Moments later there was no way out, but to surrender or go out in a blaze of glory. Cops were everywhere.

Diamond Street was sectioned off by police cars. They were calling for Saleem to give up, place the gun down and to let Shay go. He played mute to everything around him and pulled Shay closer to him, so the police would have second thoughts about shooting him, unless they were trying to kill them both. Monk, Dee and Spider drove off when they saw all the cop cars pulling up. Malik had just pulled up to drop Peanut off, after taking her out to eat and the North American Hotel.

They had no idea as to what was the cause of all the commotion, until Malik noticed a man holding a gun to Shay's head. When the guy turned his head to see how many police were behind him, Malik realized it was his brother and he was happy to see him, but not under these circumstances.

He started walking up towards him. Peanut stood there in shambles, scared for her girlfriend's life. The police officer stopped him in his tracks. Malik quickly explained to him that he knew the man and that it was his brother and he could talk to him. The officer went against his better judgment and allowed Malik to go.

"Malik what's up? You shouldn't be here," Saleem said, seeing his brother walking up on him, even though he was elated to see him.

"Leem you tripping. Put that gun down. I didn't even know you was back and why you got a gun to her head?" asked Malik, confused.

"It's a long story bro, but just know this bitch crossed me and that sucker ass Wakil. But we don't have to worry about him anymore. He's history like Harriet Tubman," responded Saleem.

"Man, what are you talking about? Wakil was just asking about you earlier and Shay," explained Malik, still not understanding the hostility towards a woman Saleem had once loved unconditionally.

The crowd had grew bigger. people were coming out of the woodwork to witness the turbulence in their neighborhood. Bryn Mawr Tower residents were on their balconies, watching the unfortunate event.

"Malik just know, Wakil is dead and he got what he deserved. He set me up for that cop's murder and he's behind Boog's death. Plus he's fucking my bitch," said Saleem, starting to cry from being emotionally drained. Malik was caught off guard by what Saleem had just told him. It was too much for Malik to take in at one time. He just put his head down in disbelief.

"Leem, I feel you dog, but this ain't the way to go out and these police are ready to blast you to mars," Malik said, still trying to convince his brother to throw in the towel.

"I'm going on death row anyway bro. I got a baby on the way and unc just checked out. That fucking cancer ate him alive," spoke Saleem, overwhelmed by all the sudden changes that were going on in his life.

"I'll get the best lawyer money can buy to pull a rabbit out of a hat, so don't count yourself out yet. And whoever your baby mom is she'll be secure. I turned my thing up since you left," Malik said.

"Money ain't the issue bro. I got more money than I ever seen in my lifetime. I can't raise my child from a jail cell," Saleem responded, with sweat dripping down his face. Shay was listening to the whole conversation. She felt guilty and like she was part to blame for him acting out of character.

"You know Leem that jail is the other side of the game. I learned that from you," Malik said.

"You're right blood. I never wanted this life for you. Now you're knee deep," Saleem said, talking as though Malik was getting across to him. The police still had their guns drawn, but they were being patient with Malik trying to talk him out of it.

"I had to get my own. You and mommy always looked after me and with you on the run, I became the man of the house," Malik stated.

"You look like you're doing good for yourself," said Saleem, proud of how his little brother matured without being in his shadow.

"Yeah, now let me play my part for you. I owe you so much," Malik responded, leaving Saleem puzzled. He stared at Malik and knew he meant every word he said.

He decided to give up and let Shay go. She ran up the steps like she was being chased by the boogie man. Saleem placed the gun on the ground and hugged his brother.

Seconds later the police rushed in, breaking up the family reunion. They gripped Saleem up with blunt force and handcuffed him. He was placed inside the patrol car, while two policemen walked up the steps to talk to Shay, but Ms. Lacy intervened for her, explaining that her daughter had just went through a traumatic situation, so the police understood and said they would return in a few days to get her statement. Peanut walked up and hugged and kissed Malik and thanked him.

Malik jumped in his car and drove off. He had to inform his mom of what had occurred because he didn't know how the police would treat Saleem due to the allegations he was being accused of.

✳ ✳ ✳ ✳ ✳

Wakil's phone rang steadily without him answering. The caller called right back. This time the answering machine picked up. "A Wah, somebody rocked Webb and his chick. The police found them shot, execution style, slumped over each other," Lil' Dizzy rambled.

"Man, I had just dropped him and Lisa off. I was chilling with my girl and the chick, Kim, called me telling me she heard gunshots and when she looked out of the window, all she saw was three guys running past her house," Lil' Dizzy responded, speaking as though he was out of breath.

"Look, we need to find out what's to that. I need you to get with me. Until you get with me, I'ma lay low. When you get this message, call me right back," Lil' Dizzy said, hanging up.

Lil' Dizzy waited for about fifteen minutes and decided to go to Wakil, instead of waiting for him to call. When Lil'

Dizzy pulled up to Wakil's apartment, police cars were everywhere and yellow tape was blocking the apartment building. In front of the building, double parked in the street, was his Benz surrounded by detectives.

He quickly panicked, knowing something was wrong with Wakil. So he jumped out of his car and ran up the street, getting as close as the police and yellow tape would allow him to go. What he saw almost made him throw up. Wakil's Benz was splattered with brains and blood in the back seat and covering the trunk.

He spotted Nell leaning against a police car, talking to one of the officers, but Wakil was nowhere in sight. Lil' Dizzy ran over to the paramedic who was pushing a stretcher with a blood stained white sheet covering a body. He asked could he see who was underneath, but they denied him his request to review the body.

Lil' Dizzy immediately fell on top of the body, knowing it was Wakil. Being fed up with Webb being murdered, now Wakil, his old head, he broke down. Not being able to hold back the tears, he wept uncontrollably.

Mimi and her girlfriend, Tasha, had just come walking up the street. "That's my husband's car!" she yelled. "That's my husband's car!" Mimi said, walking over to Nell, who was crying.

"They killed him Mi," Nell said softly. "They killed."

"Who did they kill?" questioned Mimi, seeing all the blood, but not wanting to believe what her eyes was revealing to her. "No! No!" Mimi yelled, falling back into the arms of the police officer that was interviewing Nell.

"You have to calm down Miss." Mimi only began to cry and scream louder. "If you don't calm down, you're going to hurt your baby. Please Miss, calm down."

Tasha grabbed hold of Mimi, wrapping her hands around her waist with her left hand rubbing her stomach. "Mi, calm down, please," she whispered, not knowing what to say to her.

"Them motherfuckers going to pay! I swear on everything I love!" Lil' Dizzy said, walking over to them expressing his anger openly. He was blunt about it and determined to get revenge for his old head, Wakil's and his best friend, Webb's deaths.

Tasha standing by and holding Mimi, decided to look down at her feet, being as though her sneakers were sticking to the ground. She started trembling, seeing that she was surrounded by blood and human remains. Tasha ran over to the curb and started puking. Mimi later joined her, as they both sat there staring at Wakil's car.

After the police finished with Nell, he walked over to Mimi and Tasha and sat down beside them on the sidewalk. "Mimi, I am so sorry. I couldn't do nothing. They had the drop on me," said Nell, who calmed down a lot since witnessing such a brutal murder.

"Did you at least see their faces?" asked Lil' Dizzy.

"Yeah, but I never seen them around here before," responded Nell.

"How they look? Did you see what kind of car they were in? It has got to be something, that Webb, his chick and Wakil get killed on the same day. I know one thing. It's no coincidence," stated Lil' Dizzy, trying to find out as much as possible about the perpetrators who did this to his comrade and old head.

"The one who had the gun to Wakil was a tall, stocky, ugly nigga and the other one was dark skinned, with a beard," responded Nell to Lil' Dizzy's question.

"Did they ask for money or anything else?" asked Lil' Dizzy, searching for anything that could help him find out who did this. Lil' Dizzy sent Mimi and Tasha inside the apartment while he continued to question Nell.

"The only money they took was what we had on us. They took my gun too. Man, I think they knew Wakil," said Nell.

"What do you mean by that?" asked Lil' Dizzy, frustrated and confused.

"Well, before dude shot Wakil, he said, 'Why you cross Saleem.' " answered Nell.

"You sure they mentioned Saleem?" Lil' Dizzy, standing over top of Nell, questioned, trying to connect all the dots together.

"Shit. I might've been scared to death for life, but I know what I heard and what dude said," stated Nell.

"Alright. We're going to chill for a while. I got to figure this shit out and get Mimi out of this apartment, because they know where she lives. If they killed Webb's girl, they might be coming back for Mimi," Lil' Dizzy said.

"I hear you. I'm gonna go get me a blunt and a drink. My nerves are shot," said Nell, still shaken up.

"You need a ride, right?"

"Yeah," said Nell.

"I'ma go check on Mimi and Tasha, then drop you off," said Lil' Dizzy. He ran up the stairs to make sure the girls were alright.

Tasha decided to stay a night with Mimi because she was still feeling chills through her body. Her and Mimi had been friends for a while. She knew Wakil very well. So she felt Mimi's pain of losing him. He was like a brother to her.

The police towed Wakil's car for evidence and had left the scene. Lil' Dizzy told Mimi if she needed him for anything, don't hesitate to call him. He went in the trunk of his car, got the Tech 22 and placed it on his lap, as he drove Nell towards Master Street, hoping that Nell recognized somebody.

Chapter 20

Locked Up

A week had passed and Saleem was getting out of quarantine after sitting down the district for three days. He was charged with attempted murder, kidnapping, and aggravated assault on Shay. Plus, they charged him for the murder of Charlie Edney, the undercover drug agent, on top of multiple drug charges for all the cocaine he distributed during the time of meeting and dealing with the drug agent. His bail was set at a million dollars. Being as though this was his first time being incarcerated, he had no idea how it would turn out.

He was housed at Curran Fromhold Correctional Facility known to some as CFCF which had just opened a few months back, due to the closing of Homesburg County Prison, one of the roughest county jails in Philadelphia.

His uncle, Big Slim had a proper burial a few days ago. He felt terrible that he couldn't attend the services, but was elated that Tara and Monk, as well as D-roc made sure he was sent off in style.

Saleem had moved Tara to Philly to be close to him and his family. Malik had kept his word and got Saleem one of the best lawyers out of Philly by the name of Dennis Cogan, who charged him a hundred thousand dollars for all his cases. Saleem allowed Malik to put up ten thousand dollars down payment and got Tara to give him the rest.

Saleem was preparing himself for a long drawn out court battle to prove his innocence for a murder he didn't do. He had no idea how he was going to beat the charges from the incident with Shay. He hoped she wouldn't come to court, but he was glad she didn't mention his name in the death of Wakil.

Laying back in his bed, he was talking to his celly, a dude named Sheed from the bottom who was Muslim and offered prayer five times a day. Even though Saleem was Muslim, he didn't know nothing about praying.

They hit it off from the time Saleem moved in. Alerted by the door buzzing open, Sheed jumped up to see the reason for their door opening, due to it being afternoon count.

"Yo Leem, you got a visit," Sheed said, coming back in the room.

"Alright," Saleem responded hopping down off the top bunk. He washed his face and brushed his teeth and sealed the deal with a piece of candy. The correctional officer at the desk was a Spanish old guy. He tried his best to explain the directions to the visiting room.

It was only thirty-two inmates to a pod and the jail was like Zelda, a maze to get from A to B. His block was C-2-3. There were four pods to each floor.

Saleem took the elevator down to the first floor. As he was getting off, he bumped into somebody he knew from his neighborhood. They talked for a few minutes, shook hands and continued to his destination. He had to ring the bell to be let inside the visiting room.

It was still early so it wasn't crowded. He turned his blue shirt and pants in for an orange jumpsuit, the same kind he wore in quarantine. He went to the desk and the C.O. looked at his armband ID, then she directed him to his seat to wait for his visit. Seconds later Tara and his little brother came walking through the door. Tara came straight over to him while Malik took the pass to the desk.

"Hey Boo," Tara said, reaching her arms out for a hug and a kiss. Saleem embraced her with open arms. They were excited to see each other.

"How's my baby girl and my lil' man holding up?" Saleem asked, rubbing her stomach. She was three months shy from going into labor and expecting a son.

"Missing you like crazy. The lawyer called. He said he is going to do everything in his power to clear your name with the police agent. He said the hardest thing will be the charges that Shay has against you," Tara responded.

"Oh yeah, I don't know if anybody can convince her not to come to court," spoke Saleem.

"Blood, I got you. I'll talk to her. I mess with her girlfriend," said Malik.

"How's mommy doing? I talk to her all the time, but she likes to keep stuff bottled up, even if she's alright," asked Saleem.

"She's good, besides stressing about you," Malik spoke.

"Let her know you saw me and I'm holding my head firm," Saleem stated. Ms. Cee wasn't too fond about visiting her son behind bars.

"I brought you socks, drawers, T-shirts, a towel and rag," Tara said.

"Yeah, that's on time babe. I got money, a few stacks on my books," said Saleem.

"What's to this camp Leem?" asked Malik looking around observing the visiting room.

"You know it's jail and I'm doing it like a giant," Saleem spoke.

"Don't get to Dougy Fresh. We need you and I need a plug with Wakil gone. I been purchasing garbage to hold down my spots," Malik said.

"I got you. I'ma put you on my man Monk from Coatsville. He's a good dude and loyal. He rides out, so don't worry. But I need you to handle something for me?" asked Saleem.

"Name it. I'm on it," responded Malik.

"You know Tiffany with the scar on her face?" asked Saleem.

"Yeah, black Tiff. What about her?" questioned Malik.

"Shorty did some looking out, so I promised her a gift. Give her a few stacks for me. I'll call you and give you her number," Saleem spoke. A couple minutes later the C.O. came and gave them the pass, terminating the visit. An hour went fast. He kissed and hugged Tara.

You could tell Saleem's absence was a heavy burden on her. It showed from the bags that were hanging underneath her eyes. Malik gave him a handshake and a half shoulder hug, as he whispered in his ear letting him know Wakil's funeral was today. Saleem didn't show no remorse. He didn't care about Wakil.

Malik told him Kenny was home, but he haven't seen him in a couple of days, so he's holding down Hunter Street.

The C.O. rushed Saleem in the dressing room, so he let Malik know he would call him later and that he had a horse that'll mule in cell phones and whatever else, for a small fee. Malik said he got it. Saleem got strip searched, grabbed his clothing and package and rolled out back to his cell.

＊ ＊ ＊ ＊ ＊

Meanwhile Shay was still in the bed mourning over the death of Wakil and the nightmares from that horrible night Saleem pointed the gun at her head. Ms. Lacy couldn't get her to leave the house and she hadn't been back to Head Quarters in months. Her hairstyling days were over. She thought she was losing her mind because for some strange reason she still loved Saleem. At one point, she even thought about going to visit him, but later nixed the idea. Awakened by the phone ringing, Shay had second thoughts about answering it, but did so anyway.

"Yes," said Shay, answering the phone.

"Girl, get out that bed and come on. Did you forget Wakil's funeral is today?" Peanut said.

"No, I didn't forget. I'm not going. Plus, it's a closed casket," responded Shay, getting up and looking in the mirror. What she saw wasn't her. She looked like something from a horror movie. "Alright. I'm going. Don't beat my head in. Hold on for a second," Shay said. She ran to the bathroom and started throwing up in the toilet. Peanut heard her through the phone, and was calling for her to see if she was alright. Hearing the phone pick back up, Peanut was on her.

"Ooow! You're pregnant," spoke Peanut.

"Bitch, stop calling me like I'm deaf or something. Are you crazy? I ate some fish and it messed my stomach up," said Shay, even though she had a feeling she was pregnant, but didn't pay much attention to it, even though her period still hadn't come on and broadcasting it wasn't on her agenda.

"If you say so, but I know the symptoms. Anyway, wash your ass and get dressed. I'll be there to pick you up," ordered Peanut. Shay hopped in the shower and groomed herself back to the dime piece she was. Dressed in a black Gucci skirt suit with matching black open toe Gucci stilettoes, she put her air in a ponytail.

Checking her appearance in the mirror, she threw on some Gucci sunglasses to hide the dark bags under her eyes. Peanut had just pulled up outside and Shay came down to meet her. She had no idea, she was home alone.

Leaving her car parked, she drove in Peanut's up-to-date Nisson Maxima. It wasn't Shay's cup of tea. The Q45 she drove had raised her status. But driving it brought back too many memories that she shared with Wakil. She even thought about trading it in.

✳ ✳ ✳ ✳ ✳

Everybody was rolling in packs to make it to Wakil's funeral. That was mentioned to be a closed casket. The funeral was being held at the First Resurrection Baptist Church on 54th and Landsdown Avenue, across from Heston Elementary School.

There were a lot of people who came out to attend Boog's funeral, but this one was on another level. It was more like the Greek picnic. He was loved as much as he was hated.

The majority being women who turned out to pay their last respects. Ms. Sidney and Mr. James, along with the rest of the family were sitting in the first row of the church.

The obituaries weren't being passed out until after the services were over. Due to the turnout of people who showed up, there weren't enough to give out, so more copies were being made.

People walked pass the casket laying flowers on top, along with pictures and other items. The cries were uncontrollable and tears were flowing like rivers. Reverend Scott was due to give the service which started later than usual funerals.

The organ prelude was by Sister Susan Vingan. Ms. Sidney didn't feel as though Kenny was going to show up to his brother's funeral since he felt responsible for his death for not bringing him the money and they argued over him having a Muslim "Jannaza" Islamic funeral inside a Majid, instead of a church.

But he lost that battle and couldn't do nothing about it, because Wakil didn't have a will stating how he wanted to be buried. Shay and Peanut just drove up and had to park on Hunter Street, 'cause all the spots by the church were taken.

"Girl, come on, the funeral is about to start," Peanut said, while Shay was taking another look in the mirror.

"Keep your panties on. I'm not taking my glasses off," responded Shay.

"You look good, so stop tripping. It's not like Wakil can see you anyway," stated Peanut.

"So, I still wanted to look my best. I got an image to uphold," said Shay.

"Malik told me the bullets went through the back of his head, straight out one of his eyes and his face was messed up," Peanut said, sharing the gruesome details about how Wakil looked when he got killed.

"Please, that's enough. I don't want to hear no more. You're making me sick all over again." Shay couldn't stand hearing about Wakil's demise and how he looked due to the bullets that pierced his body.

They reached the steps of the church and stopped, due to hearing somebody calling their name. When they turned around to look, it was Malik walking up on them. He was wearing a black Dickie pantsuit and some black Chukka Timberland boots. He looked like he was dressed for something other than a funeral.

"What's up yaw?" asked Malik.

"Didn't expect to see you here," spoke Shay, like she had an attitude.

"Why not? That's my old head. He always showed me love," explained Malik, caught off guard by her sudden remark.

"We wouldn't be here if your brother didn't come back with the dumb shit," said Shay.

"Now you're stepping out of your league. My brother treated you like a boss chick and you betrayed him by fucking his right hand man. So ask yourself, why shit went down the way it did," spoke Malik. He was fired up. He wanted to choke Shay to death and make it a double funeral, if Shay kept ranking his brother in his presence. Now he understood why his brother told him not to come. Even though Saleem admitted to Shay and Malik that he killed Wakil, there was no evidence to link him to the crime.

"Stop! Yaw out here arguing and cussing in front of a church," Peanut spoke. She felt she had to step in before things got out of control. So they went inside.

Two men in black suits were stationed at the door, greeting those who walked in. Malik sat in the row opposite from Shay and Peanut. There was at least a couple hundred or more in attendance. The church could seat about five hundred.

Reverend Scott took the pulpit to begin the service after Sister Whitney had just finished singing a farewell song she wrote, especially for this occasion.

Reverend Scott spoke about Wakil's shortcomings and how he helped people when he could, which brought more tears. One girl had to be carried back to her seat because she tried to open the casket and jump inside.

The tension could be felt throughout the service. Girls were giving each other evil looks. KB and Nell sat beside Malik. Ms. Sidney was suppose to say a few words in remembrance of her son, but couldn't find the strength to do so.

A family friend, Ms. Sandy Peck, who lived down the street from Ms. Sidney, took on the responsibility. Once she spoke the heartfelt words, it was pandemonium in the crowded church, but nobody was prepared for what was about to take place next.

As soon as the people thought the funeral was over, Reverend Scott made a last announcement that someone else close to the deceased, that knew him better than any of us wanted to say their last words to their brother.

Reverent Scott paused for a second before speaking and said, "It is Wakil's stepsister." People looked around like Reverent Scott was playing a prank on them. Ms. Sidney even turned back around. Her head swung sharply, 'cause she didn't know that Wakil had a stepsister. It took everyone by surprise, that nobody even noticed the two detectives sitting in the far right corner in the back of the church.

It was the same two who took Wakil down for questioning—Detectives Mills and Bradly. As the people looked around, waiting to see, no one came down the aisle.

One girl yelled from the center of the rows, "We love you Wakil," pointing at the closed casket that sat in front of the church with Wakil's picture on top.

Out of nowhere, a woman came and stood beside Reverend Scott and just looked around. Everyone stood still and it got extremely quiet. Didn't no one know who she was and why she even came. No one even recognized her until she removed her wig and dark sunglasses.

People's jaws dropped. KB was speechless. Ms. Sidney stood to her feet, then fell out. Mimi dropped her purse, covering her mouth with both of her hands. Shay threw up and ran for the front door.

They were all too familiar with the person who just revealed her true identity. No one in there could believe what they saw. Even the detectives were devastated by what they observed. The church was in an uproar. The detectives rushed to the pulpit to take the person into custody. As the detectives were leading this person away, all you heard was whispering and mumbling.

LOCK THE GLOBE PUBLISHING
Presents

An Excerpt From . . .

Hidden Agendas
Part 2 of a
Philly Tale

by

Kareem "K-Gotti" Torain

CHAPTER 1

The evening air was brisk. Malik pulled the Mark Bucanna leather closer to his body, as he looked both ways up and down the street from the steps of his apartment he shared with his daughter's mother.

As he started to walk towards his car he couldn't help but notice a white Cadillac Escalade sailing pass him. Its occupants, a lovely couple, probably in their mid-thirties. Malik's daze was broken when the police sirens wailing at full speed got closer and closer.

The gunfire erupted. The cops were chasing a black Buick straight down Lansdown Avenue, between 64th and 65th Street. A young man with braids leaned out of the passenger window and fired a few rounds at the cops.

Seeing this commotion coming, Malik quickly ducked behind a car. As the action got closer, Malik became terrified. He could hear the tires screeching, like a bat out of hell, as they took a hard turn. Then Malik heard a thump next to him. Once it sounded like the commotion had come and went, malik slowly rose to his feet and looked around. "*Them niggas are crazy*," mumbled Malik to himself, as he dusted his clothes off. Then he realized the City Blue bag laying next to his feet.

He scanned the block quickly, then he picked the bag up and looked inside. The contents made his heart flutter with joy, as he ran back to his apartment. Once inside, he locked the door and peeped through the curtains to make sure he wasn't followed . . .

. . . Black and his brother J-Rock was on the cutting edge of going out of control after one of their street lieutenants got into a high speed chase with the cops. It almost turned deadly when a hail of bullets were exchanged back and forth, causing Black to come up shorthanded on two kilos of cocaine.

"I knew we should've made that move ourselves. This is a major setback," said Black, pacing the floor, contemplating his.

"Leroy could have jumped out and ran with Biz," J-Rock spoke, scratching his nose and arms at the same time, the heroin starting to kick in, which was his drug of choice. Black knew he was using some type of substance, but never inquired about it, 'cause it didn't affect their business.

"When Leroy called from the police station, he said, he threw the bag out the window, but the cops never saw it," explained Black.

"Shit, anybody could've snatched that up!" J-Rock shot back, walking towards the kitchen.

"You're right, but he also said, he seen malik standing out in front of a car close by, where he tossed the stuff at," responding Black.

"What Malik?" questioned J-Rock, as though he wasn't familiar with the name.

"Nigga, stop acting stupid. Saleem's little brother . . ."

LOCK THE GLOBE PUBLISHING
Presents

"COMING SOON"

From

K. Gotti AKA Golden Hand
Hidden Agendas 2
Novel

⊰⊱

The Rapoetry of a Hustler 1
Poetry Book

⊰⊱

The Rapoetry of a Hustler 2
Poetry Book